The Nine Muses

The Nine Muses

Edited by
Forrest Aguirre
and
Deborah Layne

Wheatland Press
http://www.wheatlandpress.com

Wheatland Press
http://www.wheatlandpress.com

P. O. Box 1818
Wilsonville, OR 97070

Cover Design by Elizabeth West.
Disquieting Muses (1916) by Georgio de Chirico image used by permission of ARS-NY.
Interior Design by Deborah Layne
Library of Congress Cataloging-in-Publication data is available upon request.
ISBN 0-9755903-6-7
Printed in the United States of America

Contents

Come thou, let us begin with the Muses who gladden the great spirit of their father Zeus in Olympus with their songs, telling of things that are and that shall be and that were aforetime with consenting voice...they uttering their immortal voice, celebrate in song first of all the reverend race of the gods from the beginning, those whom Earth and wide Heaven begot, and the gods sprung of these, givers of good things.

Hesiod
Theogony, 11. 36-52

The Beckoning Fair Ones: Some Thoughts on Muses

Elizabeth Hand

I

THERE IS A BRIEF SCENE that has always haunted me in Peter Weir's film *The Last Wave* (1977). David, the movie's urban lawyer protagonist (Richard Chamberlain in his most affecting role) has been having apocalyptic visions: he seems to have somehow tapped into the Australian aboriginals' Dreamtime. During a visit with his stepfather, an Anglican priest, the distraught David exclaims, "Why didn't you ever tell me there were Mysteries? You sat there in your Church and explained them away!"

And his stepfather calmly replies, "My entire life has been about a Mystery."

I've carried those last words with me for decades now (though certainly not in any Christian sense). My life, too, has been about a Mystery: trying to pin down the overpowering sense of imminence and the numinous that seems to emanate from certain landscapes and certain people, trying to locate that same essence in the work of individual writers and poets and artists who also seem to have glimpsed it.

And yet, what precisely is "it"? My childhood friend Katy called it The Door; I called it the Boy in the Tree after the visionary figure I saw in a dream at seventeen. Robert Graves named it the White Goddess; his lover, the poet Laura Riding, called it "a false wall." In her brilliant, *sui generis* fantasy novel *Lud-in the Mist* (1926), the writer and poet Hope Mirrlees termed it "the Note." John Fowles knew the Mystery as the Lost Domain, the "*domaine perdu*" he encountered in Alain-Fournier's symbolist novel *Le Grand Meaulnes* (Fr. 1913; English *The Wanderer*, 1928) It is "the country of the blue" in Henry James' short story "The Next Time" (1895), as the Jamesian scholar Denis Donoghue explicates it in *Speaking of Beauty*, "the place of the imagination where it has nothing at heart but to be inventive and intelligent and to live up to its best possibility." If the Mystery evokes a sense of place, that place also contains an inhabitant: the genius loci of the Lost Domain, the Muse.

A muse! The very notion of an artist's muse has become so unfashionable as to be faintly embarrassing—like admitting to a taste for Cherries Jubilee or Beef Wellington or Ambrosia Salad, one of those outmoded culinary concoctions our parents and grandparents found sophisticated, back in an era of blowsy blondes and beefy leading men. Today the muse seems to be an endangered species, if not utterly extinct: unsurprising, when one considers that the muses were traditionally depicted as female, thereby limiting their options for procreation with others of their kind. Field guides to the species are almost non-existent, the most recent being Francine Prose's *The Lives of the Muses: Nine Women and Artists They Inspired* (2003), an intelligent and entertaining account of nine real-life, female muses, the number meant to correspond with the most popular conception of the cohort—Robert Graves referred to them as "the nine little muses" —which nowadays is less evocative of the Greek Mysteries than it is of nine hearty sorority gals, each with her own merit badge: Calliope (Epic Poetry), Erato (Love Lyrics), Melpomene (Tragedy), and so on.

Yet the earliest conception of the Muses was of three figures, not the nine who later consorted with Apollo. This Triad consisted of Aoide, Melete, and Mneme, daughters of Gaea and Uranus (and thus Titans); Hesiod's "Theogony" names, alternately, Mnemosyne as Gaea and Uranus's daughter, and the three Muses as Mnemosyne's children by Zeus. Aoide is the Muse of song; Melete of practice; Mneme (and Mnemosyne) of memory. "Mnemosyne, memory, the mother of the Muses, knows and sings the past as if it were still there," notes Jean-Pierre Vernant in "Greek Cosmogonic Myths;" and given that her sisters Melete and Aoide are related to practice and song, it is likely that the Triad Muses were, originally, priestesses or poets responsible for maintaining an oral tradition, and not merely a mythical conduit for inspiration.

The Muses may have inspired entire libraries-worth of song and story, but in their most archaic incarnation they left little in the way of a papyrus trail. The first-century Greek historian Strabo finds them on Mount Peiria in Thessaly; they then migrated south to Mount Helicon in Boeotia, a region of central Greece also associated with the cult of the immigrant god Dionysos. At Helicon the Muses' worship became subsumed into that of Apollo, at nearby Delphi.

But it is with Dionysos that the Triad Muses seem to show the greatest affinity. His cult seems to have originated in Thrace, in what is now Turkey. "[T]he Thraceians who colonized Boeotia consecrated Helicon to the Muses," writes Strabo in his *Geographia*, "and also the cave of the Nymphs called Leibethriades. And those who practiced ancient music are said to have been Thraceians, Orpheus and Musaeus and Thamyris, and the name Eumolpus [co-founder of the Eleusinian Mysteries] comes from Thrace."

Archaeological digs in Boeotia have also turned up cultic burials linked to Crete, another site affiliated with Dionysian rites (and, later, with those of Orpheus, Dionysos' legendary acolyte). I suspect that in their most ancient form the Muses are linked to Dionysos, that "womanish creature," and to what the great classicist Jane Ellen Harrison (who for some years lived with Hope Mirrlees) calls "the blind mad fury" of the God of Mysteries. Dionysos had his female followers, the ravening Bacchae, maenads whose worship of the god of ecstasy ends with them tearing Dionysos limb from limb then devouring his raw flesh. Thracian maenads slaughtered Orpheus as well, decapitating him; his head floated down the river Hebrus. Yet even in these ancient stories, there is a link between muse and maenad—

"The head of Orpheus, singing always, is found by the Muses, and buried in the sanctuary at Lesbos," writes Harrison in *Prolegomena to a Study of Greek Religion*. "Who are the Muses? Who but the Maenads repentant, clothed and in their right minds." (In an aside that resonates nicely in our current culture of body art, Harrison notes that the murderous maenads were punished for their acts by being tattooed with the image of a stag on the upper part of their right arms. The stag is one of the sacrificial animals—others being the bull, the goat, and men or male infants—associated with Bacchic frenzy.)

Even now, thousands of years later, we perceive the elusive essence of the Muse as two-fold, both desirable and threatening; at her worst, psychologically, even murderously, devastating, to herself and others—though this identification of the Muse as strictly female is, today, outmoded. The OED defines a muse as a poet's particular genius; genius in the sense of a tutelary god or attendant spirit presiding from birth. It is, I think, an eidolon not just of longing but of "the mystery of communicated knowledge," as Maud Bodkin states in *Archetypal Patterns of Poetry* (1934): "The eternal quality that belongs to the moment of vision, when the seer has lost himself within the vast complex essence of the thing seen."

The muse is the embodiment of an individual artist's obsession, and as such can as easily be male as female—though the notion of a male muse, or a female artist, seemed a dubious one to Robert

Graves (1895-1985), the 20th century's outstanding Muse mad scientist.

> However, woman is not a poet: she is either a Muse or she is nothing. . . A woman who concerns herself with poetry should, I believe, either be a silent Muse and inspire the poets by her womanly presence, as Queen Elizabeth and the Countess of Derby did, or she should be the Muse in the complete sense; she should be in turn Arianrhod, Blodeuwedd and the Old Sow of Maenawr Penardd who eats her own farrow.
> (*The White Goddess*)

Graves backpedals a bit when he admits, "This is not to say a woman should refrain from writing poems"; but his heart isn't in that utterance. If anyone could attest to the dangers of women writing poetry, it was Graves, who survived one of the 20th century's most noted and notorious Muses, the poet Laura Riding, a woman who so perfectly and deliberately embraced the witchy, destructive, protean and devouring aspects of the Muse that she might have sprung full-grown from Medusa's head (or, if she'd lived a few decades later, Madonna's).

Graves had been physically and emotionally battered by his experiences in the trenches during the Great War—he suffered from crippling shell-shock, what we would now term Post-Traumatic Stress Disorder. When he met Riding, nee Laura Gottschalk, he was married to Nancy Nicholson, an artist and feminist who retained her maiden name, a bold thing to do in 1920s England. They had four children. By 1926, when Graves and Riding actually met, the pressures of supporting a family while attempting to create art—poetry for Graves, painting for Nicholson—was for both Robert and Nancy exacerbated by depression, illness, and poverty. The success of Graves' first two poetry collections, *Over the Brazier* (1916) and

Fairies and Fusiliers (1917) was followed by the failure in 1920 of *Country Sentiment*. Graves' nephew and biographer, Richard Perceval Graves, observes that the poet "underwent a kind of personality crisis...Robert was later to reflect that by the beginning of 1926 a process of personal disintegration was well under way" (*Robert Graves: the Years with Laura, 1926-1940*, 1990).

Enter Laura Riding. She was a coldly intellectual Manhattan-born poet who had briefly allied herself with the Nashville-based Fugitive poets (she had an affair with Allen Tate) before returning to New York. There she corresponded with Graves, and at the end of 1925 accepted Graves' invitation to join him in Europe and collaborate on a volume about modern poetry. Richard Perceval Graves quotes a family friend observing that "Robert always seemed happiest when he had found someone he admired who would give him direction."

Riding was prepared to do just that. Brilliant but domineering, seemingly inexorable in her need to be the authoritarian center of any group, she possessed the exact skills needed to wrest control of the rudderless Graves/Nicholson marriage. Laura Riding was also, frankly, a nut, but a nut on the grand scale of a Madame Blavatsky or L. Ron Hubbard, able to convince intelligent but emotionally susceptible people that she had insights and powers beyond the ken of ordinary mortals. Riding accompanied Graves' family (including children and nursemaid) to Egypt, where Robert had accepted a job as Professor of English at Cairo University. Once there she declared their quarters to be haunted, and indeed for the next fourteen years the entire extended family of Robert Graves and Nancy Nicholson was haunted, by the sinister, sibylline, predatory Riding.

Richard Perceval Graves' marvelous biography gives the details of their mad and often maddening relationship. Riding, while striking-looking, was not conventionally attractive. She relied upon a combination of acute intelligence and sexual frankness; oracular pronouncements about Poetry; Woolworth bijoux, and intimations of occult knowledge to cast her spell upon a moveable feast of artists, writers, poets and their spouses, both male and female, enlarging the initial *menage a trois* with Graves and Nicholson to *menages a quatre et a cinq*. She was not above using black magic to gain the attentions of a lover, and when all else failed, she attempted suicide: in 1929, when one of Riding's erstwhile lovers rejected her and backed out of the elaborate relationship daisy-chain she had devised, Riding drank Lysol and leaped from a fourth-floor window. In a blackly comic *couvade*, the horror-stricken Graves ran down to a third-floor window and did the same. Both survived. Still, nobody seems to have learned a lesson, since Laura continued to retain her near-supernatural hold on Graves, despite her refusal to sleep with him. Ten years later, when Riding entered a relationship with the poet Schuyler Jackson (whom she eventually married), she systematically drove Jackson's wife Kit into a mental institution, an act all the more unconscionable since it was carried out with Kit's four children as witnesses.

One doesn't so much feel *Schadenfraude* as genuine relief to know that the ruthless Laura Riding has now been relegated to that long, long list of Forgotten Poets, a lengthy footnote to the life of her one-time and best-known acolyte. Of course no one expects artists to be nice people, and from the wreckage of this floating world emerged some indisputable masterworks: Robert Graves' novels, poetry, and—most important for this essay—*The White Goddess: A Historical Grammar of Poetic Myth* (1948), a book that plays a bit fast fast and loose with history, etymology, and archaeology, but which captures as no other book does that elevated, almost supernatural, sense of peril and exhilaration which accompanies the creative process.

I summarize Riding's relationship with Graves not because it is wickedly entertaining (though it is) but because it neatly encapsulates the two most crucial aspects of the Muse one finds in both fiction depictions and real life: her (or his) ineffable appeal, and her destructiveness. When it comes to the relationship between artist and muse, there often seems to be some obscure law of quantum physics in effect: both cannot occupy the same place at the same time, or one will be destroyed. Sometimes the artist consumes the muse, sometimes the reverse. Longtime, relatively stable relationships between artist and muse exist—that of Robert Graves and his second wife, Beryl Pritchard; James Merrill (himself no stranger to the occult) and David Jackson, Vladimir and Vera Nabokov, John and Elizabeth Fowles. But these are outnumbered by those creative dramas that explode (often with serial muses) like fireworks on a string: Arthur Rimbaud and Paul Verlaine, Oscar Wilde and Lord Alfred Douglas, Isadora Duncan and Sergei Esenin, Robert Lowell and Carolyn Blackwood.

The White Goddess was published some years after the demise of Graves' relationship with Riding, but her influence as Muse—oracular, fiercely intelligent, and somewhat daft—clearly informs the entire book. Graves invokes her in the dedication to the book's second edition (1952), a revision of the poem in the original volume.

> All saints revile her, and all sober men ...
> In scorn of which I sailed to find her
> In distant regions likeliest to hold her
> Whom I desired above all things to know
> Sister of the mirage and echo.
>
> ... Whose broad high brow was white as any lepers,
> Whose eyes were blue, with rowan-berry lips,
> With hair curled honey-colored to her hips.
>
> ... with so huge a sense
> Of her nakedly worn magnificence
> I forget cruelty and past betrayal,
> careless of where the next bright bolt may fall.

Graves goes on to describe the Muse or White Goddess as "a lovely, slender woman with a hooked nose, deathly pale face, lips red as rowan berries, startlingly blue eyes and long fair hair." This, minus the blonde tresses, is an accurate physical description of the woman who first sand-blasted Graves' fragile psyche back in 1926. Graves later writes "The White Goddess is anti-domestic; she is the perpetual "other woman," and her part is difficult indeed for a woman of sensibility to play for more than a few years, because the temptation to commit suicide in simple domesticity lurks in every maenad's and muse's heart."

One's initial instinct is to scoff at this pronouncement. But, in a sublime irony, after Riding married Schuyler Jackson she did at last succeed in committing suicide, of the domestic sort. As Richard Perceval Graves slyly observes, "she abandoned [poetry] in 1939 as an inadequate means of telling the final truth about things" and retired with her husband to a quiet life in Florida, where she worked on a study of language, published after her death as *A New Foundation for the Definition of Words and Supplementary Essays* (University Press of Virginia, 1997). A worthy project, but, one can't help but think, a bit of a comedown for the sibylline author of the *Covenant of Literal Morality the First Protocol*, whose followers in earlier days compared her to Jesus Christ, and who called herself Finality.

Still, numerous women artists have opted out of simple domesticity (which is never all that simple, anyway) to pursue their own muses, male or female. In fiction we find the poignant Monster in Mary Shelley's *Frankenstein*, Heathcliff in Emily Bronte's *Wuthering Heights*, Virginia Woolf's eponymous *Orlando* and Colette's *Cheri*. There is also Jane Bowles and her Moroccan female muse, "the wild and cunning, the fearful and the tough, the powerful and the childlike" Cherifa (*A Little Original Sin: The Life and Work of Jane Bowles*, by Millicent Dillon); the British writer Lady Caroline Blackwood, who could safely claim the Triple

Crown of 20th century Musedom—a novelist of some note, she also played muse to painter Lucien Freud, composer Israel Citkowitz, and poet Robert Lowell; Margaret Wise Brown who had passionate attachments to the actress Michael Strange (nee Blanche Oelrichs, once wed to John Barrymore) and James Stillman Rockefeller Jr. In *The Lives of the Muses*, Francine Prose provides a thoughtful assessment of the relationship between George Balanchine and his muse, the dancer Suzanne Farrell; yet she makes no mention of Isadora Duncan and her notorious muses, the designer Gordon Craig and especially the Russian poet Sergei Esenin, of whom Duncan said, "You know, I'm a mystic. While I slept my soul left my body and ascended into the world where souls meet—and there I met the soul of Sergei."

Today the popular image of Duncan seems risible, what with her flowing scarves and her proclamation that "All my lovers have been geniuses; it's the one thing upon which I insist". But in trading the Mystic for the MFA, artists (and their adherents) have sacrificed something:

> The sense of illumination and fulfillment that comes alike to the lover, the poet, the philosophic or religious mystic, which seems to give the clue that makes intelligible to us the poet's representation of transition from joyful love, through pain and frustration, to spiritual ecstasy, as continuous (Bodkin).

Francine Prose nails the essence of the Muse as yearning, and the relationship between muse and artist as both erotic and discursive. "The muse is often that person with whom the artist has the animated imaginary conversations, the interior dialogues we all conduct, most commonly with someone we cannot get out of our minds." What Prose misses, I think, is the mystical element, the Mystery that animates this conversation between a poet and her muse. As Anne Sexton puts it, "And we are magic talking to itself/noisy and alone" ("You, Doctor Martin").

Laura Riding, in the eerie and incantatory "Poet: A Lying Word," becomes the poet invoking herself as Muse:

> It is a false wall, a poet: it is a lying word. It is a wall that closes and does not.
>
> This is no wall that closes and does not. It is a wall to see into, it is no other season's height. Beyond it lies no depth and height of further travel, no partial courses. Stand against me then and stare well through me then. Like wall of poet here I rise, but am no poet as walls have risen between next and next and made false end to leap. A last, true wall am I you may but stare me through.
>
> And the tale is no more of the going: no more a poet's tale of a going false-like to a seeing. The tale is of a seeing true-like to a knowing: there's but to stare the wall through now, well through.

Sappho in one of her fragments (these are from poet Anne Carson's brilliant 2002 translation) gives us perhaps the most succinct description of the artist's relationship to her Muse—"I long and seek after." In another fragment, Sappho testifies to the effect of an encounter with what the British writer Oliver Onions named the Beckoning Fair One: "never more damaging O Eirena have I encountered you."

Always, the interplay between Beckoner and beckoned is fraught: the threat of one being consumed or obliterated by the other is constant. Yet it is precisely this tension, this tango macabre, that underscores the erotic nature of the relationship between artist and muse, suspended as it is between longing and dread, the yearning to possess and the knowledge that capture is so often destructive of the very object of desire.

II

I first encountered John Fowles' work twenty-five years ago. I was in the hospital post-surgery, hooked up to an IV morphine drip; *The Magus* was the sole book I'd brought with me, though friends who visited gave me John Cheever's recently-published *Collected Stories*, which I also was reading—if "reading" is the correct description for what I did in the dazed, hallucinatory state I occupied during my recovery. I'd entered the hospital not knowing if I'd make it out again, and I'm not sure why I chose *The Magus* to accompany me on what I was terrified would be a one-way trip. The novel's cover resembled that of "Goat's Head Soup," not my favorite Rolling Stones album. There were intimations of magic, which I liked; but these were very vague, and I do recall realizing fairly early on that the book contained no real magic, at least not what I called magic. I'd never read anything by Fowles, though I had notions of a successful writer who dealt in louche subjects—adultery, kidnapping; something about butterflies, a childhood passion of mine. I was on a D.H. Lawrence kick at the time, and in fact Lawrence is not a bad literary companion to Fowles, though I didn't realize that for many years.

This was all during a brief, unhappy hiatus in what was too-quickly passing for my life. I'd been forced to move back in with my parents, having flunked out of university and subsequently proved myself very bad at anything but drinking and taking drugs. Back in New York, I got a job at a bookstore, which was where I found *The Magus*, recently reissued in a revised edition. I borrowed it but never paid for it: in a state somewhere between panic and exhilaration at finding myself still alive, I quit the store and moved out of my parents' house two days after I was released from the hospital, returning to D.C. to make a second stab at becoming a writer.

I'd like to say *The Magus* was instrumental in all this, but it wasn't. The truth is, I remembered almost nothing of the book save a dreamy impression of blinding blue sky, a stone stairway, some masks; though I suspect it may have colored an iconic dream I had the night before my surgery. The fact is, I hated the book, and subsequent rereadings haven't done much to change my mind. Nicolas Urfe, the protagonist, is an insufferable prig. God knows why all the women in the novel throw themselves at him: he's arrogant and smug, and the women themselves seem tired vestiges of an earlier time, English "birds" with too much eyeliner, too-bright clothes, voices too loud or too soft by turns.

I returned to *The Magus* recently, in an effort to see what others see in it; or, no—to be honest, to see what one other sees in it. Fowles is a writer noted for his use of a muse—his late wife, Elizabeth—and I have an epistolary muse who is a careful reader of Fowles' work. My muse once commented that his side of our correspondence consisted of "gestures to evoke your response," and so when he gestured at Fowles, I paid attention. This is what writers do when their muses beckon.

Of contemporary writers, John Fowles probably best charted that perilous terra incognita where muse and artist meet, most successfully in *The Collector* (1964) and *The French Lieutenant's Woman* (1969), though also in other works, including *The Magus* (1965; revised 1977) and *Mantissa* (1982), a book-length conversation between a writer and the muse Erato. "Perhaps it is that I am hunting the woman archetype," Fowles wrote in his journal in 1954. But his quarry is not so much the Eternal Feminine, but the Mystery she represents; a mystery that, for Fowles, was often entwined with the natural world. Fowles' biographer, Eileen Warburton, notes that "Knowledge of the natural world...was a profoundly felt experience, a near mystical identification." In a 1949 entry in his journal, when he was 23, Fowles writes that "Being a poet, divining beauty, is like divining nature—a gift. It does not matter if ones does not create. It is enough to have the poetic vision.

To see the beauty hidden. As I did tonight...I felt it all exactly in a moment, such a rush of impressions that they can hardly be seized" (The Journals: Volume I).

Fowles' best work deals with the attempt to "seize" this moment of mystical apprehension, both in his life and his fiction, as evidenced, first, in a journal entry from March 1950, and then in an epiphanic scene from *The French Lieutenant's Woman*:

> The wood is deserted and I walk quietly down the paths, listening to birds, feeling content to be in the real country again and alone, after so long. I still feel the old pantheistic sympathy, the feeling that I know everything that's going on, the delight in little things, little scenes, in the ever changing atmosphere of each second. A great tit's cap, brilliantly glossy and iridescent in the day's brightness. Jays screeching, a missel-thrush, robins, singing. Fragrant blossoms, Clumps of primroses, and the sweet taste of violets.

And from *The French Lieutenant's Woman*:

> The trees were dense with singing birds—blackcaps, whitethroats, thrushes, blackbirds, the cooing of woodpigeons...Charles felt himself walking through the ages of a bestiary, and one of such beauty, such minute distinctness, that every leaf in it, each small bird, each song it uttered, came from a perfect world...He stood...astonished perhaps more at his own astonishment at this world's existing so close, so within reach of all that suffocating banality of ordinary day...It seemed to announce a far deeper and stranger reality. . .

This "deeper and stranger reality," the secret world hidden within our own mundane one, is the Mystery at the heart of John Fowles' work. It is a mystery inextricably tied to a green Eros, a woman glimpsed in the wild places, the lost domain. The eponymous French Lieutenant's Woman, Sarah Woodruff, is first seen by the novel's male protagonist Charles Smithson in "a little south-facing dell, surrounded by dense thickets of brambles and dogwood; a kind of minute green amphitheatre." Sweet woodruff is an herb used in making May Wine, traditionally drunk on May Day, the neopagan's Beltane and a day sacred to Graves' White Goddess. Sarah Woodruff indeed functions as an avatar of the Goddess or Muse, first intriguing, then obsessing, and eventually deranging Charles.

Fowles first encountered the fictional notion of the lost domain in 1963. This is when he read Alain-Fournier's short novel *The Wanderer*. As a young teenager Fournier (born Henri Henri-Alban Fournier, 1886) fell under the spell of the French Symbolists; a few years later he visited London, where he was equally entranced by the written and visual work of the Pre-Raphaelites (who helped inspire the Symbolist movement). At nineteen Fournier had the same sort of fleeting, yet obsessive encounter with a young woman that derailed the fictional Charles Smithson. In 1913, a year before his death, Fournier said of her, "That was really the only being in the world who could have given me peace and repose. It is now probably that I shall never achieve peace in this world." (*The Wanderer*)

Fate didn't give him much a chance. A soldier in the first months of World War I, he died in an ambush at Saint-Remy on September 22, 1914.

I will admit to finding *The Wanderer* thin gruel, its prose not improved by being overheated; very much an adolescent's novel, and, I think very much a male adolescent's fantasy. Seventeen-year-old Augustin Meaulnes is idolized by his younger friend Francois Seural, the book's narrator. The early part of the novel is taken up with dull schoolboy hijinks and schoolyard warfare: bullies, wicked teachers and the like. Then Meaulnes runs away, and stumbles upon a strange village that seems lost in time, medieval in its architecture and also in the dress and behavior of its inhabitants. A child-wedding is being celebrated, and Meaulnes is caught up in the excitement of the preparations. He has a brief encounter with a lovely young girl named Yvonne de Galais and immediately falls in love with her. The following day Meaulnes leaves the strange village, but he spends the rest of his life in a vain quest to find the road back to the Lost Domain, to recapture the sense of enchantment of that first meeting with Yvonne, and all the potent yearning and rapturous desire of adolescence. And while he does eventually find her—though not in the village where they first met—not even marriage to Yvonne can make him happy. The poor girl dies soon after the birth of their daughter.

Still, the novel continues to have its admirers, including the artist Jamie Wyeth, and Fowles had a profound sense of recognition upon reading it:

> *Le Grand Meaulnes*. This is the first time I have read it. A strange experience, Crusoe-like, seeing those footprints in the sand, knowing that after all one is not the first on this island. Because the green ghost behind every line in Le GM is brother to that I want in *The Magus*... the purpose is the same. Mystery, pure mystery. (Journals)

The essence of this "green ghost," the unworldly longing and sense of immersion in a deeper and stranger reality that the everyday, is summed up in a brief passage from *The Wanderer*:

> There he [Meaulnes] was, mysterious, a stranger in the midst of this unknown world, in the room he had chosen. What he had found surpassed all his hopes. And it was

> enough now for his joy to recall, in the high wind, the face of that girl who turned toward him.

"The face of that girl who turned toward him" eerily prefigures Sarah Woodruff as Charles first sees her, standing on the quay at Lyme Regis:

> She turned to look at him—or as it seemed to Charles, through him. It was not so much what was positively in that face which remained with him after their first meeting, but all that was not as he expected. . . Again and again, afterwards, Charles thought of that look as a lance; and to think so is of course not merely to describe an object but the effect it has.

This piercing look is the gaze of the Muse that transfixes the observer, Graves' "next bright bolt" hurtling to freeze the artist, Medusa-like, so that s/he returns, again and again, willingly or not, to that first inspired instant of enchantment. It is the stare of The Beckoning Fair One, who in Oliver Onions' chilling story destroys the middle-aged novelist Paul Oleron when he tries to "recapture that first impression" of "the new unknown, coy, jealous, bewitching Beckoning Fair... !" Onions' portrait of the doomed novelist attempting to do this is uncannily (I might say, depressingly) acute.

His fantastic attempt was instantly and astonishingly successful. He could have shouted with triumph as he entered the room; it was as if he had escaped into it. Once more, as in the days when his writing had had a daily freshness and wonder and promise for him, he was conscious of that new ease and mastery and exhilaration and release. The air of the place seemed to hold more oxygen; as if his own specific gravity had changed, his very tread seemed less ponderable. The flowers in the bowls, the fair proportions of the meadowsweet-colored panels and mouldings, the polished floor, and the loft and faintly starred ceiling, fairly laughed their welcome. Oleron actually laughed back, and spoke aloud.

"Oh, you're pretty, pretty!" he flattered it.

Then he lay down on his couch. (75)

Oleron has rented an old house in which to complete his novel. It is a house with an unfortunate history. The previous resident, also an artist, died a suspected suicide, though it's apparent to the reader that he has been literally consumed by the house's rapacious Muse. But there is never a sense in Onions' superb tale that the Beckoning Fair One is just a ghost, the revenant of a mere mortal woman. Rather she is a destructive, ravishing force brought to life by the artist's own obsessive desire to create; in Oleron's case, the burning need to write a novel with a heroine so winsome, capricious, adorable, jealous, wicked, beautiful, inflaming, and altogether evil, that men should stand amazed. She was coming over him now; he knew by the alteration of the very air of the room when she was near him; and that soft thrill of bliss that had begun to stir in him never came unless she was beckoning, beckoning .

Fowles best describes his own experience of writing through or about his particular Beckoning Fair Ones in his 1977 essay "Hardy and the Hag" in *Wormholes: Essays and Occasional Writings*, 1998. It's a fascinating piece of work, despite some very silly Freudian trumpery about the origins of creativity in auto-erotic attachment of the male infant to his mother, a theory which Fowles says "helps to explain why all through more recent human history, men have seemed better adapted—or more driven—to individual artistic expression than women." I can't say if I'm better adapted than my masculine counterparts, but I'll state here that I have made ample use of muses, always male, in my own work, and assume that readers can make the great leap of faith that Fowles (as well as Robert Graves) was unable to, in imagining both male and female objects of desire.

Fowles calls his muse figure "The Well-Beloved," after the Hardy novel which inspired the essay; "a young female sexual ideal of some kind, to be attained or pursued (or denied) by himself [the writer] hiding behind some male character." The writer's obsession with this ideal becomes powerful enough to have repercussions in his daily routine. "Against this constant emotional fugue must be set the real presence of the woman the novelist spends his life with." In Fowles' case, this real presence was his wife, Elizabeth, the woman who had acted as muse for both *The Magus* and *The French Lieutenant's Woman*. She was also Fowles' best reader and editor, guiding him towards the famous double endings of *The French Lieutentant's Woman*— "The mystery of Sarah ... is not answered ... In fact to my way of thinking this novel should end with no answer but only an implied one of tragedy" (Warburton 195).

John and Elizabeth Fowles remained faithful to each other during their 33-year-marriage. Still, in "Hardy and the Hag" Fowles writes about "imaginative infidelity" and the "erotic elusiveness, unattainability" of "the hunt of the Well-Beloved," that perennially doomed quest of any artist; "its attainment no more feasible than that the words on the page can become the scene they describe."

Fowles' Well-Beloved appears, in one form or another, in nearly all his works. The 19th century gave us untold examples of other Beckoning Fair Ones, including Keats' Belle Dame Sans Merci, wild-eyed and perilous, as well as the enigmatic women who filled the canvases of the Belgian Symbolist painter Fernand Khnopff,

... simultaneously near to and far from the scrutiny which tried to annex her. Always, and simultaneously, vague and precise. Always and simultaneously single and double. Always and simultaneously sensual and absent, strong and delicate. . . Motionless, even when threatened by the serpent. Threatened by it? Its accomplice, rather. (*Symbolist and Symbolism*, Robert L. Delevoy)

This sense of a creature eternally straddling two worlds—the real world, and the artist's vision embodied in its presiding spirit—is what defines the muse as a liminal creature. And through his creative process—itself a liminal experience—the artist also becomes a liminal being. I think this is what gives encounters between artist and muse their sense of psychic peril: this constant passage between the borders of the real and the imagined, with the constant threat of one or the other becoming trapped—by creative sterility or simple domesticity, by madness or murderous violence—on the wrong side of the threshold.

And if all else was falling away from Oleron, gladly was he letting it go. So do we all when our Fair Ones beckon. Quite at the beginning we wink, and promise ourselves that we will put Her Ladyship through her paces, neglect her for a day, turn her own jealous wiles against her, flout and ignore her when she comes wheedling ... but in the end all falls away. She beckons, beckons, and all goes.

Fortunately the artist has some arrows in her own quiver to keep the Fair Ones at bay, chief among them the willingness to acknowledge, from the outset, the futility of any attempt to capture and detain a muse, on the page or in a penthouse. This is creative self-preservation on the artist's part. As Fowles puts it, "the Well-Beloved is never a face, but rather the congeries of affective circumstances in which it is met; as soon as it inhabits one face, its erotic energy (that is, the author's imaginative energy) begins to drain away"("Hardy and the Hag").

I can attest to the success of this artistic catch-and-release program: if the creative endeavour is a battle (which it often is; for me, anyway), winning it—completing the novel, the painting, the performance—can be both exhausting and depressing. Ultimately no one cares as much as the artist (certainly not our Beckoning Fair Ones), and she's left like the triumphant knights at the end of E.R.

Eddison's *The Worm Ouroboros,* heartbreakingly crestfallen at the realization that their great, world-shattering war is over: NOW what are they going to do?

Fortunately a benign goddess waves her hand and, as in Valhalla, the battle begins anew. And so with writing. As Fowles notes,

The cathartic effect of tragedy bears a resemblance to the unresolved note on which some folk music ends, whereas there is something in the happy ending that resolves not only the story, but the need to embark upon further stories. If the writer's secret and deepest joy is to search for an irrecoverable experience, the ending that announces the attempt has one again failed may well seem the more satisfying. ("Hardy and the Hag")

My first Beckoning Fair One made a fairly dramatic entrance thirty years ago, in a numinous dream that transformed my life. Since then others have come and gone, and sometimes even that first muse returns—older now, as I am, but still recognizable, still unsettling, still tied to the sound of the night wind in the leaves—and takes up residence in my head, not to be dislodged till I give him his place on the page. This is a good haunting: it makes for good hunting, bringing the muse to ground.

But inevitably there comes a day, or week, or month, or year, when a Fair One does not beckon. I've learned then to heed the poet Theodore Roethke's quiet statement of faith in one's own power to create—

A lively understandable spirit
Once entertained you.
It will come again.
Be still.
Wait.

—"It was beginning winter" (*The Collected Poems of Theodore Roethke*)

Art is change, writing is change, as life is. I think the essence of the relationship between artist and muse is that it is an acknowledgement that one of us—the artist—has been changed by the latter: willingly or not; permanently, in a life's work; or for the short term, in one book, one poem, one song, one film. What remains on page or canvas is the record of that change. Muses come and go, just as artists do, but for a little while, at least—as long as the song lasts, as long as the story does—we can subvert that laws that keep the Beckoning Fair Ones in one world and ourselves in another, and shimmer briefly on the same plane.

In her life, Laura Riding fought hard to get the last word; Robert Graves stole much of her fire for *The White Goddess*, but I will give his Muse the last word here, and quote from her lovely long poem "Benedictory" —an artist's blessing if ever there was one.

The mystery wherein we
Accustomed grew as to the dark
Has now been seen enough—
I have seen, you have seen.

It seems not now distressful
Or yet too much delighted in.
It was a mystery endured
Until a fuller sense befall.

A blessing on us all, on our last folly,
That we part and give blessing.
Yet a folly to be done
A greater one to spare.

For in no wise shall it be
As it is, as it has been.
A blessing on us all,

That we shall in no wise be as we were.

(from "Benedictory in *Laura Riding Selected Poems: in Five Sets,* pages 84-86)

References

Bodkin, Maud. *Archetypal Patterns in Poetry: Psychological Studies of Imagination.* London: Oxford University Press, 1934.

Delevoy, Robert L. *Symbolists and Symbolism.* Trans. Barabara Bray. New York: Rizzoli, 1978.

Donoghue, Denis. *Speaking of Beauty.* New Haven and London: Yale University Press, 2003.

Alain-Fournier. *Le Grand Meaulnes* 1913. English *The Wanderer.* Trans.Françoise Delisle. New York: Houghton Mifflin, 1928.

Fowles, John. *The Collector* London, 1964.

Fowles, John. *The French Lieutenant's Woman* London, 1969.

Fowles, John. *The Journals: Volume I.* Edited and with an introduction by Charles Drazin. London 2003.

Fowles, John. *The Magus*, London, 1966

Fowles, John. *Wormholes: Essays and Occasional Writings.* London: Jonathan Cape, 1998.

Graves, Richard Perceval. *Robert Graves: the Years with Laura: 1926-1940. 1990*

Graves, Robert. *The White Goddess: A Historical Grammar of Poetic Myth*. Faber & Faber, London Rev. ed. 1958.

Harrison. *Prolegomena to a Study of Greek Religion* ,Cambridge University Press, 1908.

The Last Wave. Dir. Peter Weir. 1977.

Mirrlees, Hope. *Lud-in the Mist*, New York, Alfred A. Knopf, 1927

Onions, Oliver. *The Beckoning Fair One.* Widdershins. London, Martin Secker 1911.

Prose, Francine. *The Lives of the Muses: Nine Women and Artists They Inspired.* HarperCollins, New York 2003.

Riding, Laura. "Poet: A Lying Word," in *Selected Poems: in Five Sets.* London: Faber & Faber, 1970.

Roethke, Theodore. *The Collected Poems of Theodore Roethke.* Anchor Press/Doubleday, Garden City, New York 1975.

Warburton, Eileen. *John Fowles: A Life in Two Worlds.* New York: Viking, 2004.

Calliope
The Muse of Epic Poetry

The over-produced slickness of the spandex and make-up clad hair metal bands of the 80s produced a sort of critical torpor among metal listeners; heads still banged, but without much enthusiasm. Enter Calliope. Orion's down-tuned distorted guitar work, characterized by extreme brutality, intensity and speed, supported by complex drum work of Petroukas would have been enough to awaken the sleep-walking metal-heads of the day. But Calliope took the bold step of composing lyrics by riffing on passages from the Iliad. When lead-vocalist Strand growled, "Why, son of Peleus, do you chase an immortal? Me you cannot kill, for death can take no hold upon me" even the most jaded critics sat up and took notice.

Deuce McMichaels
Liner notes to ***Thrashing Troy: The Calliope Tribute Album***
Epic Records

Scraps of Eutopia

Ruth Nestvold

IMAGINE THESE TWO YOUNG women, on a cruise ship to the Old Country, destination Paris, a city synonymous with life and culture for generations of young people. They are leaning on the railing, the wind in their hair and freedom in their eyes. The hems of their dresses barely reach their knees. It is the roaring twenties, and they belong to the first generation of women who can undertake such a journey alone, especially with their ankles clearly visible. One of the women, Olivia Seton, has even left her children behind with their grandmother to go on this trip with her friend, Chloe Ramsay. Chloe had to work hard to persuade her, but persuade her she did.

Now imagine they had never gone. Chloe Ramsay never would have written her famed "Eutopia"; T. S. Eliot never would have been compelled to attack her; Virginia Woolf would have lacked much of her inspiration for *A Room of One's Own*; and Ernest Hemingway never would have written his celebrated story, "Women Without Men."

Their innocent trip changed the course of literature.
Mary Carmichael, *A Life's Adventure*

Although she was undoubtedly an excellent writer, Chloe Ramsay's work fell short of true greatness. Her most famous poem, "Eutopia," while epic in its scope, was too derivative to put her squarely in the ranks of the best and most original writers of the twentieth century. Her reputation is based largely upon the feminist content of her work and her alleged intimacy with Virginia Woolf, never proven[i]. Mary Carmichael's biography of Ramsay, A Life's Adventure, is told with a novelist's gift for plot and narrative, but is unconcerned with the literary quality of Ramsay's oeuvre[ii]. It has drawn considerable popular attention to the poet, however, and as a result, it cannot be ignored in a treatment of the subject at hand.

Charles Biron, "Eutopia Wasted"

April is only cruel to those
For whom forgetful snow is a blessing,
And the green of a Spring meadow
Too bright to gaze on.

Chloe Ramsay, "Eutopia"

It is widely acknowledged that Ramsay borrowed the structure of her magnum opus, "Eutopia," from Eliot's "The Waste Land," but in all other respects, the two works are completely different. She doesn't define herself through Eliot, she defines herself against him[iii]. The tone of Eliot's work is pessimistic and elitist, making it a

---

[i] For this type of unfounded argument, see for example Willa Armstrong, "'A Sight that has Never Been Seen': Chloe Ramsay's Influence on Virginia Woolf," LITM, 22, 2 (2002): 301.
[ii] Carmichael even goes so far as to imply that simply by going to Paris with her friend, Ramsay achieved something of literary note. See A Life's Adventure, London: Hogarth Publications, 1985: 255 ff.
[iii] Despite repeated attacks by Charles Biron, I continue to maintain that this is different than "derivative." See for example the chapter, "Eutopia Wasted," in The Lost Generation: A Reexamination. New York: Columbia University Press, 2003: 95-110.

paean to the joys of intellectual Weltschmerz, but "Eutopia," while suffused by the mildly ironic voice of the lyrical persona, is a celebration of the freedom Ramsay found in the "new world" of the old: the artistic promised land which was Paris in the years between the wars. As opposed to many of her male contemporaries, Ramsay had no fear of the joys of creativity and sensuality–perhaps because as a woman she had no need to fear emasculation.

Willa Armstrong, "Scraps of Eutopia"

We had often talked about our mutual dream while working in the lab together; our dream of visiting the Old World and seeing the splendors of Europe. It was only a dream, harmless, completely unreal, a thing to pass the time while working on a medication for the treatment of anemia or examining an experiment in a petri dish. Chloe painted life in Europe in the most brilliant colors, using her gift for words and her vivid imagination to make it come alive for me.

But then she inherited a small fortune from an obscure aunt, and suddenly the means were there to make the dream a reality.

Olivia Seton, *A Life on the Sidelines: An Autobiography*

I remember Chloe and Olivia -- everyone did, that spring. They were both pretty and fresh and intelligent, one dark, one light, and everywhere you went you would see them, they were so easy to see.

Ernest Hemingway, *A Moveable Feast*

Nothing had prepared them for the Paris they found on their arrival. Through a friend of Sylvia Beach, they were introduced to Natalie Barney's salon and from there, to the parties put on by Gertrude Stein and Alice B. Toklas. At this time, Chloe only had a few poems in obscure literary journals to her name, but she must have impressed the hostesses, because she and Olivia quickly became regulars in the Paris salons.

From Olivia's autobiography and Chloe's letters, we know that Chloe was increasingly enamored of the cultural life of the French capital, the exhilaration of the environment of like-minded, artistic people, so different from what she saw as the repressive, Puritanical atmosphere of New England. Not only that, there was a new breed of woman in the French capitol, women who cut their hair short and put on trousers, women who traveled alone and opened bookstores—women who lived with each other openly. It was the freedom and the hope of this culture which Chloe celebrated in her great epic poem, "Eutopia."

What Olivia's autobiography does not tell us, and Chloe's poetry only implies, is the personal drama that led up to Chloe remaining in Paris and Olivia returning to America, and the silence between the two very best friends which lasted for nearly four years.

Mary Carmichael, *A Life's Adventure*

While Ramsay was admittedly a popular figure in the "moveable feast" that was Paris in the twenties, it is quite a stretch to assert that her popularity could be equated with literary influence. When she and her friend Olivia Seton met Virginia Woolf and Vita Sackville-West, Ramsay had not yet even begun work on her "Eutopia," making it foolish to claim its ideas influenced two British writers of much greater stature[iv].

It is even more foolish to assert that she somehow embodied a freedom which Woolf and Sackville-West took to heart. It is obvious from Woolf's letters and journals that her enthusiasms were ardent and many, but there is no proof that any of these relationships was anything other than platonic.

Charles Biron, "Tales of Two Women"

[iv] One particularly vocal proponent of this is Willa Armstrong; see Border Crossings. Austin: University of Texas Press, 1990: 226-238.

In Paris in the 1920s, and to a lesser extent in London as well, women loving each other became a public phenomenon for the first time in centuries in Western culture. The way had been paved in the early decades of the new century by Stein and Toklas, by Colette and Missy, by Barney and Vivien. Later, numerous other literary figures joined their ranks: Radclyffe Hall, Djuna Barnes, Vita Sackville-West, Virginia Woolf[v]. A culture came into bloom during these years which would disappear entirely with the advent of WWII. Not only are many of the female figures of this movement forgotten, with standard literary histories recognizing little beyond the male authors of the "lost generation," it was not until the nineteen-sixties that women could again publicly appear as lovers.

Can it be purely chance that Virginia Woolf cited the characters Chloe and Olivia and their relationship to each other in *A Room of One's Own* as something the world had never seen before? I think not. In 1928, Woolf was in Paris with her lover, Vita Sackville-West. By this time, Ramsay had made a name for herself in the Paris literary scene, and interestingly enough, Olivia Seton, who had left Ramsay four years before to return to her children, was visiting her friend again for the first time.

Willa Armstrong, "A Sight That Has Never Been Seen: Chloe Ramsay's Influence on Virginia Woolf"

---

[v] While most scholars now accept that Virginia Woolf and Vita Sackville-West had an affair which lasted several years, some are still resistant to the notion. Charles Biron, for example, clings to the idea that while Woolf may have been infatuated with Sackville-West, there was never a physical relationship, and he flatly denies all rumors connecting Woolf and Ramsay, emphasizing the strength of the love between "Virginia and Leonard." See "Tales of Two Women," EMLA 97,3 (1999): 556-574.

I do not know whether man or woman—
I do not know!
The silhouette is freedom and hope.

Chloe Ramsay, "Eutopia"

Just as external elements can have an undesirable effect on any given tradition, so too does Chloe Ramsay disrupt the existing order in a way which goes beyond the bounds of aesthetic license. Novelty in art is not revolution; artistic innovation is foreshadowed by the works that went before it, and with the new work, the artistic order is always already changed.

T. S. Eliot, "Crimes Against Order and Art"

Given Ramsay's ultimate fate, even the rumors of her life-affirming attitude must be said to be greatly exaggerated. What precisely is left of her life and her oeuvre when one strips away the unfounded tales and claims? She was an American in Paris in the 1920s and '30s, one of many, a minor figure in the major movement of the Lost Generation. While Hemingway and Fitzgerald were said to admire her poetry, Virginia Woolf never even reviewed her work; by contrast, she actively promoted the work of T. S. Eliot, she and her husband publishing his masterpiece "The Waste Land" in the Hogarth Press. Woolf was obviously as aware as anyone which of the two was the better poet.

Charles Biron, "Eutopia Wasted"

Shouldn't we ask ourselves why an anti-Semitic poet with a fascist cultural understanding is regarded as more serious than a poet who celebrated an island of freedom in the midst of millennia of oppression? Why the aesthetic principles promoted by such figures as T.S. Eliot and Ezra Pound and Paul de Man have become an accepted and coherent intellectual tradition? Certainly, Ramsay was indebted to Eliot, and "Eutopia" would be inconceivable without "The Waste Land." Nonetheless, I think the question still deserves consideration: what does it say about our culture, about our literary institutions and aesthetic values, when fascism and cultural elitism hold more interest and sway than hope and pluralism?

Willa Armstrong, "Scraps of Eutopia"

Chloe could not imagine returning to the United States, even when the situation in Europe grew dangerous. In Paris, she had found a life she had not even dared to dream of before we arrived there, despite her vivid imagination. To her, America would always be associated with the straight-laced, Puritan, New England family she had escaped, and no matter how much or how often we assured her that things were changing here too, that she could make her own Eutopia in a city like New York or Boston, she would only say that she had found her home and there she would stay.

Some will perhaps say that the choice she made betrayed the principles of hope she upheld in "Eutopia," but they cannot understand how much she invested in "her" Paris, how much a part of her it had become. And even in the end, I do not think she allowed bitterness to poison her attitude. Initially, she worked with the resistance movement against the forces poised to take over her beloved city, while all the other literary figures she had shared Friday evenings with except Gertrude Stein had fled. Even her suicide note contains thoughts of hope and affirmation:

Eutopia is and must be utopia, a place that can never be. But that is why we must create it again and again. And it will be created again, of that I am sure. It will not be perfect and it will not last, but it will be a place of freedom and tolerance, a place where others can be as happy as I have been here.

Olivia Seton, *A Life on the Sidelines: An Autobiography*

Chloe Ramsay's suicide was a logical consequence of the developments in Europe at the time. She could have left; she had an American passport as opposed to some of her Jewish friends, who were unwanted anywhere in the world, even the United States. But America was no longer home to her, if it had ever been. When the brown menace began to sweep across Europe, all that was left her were scraps of Eutopia.

Willa Armstrong, "Scraps of Eutopia"

Even prisons have keys.

Chloe Ramsay, "Eutopia"

Clio
The Muse of History

And Clio Wept
1917
Alphonse Josephe de Chiodo
28 by 42, Oil.
Private collection.

Third in a series of oils depicting scenes from the Homestead Steel Strike of 1892. De Chiodo shows Clio, the Muse of History perched atop one of the makeshift ramparts of steel, pig iron and scrip iron which shielded the workers from the Pinkertons' shots, her white robe freckled with rust and soot. In lieu of the traditional scroll she brandishes a hammer. Her gaze reaches the Pinkertons. Tears of fury and sorrow trickle down her dusty cheeks.

She Who Remembers

Dianna Rodgers

MY MOTHER TAUGHT ME that in the beginning of time, all the people knew each other. They lived the same lives, ate the same thing, spoke the same language. And everyone remembered each other's stories. They dwelled in a land of green grasses and sparkling waters, sweet honey and mountain buffalo. They hunted and wove baskets and made love. And though they loved their land, they grew curious about the land in the skies.

So they decided to rise up to the heavens and see the lands where Achafa Chito, the Great One, lived. They piled gray stones to build a pillar that would reach unto the heavens. Four days they worked, each night lying down exhausted next to their labors, each morning rising to find the rocks scattered, the pillar gone. Still, they longed to see the Great One's lands and each day they rebuilt.

On the fourth day, in his anger, Achafa Chito scattered not only the rocks, but the people as well. And when they awoke, the people no longer recognized each other. The language they spoke had changed and was now shared by only a few. Few could remember other's stories and only fragments of their own. Some of the people fought each other and some wandered away. Thus, the different tribes were born.

My people, the Oklans, stayed with the bones of the pillar,

loving Hashtahli, Grandfather Sun, and still longing for the beauty of the skies. Over time, the sacred hill of Nanhi Waya grew from the gray rocks. Without their stories, they forgot why it was a sacred place, and even forgot about Achafa Chito. But the Oklans did not stop loving the land, and knew that it was home.

Still, without our stories, we could not find our way back to the spirit and the beauty of what we once had. Achafa Chito loved his children and wanted us to remember what we had lost, so he found a worthy maiden who longed for a child. He took her to the river close by Nanhi Waya, where the soil spread black and fertile and the rocks shone gold and silver and the water ran sweet and cold. From these things, together they made a daughter and named her She Who Remembers. Her gift and her duty was to know the history of her people so that they might survive and learn and prosper and one day regain the full spirit of their ancestors.

Achafa Chito blessed her and said, “Through you, if you are strong, the Oklans will survive.”

Unlike her sisters, she did not grow tall as the willow blowing in the breezes. Still, her dark and wiry body served well as a vessel to hold all the memories of the tribe. The others teased her, calling her Shakchi, the crayfish, for the muddy color of her skin was so much darker and richer than their own. But her hair grew to her knees, black with shimmering rainbow colors glowing amidst the shiny strands.

Like the tree-climbing gray fox, she learned to spend the days high in the branches of a sweet gum, watching and learning and remembering all that each person did. And at night, she would come to the fire and spill forth the stories of the day to the people of the Oklans, or the Long Hairs as they came to call themselves.

But the people’s faces burned in shame at her tales. Shakchi was no longer welcomed at the evening fires. She learned to swallow each memory, keep it inside herself. The gentle memories of a mother nursing an otter-brown babe, or a man stroking a woman’s cheek slipped down her throat easily and soaked into her bones.

But other memories were sharp like the edges of a shell or the prickly spine of a catfish and they caught in her throat and rubbed holes in her belly. Still others were heavy like river stones and weighed her down so that she would never grow tall.

Some memories even burned like the sting of a scorpion and she told me, "Often I wished I could take my good hunting knife and cut them out of my body."

She learned to speak only when someone called upon her to share. Her own mother despaired that she would ever find a man to take a girl such as her to wife. And indeed, the young men would prance and wrestle in front of her cousins, but stop when they saw her watching them from her high perch. They knew she would remember who won and lost and who ran away in shame. Many people began to avoid her, for fear of what she might remember of them. Only when they wanted the glory of their actions recounted did they call upon She Who Remembers.

On a spring night in Hashninak, the Panther moon, loneliness filled her and she crept from her furs and wandered by the far stream where the best reeds grew for her mother's baskets. She sniffed the air, and tasted the tang of the paw-paw blossoms that would bear fruit in the month of the Blackberry moon. She smiled and this memory melted into her.

Grandmother Moon shone down, bathing her in light. In that light, she felt as beautiful as a young doe. To honor her Grandmother, she danced and sang, her voice low and honey sweet. In the grace of that night, she forgot herself.

She let her dress slide down her thighs and wrapped herself in the thick cloak of her hair. Then she swayed back and forth, back and forth to the rhythm only she could hear pounding inside of her. For each painful memory she bore, she made a dance, weaving the beat of her heart together with the sting of hurt or shame. She could feel the song of memories binding inside her, like her mother's braided baskets, the colored reeds weaving into the pattern of a story.

As each moment of joy bubbled forth, she twirled with her arms stretched out. Her hair swirled around her like a raven wing. Her heart soared above her. Her sorrows drained away and the memories were a beautiful song within her. For once, she reveled in her gift.

She thought nothing of it when it began to rain.

Spears of light struck hard across the sky, and Hilohachi, the Spirit of Thunder rumbled out of the night and stood before her. His beauty hurt her eyes. She trembled as he reached out to touch her.

"Your dance has won my heart," he said. "Long have I waited for you." He tugged on her hair and pulled her down with him. In the darkness of the night, she lay with him and became his wife. His eyes, dark coals of heat, loved her. She shuddered with his touch, feather-soft along her ribs. His lips covered her with ferocious kisses, tearing at her like the panther at his supper.

These precious memories settled in her bones and she felt their strength. Each moment with him filled her to bursting. His touch washed away the burden of the people's memories and gave to her new memories—memories that were hers alone. Never would she forget the gentleness of him, nor the fire he left burning inside of her. "Thank you. You have brought my life joy as well as duty," she whispered in the darkness.

Grandfather Sun peeked over the ridge the next morning, and she feared he would not be happy that she had created her own story. She hid her nakedness from him. Hilohachi laughed, a small rumble that shook the ground, and offered her his hand that she might go with him. Instead she ran away, shamed that with him, she had made memories of her own.

In her fear, she hid from her husband, shuddering as he called to her with his lightening and thunder. She could not bear to stand beside him in his glory. Still, when she returned to her people, she told her mother, “No longer need you worry about finding a husband for your difficult daughter.”

She could not hide from the stabbing pains of that long, first birth, for Thunder rolled through her belly, reminding her she belonged to him. And then, another memory dripped into her marrow as she felt her daughter wriggle in her arms. The baby smelled of the dew touched by early morning sunlight and when kissed, her skin tasted of the petals of a climbing rose.

The child glowed hot and bright like a star, and when She Who Remembers looked into the night sky, it seemed diminished somehow by the light of her daughter. With awe, she carried the child out to be kissed by the sweet rains sent from her Hilohachi. “Thank you for this blessing that we brought into the world,” she said.

Afraid though she was of making memories that were hers alone, again and again desire drove her out into the night to lay down with her husband. “Stay with me,” he would say to her.

Much as she wished to remain with him, she could not take his outstretched hand, knowing her task for her people was not yet done. Again and again, she brought forth a daughter, until she was blessed with nine beautiful girls, all filled with a glow of light. With the birth of each child, the sky darkened just a bit. Her love for her daughters eased some of the pain that she felt upon refusing her husband.

The daughters grew into their beauty, strange and unique and separate from the tribe. She Who Remembers knew the pain of being set apart, but her daughters found comfort in each other and in the gifts their father shared with them.

Her first daughter She named Anumpa Ikbi, the storyteller and the girl spun beautiful tales of the heroes of the Long Hairs. The second became Anoachi, the Proclaimer who told stories that reminded the people of their history. The parents would send their children to her that they might learn the old ways. Third in line, beautiful Aiukli Ikbi shared pleasing tales of love. Yakoke, the giver of pleasure taught the music of the flute to the young men so they might woo their chosen loves.

The sweetest voice came from Taola Ikhanachi, who sang songs so sad that a man's heart would ache inside his chest. Words of the spirits poured out of Ataloa Ikbi. And none could keep up with Fali, the Whirler as she danced amongst the sweet grasses. Laughter spilled from Hatak Yopula, for she brought joy wherever she stepped. And the baby girl, Aba, was named for the Heavens, for her eyes never left the stars where her father dwelt.

For time untold, She Who Remembers and her daughters lived by the water and the Long Hairs would call to them,"Come share your gifts with us tonight." My people rejoiced for the blessings of stories and songs and dances the daughters brought. And good fortune to came to the people of the Long Hairs. For many years, the people flourished and She Who Remembers was again welcome at the fires of the Oklans.

But She Who Remembers always looked to the sky, missing her husband. She had resisted him too many times, knowing her duty still lay ahead of her. The last time she had lain with him, he begged her to follow him, whispering to her of a time of hardship to come, of pale people who would crowd out the Long Hairs like the young cowbird shoves the fledgling blackbird from its nest. But again, she ran from him, torn between love and duty, holding her memories of her love tightly to her chest..

"I will not come again, not until you are ready to join me," he called after her. And he did not.

My mother had gained her children but missed her husband. In the dancing rays of the sun, she rejoiced with her daughters. But when it rained, she would retreat into her cave deep in the earth and cry for what she had let go of.

Over the long years, her greatest wisdom became the knowledge that happiness seldom lasts.

The good times flew by too swiftly. Then the white men came, greedy for land and slaves and women. In fear, Shakchi hid her daughters from the eyes of those men, especially the soldiers in blue coats, for in her heart she knew they would yearn to own Thunder's daughters just as they yearned to own all the land.

The day was hot when the blue coats told the Long Hairs they must leave their lands. The Lieutenant in charge had hair that gleamed red and gold like leaves during the harvest of the Blackberry moon and wiry curls that grew down the sides of his cheeks and over his top lip. His eyes, the muddy gray of the rocks at the bottom of the riverbed, drove cold fear into Shakchi's heart, for they showed hunger for more than a good night's hunting.

The Long Hairs wanted to keep the land of their hearts, where their children had been born and their elders had died. The young men shouted and beat their fists on their chests. But in the end, they listened to their chiefs who said it was "better to leave and live another day".

A thousand Long Hairs, many elders and children among them, gathered for the trek to the new land they were promised. Many fine gifts were also promised; wagons, blankets, food. But the lies fell like water from the tongues of the Blue Coats and the promised supplies did not appear.

One after another, the Long Hairs wore through their moccasins. The creeping sickness stalked them, laying many low, taking others to pass over into the lands beyond. Tears glistened on the face of Thunder's daughters, yet they sang and danced each night, telling stories and cheering the people onward. From their stories, heroes grew on the trail, fine singers learned to lift their voices and new tales were born. But with each blessing, the sisters lost some of their light and faded more into shadow. Many Long Hairs died, heartbroken that they would never again see the sacred mountain, Nanhi Waya.

Then they came to the Arkansas River. Its waters raged dark and nasty. Shakchi listened to the waters and knew they did not welcome a crossing. Only she stood up against the chiefs, those who had sold their lands away. “No, we cannot defy these waters. We must wait until spring when they are calm. Let us rest here and bury our dead.”

The Lieutenant rode up on his fine prancing stallion, showing no regard for the elders required to walk while he rode. He demanded to know what held them up. His eyes were hard gray ice, but his mouth forced a smile.

The Chief strode forward, ashamed that a woman would have to take a stand for his people. “We will rest here. We must care for our elders and our sick. We must make a path for our dead. We must rest and hunt and make new moccasins. This we will do.”

He turned away, his fine shirt, a gift given when he signed the treacherous treaties that gave away our lands, hung loose on him, showing how feeble he had become on the long journey.

“No,” the Lieutenant commanded. “Ford the river and then you may rest.” He stroked the yellow hair on his lip, and waited to be obeyed.

But the Chief said again to the people, “We will rest here.” And he walked away.

The Lieutenant swore. He turned to one of his bluecoats and told them to get the people back on their feet.

The Corporal was a dark man, with a full beard and a tobacco stain running through the coarse hair on his face. He stood up and spat. “They ain’t going nowhere. When the Chief says rest, they sit. When he says hunt, they scour the countryside.”

“But we have food for them,” the Lieutenant sputtered.

The corporal spat again. “Worms in the flour and maggoty meat. I wouldn’t feed that to my dog. The way we’re going, most of this bunch ain’t gonna make it anyway. Maybe we should let them rest, sir.”

The big stallion danced in a circle and the Lieutenant struggled to rein him in. Anger flared in his eyes. "This will be their last rest, then. Make camp!" He kicked his claw-like spurs into the horse's side and leapt away.

After too few days camping on the shore, the Lieutenant ordered movement and this time, the Chief agreed, though the River roared wider and deeper than ever. Many died in the crossing. For seven days they toiled through waist high water in the Arkansas swamp under leafless cypresses. Heavy sleet beat upon the trees, breaking all the small limbs and lashing the Oklans with the downfall. The little children and the old women wore nothing but cotton under-dresses, their warm deer skins long ago discarded for the dress of the whites as a way to prove their friendship with their white brothers.

On the fourth day after the river crossing, they came upon a small field of *isitos*, pumpkins gleaming red and yellow in the brown ravages of the meadow. Longing swept through their hungry bellies, but the people would not step where they had not been welcomed.

But a good white man owned that land, and pity moved his heart to let the starving people harvest his leftovers. The Long Hairs fell on the pumpkins, broke them apart and ate them raw, orange strings catching between their teeth. The women saved the seeds. That night they roasted them in the fires and counted them out to the children for the next day.

Toward the end of their journey, the nights grew longer yet. Each evening in front of the fires, Shakchi's daughters shared their gifts of stories and dances and songs with the Oklans. Anoachi Anumpa, and Aiukli took turns regaling the people with rhyming tales of lovers, the spirits and great heroes. Those three were always together, supporting each other; three bright and shining stars who made their mother's heart ache with their words. The others shared dances and songs that made the skies weep with rain. Their father rumbled his anger high in the skies as he looked down on the sad state of his children.

Shakchi watched in pride and put to memory the glory of her daughters shining lights that so filled her they burned through her skin. As she looked up, she saw the Lieutenant, his eyes gleaming in delight as he looked on Anumpa. Fear burrowed deep into Shakchi heart like the bole weevil burrows into a ball of cotton.

Every night, the Lieutenant haunted the Long Hairs camp, bringing choice bits of meat and sweet honey with which to woo Shakchi's eldest daughter. But she would have none of his gifts for herself. Instead she used the meat to make broth to feed the sick, and the honey for the coughs of young. Her sisters clustered around her, shading her from his sight.

Still, for all their generous spirit, Thunder's daughters grew weaker. Their limbs faltered as they danced and their sweet voices sank to murmurs as they sang their songs and told their stories. Their skin grew pale as that of the Blue Coats. Fear crawled through Shakchi's belly. She knew that not much time remained for them unless Anumpa succumbed to the Lieutenant, something she would never do. All the people suffered. But to see little Aba so weak her sisters had to carry her, this Shakchi could no longer bear.

In the dark of night she went to the riverside and with her knife she cut nine slices on her arms, one for each of her daughters. Then once more she dropped her dress and in her nakedness, she danced and sang with all the memories within her, tears rending her voice harsh and pain making her dance lifeless.

Finally, her husband came to her, catching her as she fell under the weight of her burdens. The ground shook with his anger. Streaks of fire danced across the sky. The rain fell heavy, each drop a painful statement of his displeasure.

"Our daughters are dying," she said, looking up into the blackness of his eyes. "I would have you save them."

He stared at her, then kissed each wound, healing the skin with his touch. In his arms, she finally felt safe, yet so tired, she wanted to curl into him and never let go. But she could not think of herself for her children were at stake.

His voice rumbled low in her ear. “I would have had you come and live with me, but time and again you refused me. And you have brought our children to this. It is time. They must come home.”

“And me as well, husband?” She trembled, knowing too well the answer she would hear.

His denial cut her to the core. “Many times you have refused me. You were the strong one then. Now I must be strong. You are truly needed here.

“Our daughters will come to live with me and I will create a place for them in the skies. But when they leave, they will take their gifts with them. For a time, some of the people will remember the stories, the songs and the dances. But those memories will fade. The Long Hairs, who would not fight for themselves, will survive by learning to live in the white man’s world, just as a fox takes refuge in an old badger’s den in time of need.

“Survive they must. So you must stay here, for your duty is to remember when they cannot. You will watch and wait until the chosen one cries out for the path to these memories. Only then may you come join us, my wife.” His lips seared her as he kissed her one last time. And then he was gone with a horrible clap that shuddered through her bones.

The next day, she walked hunched over and weary, knowing that too soon she would lose all that she had loved so that she might save our people. Anumpa, Aiukli, and Ataloa could barely stumble down the path, so weak and weary were they. But for the first of many days, Grandfather Sun shone down on the Long Hairs and warmed their path.

That night, the Lieutenant came. Fever burned in his eyes, but she knew it was lust for her daughter and not illness that made them smolder so. “I will take Anumpa into my tent and tend to her,” he said. “I have powerful medicines that will heal her and a soft bed in which she can sleep.”

Wearily Anumpa she shook her head. And with dignity, the sisters stood and began a chant, shuffling their feet in time to the beat of the drum and flute.

"Stop it," he screamed. "It will kill you. You must stop these heathen rites." And he strode forward to break the circle they had created.

Shakchi took a deep breath and jumped at the Lieutenant. He towered over her but he was unprepared for her determination. They fell, rolling over and over toward the fire.

"Crazy squaw," he cursed, trying to grab her arms. "I'll kill you for this. No one will care if one more of you die."

But that night Brother Bear must have lent Shakchi his strength. She found the long knife the lieutenant wore at his belt and pulled it as she pinned his shoulders with her knees. "I do not fear death. Nor do I fear you."

She held the knife to his neck, a thin gleam of red welling up from where she drew it across his pale skin. "We have sacrificed much to live another day."

The smell of his fear brought a smile to her face. She would have liked to kill him, then and there, but she had a job to do. With the knife, she reached up and cut off the shining cape of her hair, the glory that had originally drawn Thunder down and threw it into the fire. The blaze called forth her husband. Lightening danced across the sky and thunder roared and the stars fell from the heavens to form a path.

Anumpa, Aiukli, and Ataloa clung to each other, whirling faster and faster up the passageway of stars, until they joined together and became the brightest star in the heavens. The other sisters danced harder and faster until they too became twinkling lights that grew to a crowd in the sky. And the darkness that had been in the sky since their birth was no more.

The people fell down in wonder, proclaiming them Fichik Watalhpi, what the whites called the Pleiades. Shakchi rolled off the soldier, her heart heavy. She cared not what he did to her then, knowing only that she would survive as her husband foretold. The Lieutenant scrambled to his feet, reaching for his gun, but as the men of the Long Hairs stepped forward he hesitated. Then he spit on her and stormed away.

They traveled many more moons until finally they reached the place where the Red River met the Arkansas, where they would now have to make their home. More than a third of the Oklans had died, for they ate only acorn meal and rotten pork that the soldiers gave them. They cleared the land of tough grasses, tangled roots, and wiry post oak. They planted corn on the land where the Arkansas and the Red River met, under the watchful eyes of the Blue Coats. But the Green Corn dance had no heart without Fali there to lead them. Angry at loss of the ceremony, the Arkansas punished the people. She overflowed her banks and swept away both homes and crops.

After the flood, the Lieutenant came to look at the dead animals that lined the river and shook his head. "You have been ruined as you deserve," he said. He laughed as he rode away.

For years upon years, She Who Remembers waited by the banks of the Red River. She shrank in upon herself, developing a hard shell and burrowing in the bank like the crayfish that they had called her. Soon she became like a rock, waiting and watching for the one to come.

She slumbered, waiting for something to wake her from her half-sleep while she watched the remnants of the Long Hairs. So many of the old ways were lost when Thunder's daughters went into the skies. Only Shakchi carried their memories close, only Shakchi could still hear the sweet songs and feel the beat of the drum and the call of the flute.

Sometimes, an old one would come and offer a prayer to her, but they did not have the will to challenge what had become of the

Long Hairs world. She could tell they could not bear the memories of their people couldn't bear, to breath them and feel them beat like a hundred drums in their blood so that they had to sing and dance or die. When she cried the skies cried with her.

Then on a hot summer day, he came. He was an old spirit who smelled of the mountain buffalo and catfish that had fed his people long ago. She knew this man, had seen him as a small boy, playing with smooth white pebbles by the river. Saw him again as a teen whose spirit was strong when the elders had anointed him a warrior and honored him with one of Brother Eagle's feathers. The last time he had been here, he'd worn the blue uniform of a marine and he had shed tears for his grandfather's death. His grandfather had planted a love of the old ways in this grandson.

She watched him. It had been many years since the warrior had returned to this place. He was a man now, on the far side of his warrior ways, his eyes cold from seeing too many lives tossed aside for greed and desire, too many battles lost. She saw his memories of the horrors of a place called Viet Nam, smelled the rotting jungle, felt the blood of his men on his hands, watched as bullets stalked him as prey.

He limped to the riverbank and took some shiny medals from his pocket. He stroked each one lightly, perhaps recounting the battles which had brought him these honors. Salt tears fell down his cheeks and her heart ached for him. How many deaths had he seen; had he caused? And what had he come home to?

She Who Remembers looked deep into his weary heart. He had been a warrior for so long now he hardly knew any other road. But he was done, had left that life. To acknowledge this passing, he threw the medals into the river. The Arkansas accepted them as her due, and accepted him home. Not the home of his people of old, the holy hill of Nanhi Waya, but the new home of the Oklan's, the home they had carved out of this place forced on them by the whites.

Too long his voice had been raised in a warrior's cry. Now it was cracked and hesitant as he spoke a prayer in the old words. "Achafa Chito, Great One, hear my plea. I am of the Long Hairs, of the Okla, of the Choctaw and I have come home. Remember us, for we are still a people, we are still alive, though our blood grows faint and our ways are now mostly one with our white brothers. I call on the sisters, the Pleiades, Fichik Watalhpi to help me bring back the essence of our people."

Shakchi's heart broke to hear him call out. He knew them. Here was one who was worthy to return the gifts of her daughters to the people. She called Brother Wind to bear this man's prayer to Anumpa. And the breeze came and carried it away along with his tears. She had watched long enough. It was time. She would help this warrior bring joy back to the Long Hairs. "Please," Shakchi whispered. In the distance, thunder rumbled and she knew her husband could hear her prayers as well.

She Who Remembers shook herself, cracking off the shell of many years and once more became a woman, vibrant and alive.

His eyes widened when he saw her, legend come to life, for his grandfather had told him of her. He fell to his knees. "Grandmother," he said. "Are you the one they speak of, She Who Remembers?"

She smiled at him and reached out her hand. She had forgotten the soothing coolness of the water and rejoiced as she led this warrior into the river. He did not resist and she washed away the traces of the warrior world he had left behind, like one would wash a child. He cried in her arms. Never had she born a son, but as she cradled him, she knew that he belonged to her as much as if she had pushed him out of her body.

Together, they bent willows into half circles and tied them with strong reeds, making the lodge. Of old they would have used the hides of the buffalo and the deer, but now calico quilts and woolen blankets sufficed for a covering. She guided him to choose his rocks well, for they must be strong enough to hold the heat needed for purification.

They built a fire of hickory and oak. The smoke smelled sweet and she remembered those fires long ago when her daughters told the stories to the young ones. When this fire burned hot enough to sear her lashes, the rocks were ready. With red ocher she painted his face. He stripped, and his body bore the scars of war. She kissed each wound, with a mother's love, knowing that she could never completely heal the pain he'd suffered, but knowing too that the skin there was stronger for all that it had been torn apart.

For four days, her son fasted and prayed and cried for a vision so that he might better serve his people. The first day or two his sweat smelled of old hides burning. She stoked the flames to make the rocks sizzle so that the poisons would leach away quicker.

Finally on the last night her daughters answered his prayers. They trailed out of the sky, brilliant lights streaking to the earth and into her arms. Tears danced on her cheeks as she touched her daughters once more and soaked in the memory of their lilting voices. The river inside her thawed with the promise of spring. "Long have I waited for you," she cried. "Come meet your brother, who will bear your gifts back to the Long Hairs." And she ushered them into his lodge that they might bless him.

Afterward in the light of the full moon, I was born again into the sweet night air, for I am that man.

I stumbled into her arms, weak as a babe. She put me to her breast so that I might drink of her gift of memories. Much of the milk was sour and I balked at the bitter taste. But it also tasted of prairie skies and children's laughter and the joy of stick ball games that went on forever. Each suck lightened both her soul and mine, and yet she grieved for all that she had carried for so long. I nursed that night, starving for the knowledge of my people, then slept the deep sleep of redemption.

When the sun touched the sky, I arose, a new man with a new

purpose. We met at the river's edge. Then my mother gifted me with the last thing she had to give. I took the drum she had made for me during those days that I had fasted and prayed, and I knew I was her son now in truth. I honored the drum's life and death and life again; the deer which had given of it's body, the tree grown tall with the mother's earth to nourish it, the fire which had dried the skin and the smoky air, which made it pliable and vibrant. I smiled, showing the tooth I chipped as a child while I beat out a song. My feet moved in patterns I did not know and my lips formed words that I had never heard before.

She watched and smiled and laughed as I jumped into the air and then crouched down, imitating Brother Eagle. I had learned my lessons well. All day, I danced and sang, my feet moving to the rhythm of Thunder's daughters, my voice hitting notes not on the white man's scale.

That night once again lightening crackled amongst the stars and thunder rumbled. The stars shifted and moved. This time, they made a path for She Who Remembers. Finally it was time for her to go home. And I, as her son, sang her into heaven because her job here was done. Now, I am the one who remembers. Now I am the one who teaches the people to sing and dance and tell stories. Now the Oklans are a whole people again.

Euterpe
The Muse of Music

Launched on November 14, 1863, *H.M.S. Euterpe*, named for the Muse of Music, was a full rigged iron ship under the command of Captain Benjamin Case Wrigley. On her maiden voyage, she collided with a Welsh vessel and had to turn back to Anglesey for repairs. While in port, the crew reported seeing the ship's namesake, first in dreams, then in visions upon the deck of the ship. The captain discounted these reports as mere diversions fabricated by a mutinous element within the crew and ordered a third of the crew gaoled. Within hours, his body was found floating in the harbor alongside the *Euterpe*, dead of estrangulation by the wire of a harpe.

Wesley Bentonhurst
A Brief History of Haunted Sailing Vessels of the United Kingdom, 1923Edition

Melody

Catherine Kaspar

SHE GAZES INTO HER lap incessantly humming something unrecognizable. It's a weary tune and it goes nowhere. Never into dismal, minor digressions or familiar refrains, never picking up tempo or lapsing into marching band rhythms. She sits with half-closed eyes, her short hair carelessly brushed into place, and her clothes skewed, inside-out at times, with the buttons misaligned. Her hands slowly spoon food into her mouth, always mashed food, that she slowly swallows while she continues. She hums to keep them at bay, the doctors, the nurses, the other residents, even her family. How could I know, you ask? After all, I can't get inside her brain. I've just sat with her every day now, at every meal—that's three a day every day for four years, and twice a week at cards or bingo, always the same thing.

You add those numbers up—humming—never a word hello or goodbye. She's keeping them from overflowing onto her, overwhelming her with their inappropriate grief, with their guilt. They tell me that I don't have a clue. After all, maybe she's humming with happiness, or humming to get through the pain. Most of the family wants her to be some sort of martyr, but it's them, looking at themselves in a mirror. They want a badge for having to visit once a week, sometimes a half-hour sometimes less. Because the humming gets to them as much as it gets to us. Do the math, I say, add all those meals up, each one an hour until they get around to wheeling us away. If anyone could talk about unbearable humming, it would be me. But that's not what I'm saying.

I'm saying that some of the nurses say she's found inner peace and we should be so lucky. I often think she's overmedicated, but they just shake their heads at me like I'm a child. After all, what would I know about medicine? I've only lived on this planet eighty-seven years, during which time, I've taken a good share of those medications and I've seen what they can do to people. Because everyone is not the same. I don't care if the rats or guinea pigs are. Once they gave me medication for a "woman my age and weight" and it almost killed me. Put me into an underwater fog I couldn't swim out of, not unlike living all those years in the Depression, with nothing but another world war around the corner. Turns out it was more than twice the dosage my body could tolerate.

Inner peace. I'll believe it when I see it. This woman is no dummy. She's humming us away into the corners of this room, humming away our boring conversations about how bland the food is, and chit-chat about the weather, and you-know-who isn't down for dinner again, and who got carted away in an ambulance this week. There's no on-floor romances, no millionaires amongst us ready to give their money away, no scoundrels who have lived cinematic lives. We're a bunch of TV watchers and paper pushers. What we used to call "plain folks" who raised our families and paid our bills and never dreamt for much more than a nice restaurant meal now and then, and a regular paycheck. I'm happy to have a roof over my head, and worked hard to get one. I deserve a little relaxation the way I see it.

But Sis over there, she could be more than that, residents here say. Abigail thinks anyone without a name must either be royalty or have a prison record. What's her name? I've demanded of the nurses over and over again, and all I get is, Mind your own business, or

She'll tell you when she's good and ready. Deary and Honey they say, You there and Darling. I want to gag. It's been four years and I will say with utmost confidence, that "Sugar" over there is never going to tell anyone her name.

That's fine by me, I've come to terms with it. After my second year here, a few of us were going to try to steal her records, find out the stupid name already, and maybe get things fired up around her. After all, even if she doesn't speak, we wanted to be able to call her something real, treat her like a human being. We even came up with a plan. Colonel Vasquez was going to stage a fit for distraction and Abigail and I were going to wheel into the record station from the rear. We knew the times when they were extra-short staffed, when they were putting us to bed for enforced afternoon naps so they could have their ritual coffee. Well, we had the plan, but after that, we just got too tired. It seemed like too much work. Abigail had a cramp in her leg, and I could feel the arthritis acting up. The colonel kept talking about a nap.

Her family was already coming by less and less: a bland divorced daughter, overweight and in her late fifties who looked like she'd like to exchange places with her mother. Sometimes she came with a teenage boy and girl who both rolled their eyes a lot, giggled and left without saying hello. They'd wait by the car, where we could see them through the lobby windows, or they hung out in the vending room, their mother always apologizing for them to the air. She meant to be nice, I guess, but she usually talked to us like our eyes were up by the ceiling or air molecules floating around her head. She never listened or we might have been able to get the name from her. She'd talk to her own mother a little bit, but the infernal humming just continued and that made us laugh. What else could she do? Never asked us who we were, never introduced herself properly. There was a dapper son, also in his fifties, who tried not to touch anything and turned up his nose at the food we ate. He always had a fancy suit on and thick, gold watch, and rings, although we didn't think he was married. He came alone, and when he did, he spent the whole time talking about his work and how busy he was, and what accounts he was working on. I never found it very interesting when I was in earshot, and after a few years of it, I prayed his mother would drown out his soliloquies.

Where's the volume control? Mrs. Buentello said when she first arrived. Every meal after that she'd say something similar. Time to change the channel, she'd yell at the woman who hummed, or Can I put in a request? Got any Sinatra on that turn-table? The woman who hummed never looked up, of course, and never changed her erratic tune, whose melody-less sound was in harmony with pumping oxygen machines, farts, and slurps from dentures.

I wondered why anyone's family came at all. How did I end up here, I'd say to myself, with all these old people? There was a table with the paralyzed who had to be spoon-fed and who drooled like babies. There was the memory loss table next to ours, where someone was constantly asking what time it was and where were they? Or worse, someone would be asking for his wife or her husband who needed to come and take them home. We'd exchange glances then, knowing said spouse was six feet under and no one was going to get out of this place. It was a relief that no one I knew was here to see this, even though I'm at the better-off table. Here, people can generally feed themselves, and I have learned to manage with my right hand.

Lucky I'd say to Abigail, it's the right one that works. If it were the left, I'd be with the veggies.

We have lots of jokes like that, but I don't think it gives as much satisfaction as your own personal weapon, as a permanent, invincible tuning-out system. When you can't do things for yourself anymore, and you have to rely on others—and it makes no difference to me whether it's complete strangers or my best friend, it's still humiliating—it takes something out of you. I don't like to think about how two people need to lift me into the shower, and that someday, those same two people, as I tell Abigail, might throw me down a laundry shoot. Sometimes I dream that I'm flying though the eye of a tornado, a tornado of bleached cotton and worn-out gingham, corsets and underpants and the bright flowery tablecloths from the dining room. I wake up tangled in my bed sheets, hearing the endless, nagging voices: Did you eat your beets? and Are your pants wet? and Now, wipe your face, like a good girl! As though we were pre-schoolers. Take this and take that and don't ask questions. They're just waiting for the right moment.

You can't think that way, Abigail says, you have to have faith.

You're right, I say, You're absolutely right. After all, at least I can still have a decent conversation.

And you can feed yourself as well.

Yes, and punch someone in the face if I have to.

Still got a good right arm. . .

You'd better believe it, I'd say, and someone's going to feel my wrath someday!

But between you and me, I lost my faith. Lost my faith along with whatever brain cells checked out from the stroke. So I feel I know somewhat what the woman who hums is doing since that's one thing they told us, she's had a stroke. She's just hanging out in there, instead of coming back to this half-life like some of the rest of us. She's smarter than me that way, keeping the voices from this world out, and protecting a place where the moldy smell of old chipped beef can't wear you out anymore than the morning call to breakfast. In there, you don't have to figure out who's going to have to get you onto the toilet, or who's going to throw up in the dining room. And you aren't able to count how many days have passed and take bets on how many days are ahead that are exactly the same, without any way of changing. I've thought it over, studying her immobile face and her stoic lips. In there, maybe there's an orchestra playing up on stage, the men and women in proper clothing like they used to wear, neat and clean in their formal black and whites. Maybe she's got herself a nice table, with a solid white tablecloth, candlelight, and a decent cocktail, or maybe she's in a great gown, dancing with some handsome soldier. One of the good-looking ones from the airforce. Now that's somewhere to be. If I wasn't so tired, I'd be humming along with her until the all-clear.

Melpomeme
The Muse of Tragedy

While Melpomene's worshippers gave audience to the muse's joyous singing, the Althakian footmen had wheeled southeast, taking positions on the other side of the hill from the theater at Hykassus. Little did the audience know that a new act of the play was about to commence. An act without stage directions, save for the hillcrest appearance of the Alkathian pikes gleaming in the moonlight.

Phinneaus
Histories

Cue the Violins

Toiya Kristen Finley

Friday—When the strings strain against bows

The boy next door threw his girlfriend across the bedroom again, and the minute hand on the wall clock of Jasmine's apartment fell back from the 7 to the 6. Jasmine was startled. He wasn't due for another outburst until next month. She would have been better prepared if he'd followed his pattern, and she wondered if it had taken the girl on the other side of the wall by surprise. Jasmine thought of calling the police, but whenever she did, they were of no use. They asked the girl if she were okay, she'd lie, and they were gone in under five minutes, allowing her boyfriend more time to stew. Another jab shook Jasmine's bedroom wall, and the dream came thundering back.

It was one of those half-remembered, forever vanishing dreams. Not quite a dream you tried to forget, but one of those slippery ones running back to the unconscious as soon as you woke. And you were never going to remember the whole thing. Only a glimpse returned to memory again and again, with the greater message staying lost. Of all the sense Jasmine could make of it—it was longer than most and strange, especially for one of her dreams. But she could not understand why her neighbor brought it back.

No, that wasn't quite right—it wasn't the boy next door's fault. It was her mother's. That voicemail message she found waiting for when she got home last night:

Hi, Jazzie. You'll never guess who called today. It was really nice talking to Priya again. She said Jason's throwing a party here July 21, and you are *invited. I really hope you'll consider coming. Okay?*

No, it *wasn't* her mother's fault. It was actually Jason's, which led to him calling her via her mother, which led to the dream. It was only the boy next door's fault for reminding her.

Jasmine fought to pull anything from the dream back into consciousness. Lots of wisps of smoke and grey and murkiness, but not a nightmare. Jasmine had not thought of him, had not bothered him since they were in high school, and, suddenly, Jason's face challenged hers. She hadn't seen him in two years. Not *physical* Jason. Dream Jason materialized every now and then as he did last night, when Jasmine's mind couldn't erect barriers and banish him from thought. His eyes were huge and pulling at her with desperation. The same wide-eyed desperation of fish struggling on land, their gills fanning out wildly, waiting—hoping—for someone to drop them back into water. Just at the moment Jasmine thought he'd reach out, snatch the strength from her eyes, Jason smashed his forehead into the glass.

Jasmine took a step back and bit down hard on her toothbrush. Jason banged on her mirror while she stood in front of the sink brushing her teeth. Jason didn't say anything. He pounded on the other side of the glass—not in anger, at least—but he kept trying to get at something he saw in her eyes. And that's when Jasmine felt the thread pull tight in her stomach. And that was the only part of the dream wanting to be remembered.

So maybe the dream came back when the boy next door swung his girlfriend into the wall because Jason knocked maniacally on the other side of her mirror. She took some consolation in being able to blame her neighbor.

Jasmine was going to call the police when she heard him plodding up to the front room. The girlfriend slammed the door to the bedroom, and Jasmine heard the tonal dance of the girl's fingers dialing a phone number.

Jasmine listened to her mother's message again. Just hearing Jason's name transmitted across thousands of little fiber optic wires summoned another tug from the thread in her stomach. How could he invite her to a party? Was he crazy? There was only one thing to be done, really. There was nobody here Jasmine could really talk to about it, either. The other sophomores she knew didn't understand things like this, didn't want to. The freshmen and juniors didn't either, for that matter. When they weren't busy torturing themselves over obsessive studying during the week, they mixed escape with alcohol and sex on the weekends. Jasmine had nothing in common with them. She was content to stay locked away in her apartment from Thursday to Monday playing video games or reading until the words blurred on the page.

The only person who'd understand was the senior she worked with in the Admissions Office. "Understand" wasn't quite accurate, but she was as close a connection that Jasmine could make. She listened because she was nice. They could have any conversation they wanted, no matter how wild she figured Jasmine's imagination. Sometimes, only sometimes, Jasmine felt the slightest guilt because she hadn't learned the girl's name. One of these days, Jasmine decided, she would make the effort. But her name didn't fit her face, and that made it hard. A name should always fit the face. A name should always be able to represent the person, whether she were present or not.

The eruption next door quieted for the moment. Jasmine went into the bathroom to wash her face. When she turned on the faucet, the door to the medicine cabinet jiggled a little. She tapped the glass with her index finger, and cracks like spider webs splintered from the center of the mirror and extended out.

"Jason, you broke my mirror!" she yelled. Monday could not come fast enough.

Fragments of the glass tumbled from the frame, falling into the sink and onto the floor. Where the mirror had been, a black film stared back at her. The gaping shadow breathed out a few strings of pearly, white smoke. Jasmine jumped back and nearly fell over the toilet. The steam burned her cheeks.

"So, are you going?"

"I—I don't know. Nashville summers are *nasty*. It's weird he even invited me."

"How come?"

"Something really weird happened—not to us exactly, but me, and him, and a friend—we all witnessed it."

"What?"

"..."

"Now, now. Don't get all secretive."

"We saw a girl die. She was shot right in front of us. Well, I shouldn't say *we*. *They* did, but I was there when it happened."

"The girl shot wasn't the happening?"

"You ready? You're gonna think I'm weird."

"Jazzie, I already *know* you're weird."

"...We saw her spirit leave her body. Reina and I did. Jason couldn't see it."

"You can't go to Jason's party because you saw a girl's spirit leave her body?"

"No, but it just makes it...*awkward*. Since then, Reina, Jason, everybody we used to run with, everybody except *me*—they just think Death follows me and Reina and Jason around. Of course, *we* never die. It's always someone close to us, or supposedly close to us. Heck, we don't even have to know them. The whole thing is highly irrational."

"Just 'cause you saw someone die?"

"I told you something happened. I think on some level, Jason's aware, but Reina and I...we could see it, we could *feel* it."

"Women are more intuitive when it comes to these things."

"Oh, come on! Don't stereotype us like that! What is this—two hundred years ago? You're the *second* person to tell me that. 'Women are more spiritual, intuitive, whatever, because they don't have the same brain capacity as men. Since they're ability to reason is shut off, and they're less intelligent, they have to be good at something! Wait! Superstition! Touchy-feelyness! They're good at that!'"

"Aw, come on. That's not what I meant. It's just that women seem to be more *aware* about these things than men are. Where would men be if we weren't? You know how many times a woman's stopped a man from doing something dumb because he decided to go with her 'bad feeling about this'? 'Oh, no, honey. Don't press that little button. The whole world might end.' Stuff like that."

"Know what would be nice? If I could keep Jason from throwing this dumb party. *There* would be some helpful intuition...."

"..."

Saturday—she'll appear in darkest light, and

"Stereotypes, especially *living* stereotypes, just really piss me off."

"Living?"

"Yeah, like the guy in the apartment next to me. He might as well tattoo 'Jungle Bunny' or 'Oversexed Black Ape' on his forehead. Let's forget he's under house arrest with a little black box taped to his ankle and smoking up and buying ganja and stinkin' up the whole apartment house—this fool flips and beats up his girlfriend about twice a month. And the police? They don't do anything. He just beat her up *again* Friday morning. I'm not saying she's innocent—far from it. But she doesn't deserve him."

"And the girlfriend's white, of course."

"Of course. A violent, Oversexed Black Ape doesn't fit the full description unless he's messing with a white chick. And you know he's a trophy for her too. All the whiggers got one....Why in the world would anybody want to be a living stereotype, ruin it for the rest of us by making us look bad and dragging us down in the process?"

"They don't know they're stereotypes. I'm sure they don't care....So, this death thing you're dealing with? What *other* thing happened when you saw this girl die?"

"I don't really know how to describe it. I can tell you what it *felt* like. I can try to give you some picture of it, but it's one of those things you can only get a handle on if it's happened to you..."

"I've been through lots of stuff—"

"But have you had Death stoop down next to you?"

What was Jasmine thinking anyway? That poor girl would finally get it and leave the bastard? Yesterday morning, she moped around for a few hours in their bedroom while he fumed and paced up front. Jasmine heard him muttering to himself, a series of veiled half-threats tumbling from his lips. His girlfriend went with her sister last night, and, a few hours ago, she was back. By 11PM, they had made up. Jasmine would spend the night in the den, away from their bedroom wall, if she wanted any sleep.

Jasmine couldn't understand how that girl tolerated him, lived with the threat of his impending furies from day-to-day, week-to-week. A chorus of bruises to greet her every morning mapped across the places nobody could see when she wore clothes. Promises of again and never again and once more to be shattered every other time he opened his mouth. This girl was too young to be caught up in all of this—Jasmine's age. But the women who would live tormented for years? These women were strong. Maybe not the girl next door, but most of them were. They had to be. Jasmine had heard of that rare man who allowed his wife to beat on him and never struck back, but with women? The illusion of love must have been able to dig deep to keep sustaining the body and the mind.

When that vase broke, I just snapped because I paid so much for it, you know? he said through the bedroom wall. *That's why I got so mad. I just snapped. But I know you take real good care of this place. You take good care of me. You're a good girl. I couldn't ask for a better girl.*

Jasmine wanted to take a needle, take the thread deep on the inside of her, and puncture some common sense into that girl next door. Send her a message. *You've heard that how many times now? Go back and live with your mother.* She does *love you, even though you fight so much. How do I know about that? Why should I care? What would you do if* you *were on the other side of this thin wall?*

I know, the girl said. *I know. I just get tired of dealing with this.* But she would deal with it again and again and again, because the pattern would spiral on forever, and she would run along its sequence waiting for it to end until she burned out, or he (or even she, with her equally explosive behavior) was in jail. Patterns. *I hate you I'm sorry I love you I hate you I'm sorry I love you I hate you I'm sorry I love you I hate you I'm sorry I love you I hate you I'm sorry I love you I hate you I'm sorry I love you I hate you I'm sorry I love you I hate you I'm sorry I love you.* As long as that final I love you reared its head at the end, there was a little hope still.

The girl who died, the girl who lay bleeding to death under Reina, Jason, and Jasmine's awe while help came too late—there was no pattern with her. Her death revealed secrets more easily kept while she was alive. The puzzling thing was that she helped to keep them. Back when Jasmine used to hang out with her, she never mentioned what her mother was doing. She bitched about her mother constantly, but it wasn't like she couldn't run away, or fight back. She dwarfed that woman. Jasmine decided the girl must have stayed for the drugs. Her father gave her an allowance.

"..."

"When her spirit left her body, somebody knelt down there beside us. I can't tell you if it was a man or woman, or whatever. But it was something like Death, and Death threaded me and Reina and Jason together."

"Threaded?"

"Yeah. It was one of those things that went so quick you kinda say 'Oh my God! What just happened to me?' Something pricked me on the inside. Not that it hurt or anything—it was this quick little prick in the hollow of my stomach. And then I could feel this line going out my stomach and through my spine. You know like you pull a rope? It went through all three of us, and then I felt it pull, and it locked me tight with Reina and Jason."

"Sooooo, you're bound by death?"

"Yeah."

"And nothing ever happens to the three of you, but it does to other people?"

"Yeah."

"That's some weird karma."

"Nnnnnnn...that's not karma....Jason's pretty scared of me and Reina. He doesn't know about the rope holding us all together, but he didn't talk too much to us after that. Actually, neither did me and Reina."

"Maybe everybody else dies around you because they don't know how to live, and you do."

"....That? Made no sense. I don't leave people dying in my wake."

"Well, maybe that's how Jason sees you."

"But seriously—"

"Must be *some* reason he invited you."

"It's not love, and it's not physical, but Jason's had this thing where he's always depended on me. Like when he was down or something, I'd always catch him looking at me—"

"And then he'd quickly look away?"

"Of course. Now that our spirits are connected—"

"Hold on. Wha—"

"My spirit with Jason's spirit. They're connected...because of the rope. You know what I'm talking about, when you don't even have to ask somebody, but you know something's wrong? Or you get this sense that jolts you out your sleep or whatever it is you're thinking about and you need to call someone up?"

"No, no. I can't say that I do."

"Well, it happens. Jason must need me, even though we're going to both feel incredibly uncomfortable around each other. When you can draw strength from someone on that level—on the spiritual level? —you can get pretty desperate."

"..."

Sunday--the chord will finally end.

"So, I'm going."

"I knew you were. When'd you decide?"

"Eh, I think I always knew. I thought I'd give you a chance to talk me out of it, though. Couldn't you try a little harder? I was really counting on it."

"Who died?"

"What?"

"You said people died around you. If you go, people might not go to the party. They might be afraid they'll die too."

"Oh, don't even joke that way. I'm not telling Jason I'm coming. I'll just show up....Both of Jason's grandfathers died his first semester in college *a year* after all of this. *A year*. But the argument is they were young and healthy, blah blah blah, so obviously it was because of Jason. Like I said, I didn't keep up with Reina, but something happened with her cousins—and it wasn't around the time Death knelt down next to us. I don't have the details, but they died kinda violently."

"How can you die 'kind of' violently?"

"When I don't have all the details, 'kind of' is about as good as you'll get from me."

"What's your story?"

"Really peripheral stuff. Honestly, I never should have e-mailed Priya about it, 'cause I know she made a big deal over it with Jason. Last year, I had a suitemate who moved out. This girl couldn't get along with any of us. She was always so pissy, always shouting about something and carrying on. Everybody else would run to their rooms, but I'd listen and then go call my mom. Man, it was draining. Turns out she had some kind of chemical imbalance. She jumped out of a Geography Department window."

"Oh, yeah! I remember hearing about her! She was your suitemate? No wonder you've sworn off dorms."

"But her death has *nothing* to do with me. I didn't even know her that well. Anyway, nobody else has died on my watch."

"That you *know* of."

"It's all nonsense...."

"Jason must be pretty desperate to see you. Maybe he's having a rough time right now. Maybe it won't have to be so awkward and you won't have to speak to him. Maybe your just being there will be enough."

"Well..."

"What?"

"Mmmmm—"

"There's something *else*?"

"Don't worry about it. It's nothing to worry about, okay?"

She would have liked to have slept in a little later and struggled to get back to sleep, but for the past half hour, the waning festivities of another drug party shook the old apartment house. Jasmine threw her sheet off the bed and considered calling the police just for spite, but she found something poking through her navel.

A thread red as coral led out from Jasmine's stomach, drooped off the edge of the bed, trailing out of the bedroom door. Jasmine followed it into the bathroom and bunched it up as she walked. The thread hung down from the gaping shadow where Jason had broken her mirror and piled into a coil in the sink. Jasmine sighed. As far as she could tell, Jason wasn't going to leave her alone, and July was too far away. If she could appease him somehow, maybe she could get her mirror back.

Jasmine stood up on the toilet and took one step onto the sink. The old porcelain didn't give way, so she reached out with the other foot and balanced herself. She grabbed the red coil from the sink and threw it through the hole in the mirror, her head piercing the shadow. It was sauna steamy, but not black-hole black like she imagined it to be. In the darkness, Jasmine saw the thread leading down the wall and disappearing. There was no floor that she could see, but she knew Jason had stood on *something* while he was peering at her Friday morning. She wriggled through the narrow square and squeezed her knees through, but she lost her balance and tumbled over.

She landed on her left temple, and it did not hurt at all. The thread twined around her shoulders and torso. Jasmine didn't bother unraveling it. Behind her, the bathroom on the other side looked like it had been magnified under a dirty microscope. She read the ingredients from a shower gel bottle hanging over the toilet. Not only did Jason break her mirror, but in the process, he probably took the opportunity to study all the flaws of her face.

Jasmine fumbled for the thread in the darkness. Her hair clung to the sides of her face in strings. The square of the mirror growing smaller behind her, the way cleared in a bronze half-light. Each step felt like a thousand miles. Each cell of her body hummed with the frequency of the light.

There he was. Jason standing in front of his own mirror in a cave of heat and dark light. He had stripped off his pajama tops. His hair, wet and slick, ran endless drops of sweat down his stomach and back, collecting in the hem of his pants. Jasmine thought she would find the end of the thread here, connected to Jason's navel, but it kept traveling beyond him in the darkness.

"Jason?"

At first he didn't respond, too preoccupied with the thin wisps of white smoke twirling around his head in the mirror. Jasmine tapped the end of the dresser with her fist. Jason turned to her with hollow eyes.

"Jazzie, what you are you doing here?"

"You summoned me? In a dream? I'm paying you back. You broke my mirror, by the way. I'm going to have to take care of that on a student salary."

"A dream..." Jason said.

"This...this isn't your dorm room. Why aren't we in your dorm room?"

He looked around. Everywhere the same dark brown with a bed in one corner and a chest of drawers in the other. The smoke rose like heat vapor.

"Oh, no, this isn't my dorm room. This is my bedroom...at home. I've got roommates at school."

"Why are we in your bedroom at home? Never mind, never mind. You're not going to remember any of this, and I'm going to have bruises from where I had to crawl through my mirror."

"It's the day she died, Jazzie."

"What?"

"It's always the day she died." He beckoned to her, and she stood with him in front of the dresser. The smoke around his head tasted of gunpowder. Jasmine couldn't see herself in the mirror at all, but a younger Jason with a softer face stared back at the older Jason, both with their hair sticky on their foreheads.

"It's always been this way," he said. "It's like this every day."

"You sent me a really disturbing dream. Well, okay, maybe it wasn't so disturbing. Why did you contact me?"

He never looked at her. "You always see what I can't see."

He'd said that same thing to her, or something very similar, a few nights after the girl died. He called late, embarrassingly late, late enough that had the situation been different, Jasmine's mother would have thought ill of him the rest of her life; she wouldn't have been so ready to pass along the invitation. And when Jasmine finally took the phone after her mother woke her from a solid sleep, Jason sounded so *clingy*, as if his very life depended on the words Jasmine chose to send through that phone. He *said* the only reason he called was because he wanted to know if she and Reina saw something else—something besides watching the girl's spirit rise from her body. And Jasmine said no. And she asked if he saw something else. And Jason said no, and they both were aware that this wasn't quite true. Jason ended the conversation with him and her knowing he would never admit to calling.

Jasmine fidgeted with the thread. "Sooooo, the last time we talked?" [Because that *was* their last significant conversation.] "What was that all about? Or do I really wanna know, 'cause something really creepy felt like it was coming through the phone."

He still didn't bother to look at her but grabbed her hand. Her skin absorbed his sweat.

"Oh, that. She was there, in the room with me."

"Nnnnnnnn...the dead girl?"

"Well, yes...no. Not the dead girl. Parts of her. Something from her. *They* were there."

Jasmine wanted to wrench her hand away and wipe her palm against her pants. "Jason, you haven't talked to me in two years, you send me a dream, and instead of keeping me from wasting my time, you're telling me pieces of a dead girl were floating around in your room?"

The boy in the mirror, Younger Jason, reached for Jasmine. When his fingertips grazed the glass, his eyes widened in desperation. The same futile desires glaring at her when the dream came roaring back. His outstretched arm shook, his whole body stiffening as if he dared to fight off rigor mortis. "Why can't I ever see what you see?" he said.

Jasmine inched closer to this boy, the clingy one she'd talked to the night that seemed like a decade ago. Way over his shoulder, against another wall, two figures stood with their backs to Younger Jason. Neither of them that tall, one a little shorter than the other. To their left, a thin line the color of drying blood snaked its way into darker light.

"Give me a break," Jasmine said. She tugged the thread wrapped around her shoulders. The maroon line behind Younger Jason wiggled. She turned around and saw nothing there. She watched her reverse-self in the mirror and backed away, walking in the direction of the reflected thread.

"Gotta go." She patted Older Jason. Sweat sprayed off of his shoulder.

"Yeah." He remained fixated on his younger self. At least Jasmine *thought* he was staring at his younger self. "I'll see you at the party," he said.

The thread her guide, Jasmine backed away from Jason until he faded and her feet stepped into warm, shallow water. The strange amber light dissolved, and a clear, spring night embraced her. The last time she talked to Jason, when the girl died, it had been much colder. The seasons were changing, and winter still tried to hold on. Jasmine turned and faced the thread. It ran underwater through a wide strip of creek and out on the opposite bank. No wonder Jasmine hadn't recognized it at first, because in her neighborhood, no one could remember when they could see through to the bottom. Parents stopped letting their kids swim when she was ten, and the few times she passed by the banks since then, the only things seen surfacing were the lines of shoe laces attached to sneakers wedged between rocks. Or snack cake wrappers. Or the bubbly, greenish-white film nobody could quite explain but knew shouldn't be touched.

On the opposite bank, the white side of the creek, a girl stood with the end of Jasmine's thread in her hands. Jasmine had not seen her in a long time, not since the day she died. When they were little, she and Jasmine used to meet here all of the time.

The wide rock tables weren't slick under the water, and Jasmine walked the path over to the other side. The girl grinned.

"Well, nice to see you, I guess," Jasmine said.

The girl twined her end of the thread around her fingers. She was taller than Jasmine remembered. She used to slump over, but her shoulders were broad and her collar bone prominent. She wasn't skinny, but her chest and waist tapered down into an almost perfect line, with only a slight rounding at the hips. Jasmine had always thought of her as attractive, but never so statuesque. Her hair was quite blonde even in the dark, the curls rolling past her shoulders looking like they had been individually sculpted. This was not some fond memory Jasmine drug up. She always thought of this girl as a bit of a wreck, especially during the later years of her life.

"Hey. What've you been up to?" she said.

"You already know that, right? Trick question?" Jasmine said.

She fashioned a cat's cradle around her fingers with the coral thread. During the early evenings when they got home from school, they used to play the game with a ratty piece of string. "You mean Jason?"

"He's been reliving your death since the day you died."

"Yeah..."

"I know you're not a ghost, and even if you were a ghost, you wouldn't be into haunting. What's going on with these pieces of you lingering with him?"

"All different kinds of haunts, Jasmine."

"Oh, okay, okay. Fine. Be like him. Don't tell me anything."

The girl passed the cat's cradle on to Jasmine. Jasmine began to lace diamonds through her fingers.

"Sometimes I wish you hadn't gone to private school, although I know that was best for you. You forgot all about me. The last time we talked?" the girl said. "It meant a lot to me. You probably don't remember that either."

Jasmine hadn't, until it was mentioned. A party she only went to because her father begged her. "Oh, yeah. You were drunk."

"*High*."

"Sorry. *High*."

"I know you were thinking what the hell I was doing, but you never said anything about it. That was nice. After my mom always yelled at me for whatever, or my dad, or my stupid siblings, it was nice to just...talk."

Two solitary figures standing at odds with each other formed themselves within the thread in Jasmine's hands. They looked away from each other, one slouched over. The other standing tall and defiant. Jasmine held her work up for the girl to see. Her neighbors on the other side of the wall moved in towards each other, their bodies dancing and tangling together. Then they freed themselves and separated again. "How could you let your mother hit you? I didn't even know until you died." She passed the thread back.

"How come you don't use my name anymore?" The girl worked on a manger with the thread. "....Where do you find the strength to deal with all the clingy people and the energy vampires?"

"*What*?"

"You know? All those tragic cases? Jason? Your next door neighbor?" From between the gaps in the string, the ex-suitemate stared at her. The stress of the past year clipped Jasmine's shoulders as the girl's taught lips and wild eyes emerged. The sudden clap of slammed doors and ranting about this friend's betrayal and that boyfriend's stupidity escaped from the fog of Jasmine's unconscious.

"Look, I had nothing to do with her committing suicide. It would be really nice if you could let everyone know that Death doesn't follow us around, 'cause you have nothing to do with it."

The girl smiled. "Of course not, Jasmine. You're the one lured to *them.* Somehow, you're always there when they need you. You always find your way to them. You've gotta special intuition, a gift. Letting that psycho girl ream you out. I never would have done that."

"You are making about as much sense as Jason."

She wrapped the thread around her fingers a final time, returning the red lines to the cat's cradle. "I can't make any excuses for my mother--I won't. She never liked me very much, and I always resented her for making me take care of all her kids. But I did understand her, you know? My dad was an asshole, too, not that he ever laid a hand on her. He stressed her out, so she stressed me out. But she's not that big. I let her do it, you know? Nobody else cared."

"Yeah, but—"

"We're not so much different that way."

"You're not saying I'm going to die violently?"

"No. Not at all." The girl whispered in Jasmine's ear, "She knows you call the police. She knows you watch out for her. You do it anyway, even though she's not going to change, and you know how her story'll end."

"You might as well cue the violins for that girl."

"You knew I wasn't going to make it either, didn't you?"

"I didn't think you were going to get *shot.*"

"It's okay," the girl said, airy skin brushing against her old friend's hands as she transferred the interlaced thread around Jasmine's fingers. "I knew I was a wreck too. But do me a favor, will ya, Jazzie? You can take abuse better than anybody. No matter how frustrated you get, keep watching over us fuck ups. Nobody else does."

The dead girl went up the bank, back to the white side of the neighborhood through the deep underbrush. Jasmine walked the granite table down the middle of the creek, thinking of the girl's name and gathering the thread as she went. That name filled a hollow place in her memory, a place better left untouched. Names took the places of people, stood right there for them even when they weren't present in body. It was easier for her to stay dead on the pavement, without a name carrying so many thoughts of their childhood. Sure, once upon a time, Jasmine knew you might as well have cued the violins for the dead girl too, but she recognized it much too late. Missed the opportunities to let her rant and rave about whatever, clear-minded or high. Maybe it didn't have to be that way for Jason.

The rock ended, and Jasmine went down the slight hill underwater. Even below the surface of the creek, the sky burned splendid as the glow of early twilight. When she rose to the top of the water and exhaled, the little square of her medicine cabinet greeted her.

Water puddles fell with heavy thuds as she walked out of the bathroom and back to her room. She was too exhausted to dry off. Pools of water seeped into her mattress.

The neighbor girl's giggling woke Jasmine up in the afternoon. She promised to make her boyfriend his favorite breakfast, sausage and Belgian waffles with strawberry syrup. He said something, and Jasmine heard the loud smack when he kissed her on the cheek.

Jasmine rolled over in her damp sheets. The entire coil had retreated deep inside of her, all of it except a thread of coral cat's cradle clinging to her long, tired fingers.

The Day After Tomorrow

Tamar Yellin

THIS IS HOW THE ACCIDENT occurred: driving at fifty miles an hour along the Great North Road, Maxine was fast-forwarding her radio cassette. Twenty-five yards in front of her a lorry pulled out. By the time she saw the lorry it was too late. If she hadn't felt the overwhelming need to fast forward the tape she would have kept her eye on the road. If Johnny Cash had not included 'I Still Miss Someone' among his greatest hits, Maxine would probably still have been alive today.

Two hundred and eighty-two miles away, in a restaurant in Paris, a woman reaches over and kisses another woman. On the lips. It is what she has dreamed of doing. The kissing woman is Suzanne. The woman kissed is Elena. Suzanne upsets Elena's cappuccino.

"I don't know you," she says.

"What do you mean, you don't know me?"

"Just what I say. I don't know who you are."

They are in the kitchen. It is dark outside. Their forms, the shiny sink, the whole kitchen are reflected into the darkness.

She is drying the dishes; he is washing up. There is a strangeness about the familiarity of the kitchen, cast in, perhaps, by the darkness of the night. Perhaps it would be better if they drew the blind.

She shudders a little.

As he places a plate upon the drainer, she waits a moment, then she lifts it out. How well they work together. How methodical they are. Usually she washes, he dries. Sometimes they change over, for variety.

"Maxine," he says. He reaches out a hand towards her.

She starts back. "No, it's no use, Nathan. You can't pretend any longer. Don't talk to me."

The kiss is unexpected. But just as unexpected is the sudden splash of hot coffee in her lap, causing her to start back. The movement is unfortunate; Suzanne considers her caress unwanted. The next few minutes are taken up with napkins and waitresses.

Elena excuses herself and disappears behind the door that says Dames.

Alone at the table, Suzanne sits frozen and reflects on the train of events. It was a mistake, she thinks, to act so suddenly in a public place, but then, the frisson of danger added to her lust. The moment before the kiss was the most delicious: the sheer welling up of passion beyond restraint. The kiss itself was something of an anticlimax. But as for the coffee—that had ruined everything. If Elena had laughed, if they had both laughed, it might have been all right. But Elena had not laughed; she had disappeared. Now Suzanne is uncertain what to think. An accident has robbed her of her full desire.

When she goes upstairs alone, when she lies in the bath, when she goes from the bath to the bed and lies naked in the pure warmth, she thinks of how it was, for a brief time, when they loved each other. How delicious that was. All right, perhaps they weren't in love but in lust, but it felt good, it is good to remember it, the way it feels good now to run her hands down the smoothness of her hips, under the softness of her breasts, along her own ribcage which is so delicate yet resilient... She prefers to be alone these days, she thinks she might almost be in love with herself; the realisation is a little mournful. But one thing's for sure, your own love won't betray you. You're sure to stay true to yourself no matter what.

She turns over on the bed and admires the line of her thigh, the creaminess of her calf. The body beautiful. She smiles to the ceiling, conspiratorially. Yes: that much is certain, she addresses her body. You won't go off and sleep with another woman.

Down in the kitchen he gazes out of the window into the dark garden. Forty-five minutes ago she went upstairs to run herself a bath. Now he is alone with nothing but the dripping tap for company. He doesn't realise how long he has been standing here, motionless, gazing at and beyond his own reflection in the window. He knows that, essentially, this is how it has always been, that he has always been lonely and alone like this, or feared it, at least, known that it would come. That was the nature of his orphanhood. Before she entered his life he was lonely, after she leaves he will be lonely too, and all the way through, he was probably alone, except perhaps on a couple of occasions.

Always his actions were numbed, his feelings deadened. His whole life has been lived in the prison of himself. For a while he thought she could reach him but now he wonders whether it wasn't all a delusion. They met by accident and they will part casually, accidentally. He wonders if he was ever really in love with her.

Moonlight silvers the girders of the Eiffel Tower; moonlight lies coldly on the Tuileries. Broken moonlight mars the surface of the Seine. Out in the suburb, in the quiet house, Suzanne lies in contemplation of the bathroom ceiling. An old cobweb runs across it which she will probably never remove.

Her body is at rest, but her mind is racing. Her mind is filled with the memory of the kiss. She still feels on her lips the imprint of its pressure. A dangerous moment lies upon her lips.

When Elena returned from behind the door marked 'Dames' she was smiling, distant, formal, still brushing at her skirt as though that was the thing that mattered, as though the damage to her business suit was all that had occurred. She fussed over payment, flourished her credit card, glanced three times at her wristwatch and was gone.

Now Suzanne is left with that sense of slowly melting unreality which follows a great act of rashness. She cannot believe it happened. She tells herself that in fact it did not happen. The kiss was never achieved; the upset coffee cup prevented it. She dips her head under the bathwater, passes her damp fingers across her mouth. It is all useless. The more she tells herself the kiss was unconsummated the more she senses its remembered weight.

He hadn't slept with her with any conscious intention. That is, he had had no conscious intention of hurting Maxine. Perhaps, in some distant way, he had thought of hurting himself, of stinging himself alive out of this numbness and torpor he had slipped into. Briefly, momentarily, he had achieved that. But the cold had closed in again, and worse than before. The contrast between feeling and not feeling was so poignant.

As for her, she might have been provided, like a stage prop to the circus of his aberrant whims. She had encouraged him to return with her to her small flat after dinner. She had half-undressed before he had unlaced his shoes. She was swift and businesslike, almost too efficient, as though she expected to be made use of, to make use of him.

One thing that had occurred to him, at the moment of consummation: having sex with a woman he barely knew and cared less about was very little different from not having sex with Maxine. Both experiences were a kind of absence. Both were filled with the sadness of his loss.

He realised there were few routes by which you could escape the reality of grief. Every fresh blow brought it back again. Whichever way he turned he came face to face with his abandonment. The death of his parents was no different from the death of love.

Lying on her back in the dark bedroom, a song playing softly on the stereo, she remembers how it was, for a brief time, when they loved each other. How innocent, how exhilarating that was. They were so young then; they felt things so intensely. A patina of newness lay upon the world.

Once, in one of the alcoves of the municipal park, half-screened by hanging ivy, they had kissed suddenly, impulsively: a passionate, half-frightened, mutual kiss. An act of ecstatic union, almost a collision. They were thirteen years old. All these years later, she still remembers it. It was the pure and original, the first and best.

She had been nervous then, afraid of being noticed; even as they embraced she had tried to protest: "Maxine!" And Maxine had laughed, had looked into her eyes: a half-laughing look of penetrating love.

She has had many affairs since then, she has loved both men and women; women and men have been in love with her. They didn't embrace her in alcoves, they didn't laugh at danger. It never touched her, it was never true. Nothing since then has been able to match that moment. Her whole life she has been seeking to retrieve one kiss.

She wonders what on earth she is doing here. Why she is still clinging to this cold Englishman.

Rain is flung like rice at a dark wedding, night hangs scattered with light at the black window. She sits by the dressing-table, combing her long hair, watching her own features in the mirror.

Is she still capable of love, she wonders. How many times can the human heart be broken? The history of her life is a string of bodies. Beyond the carnage she sits magnificently alone.

The face in the mirror is hers, but search as she may she cannot see in it the face of the child she once was, nor that of the old woman she will one day become. The more she examines the less it makes sense to her, like a word read over and over turns into a jumble of letters. The face she possesses now is a visitant: shifting, provisional, the face of a stranger.

Downstairs is a person who once claimed to love her and is now unknowable. Who on earth is there who can still be trusted? She must keep faith with herself; all this way she has come she has found no other. From Dijon to Paris to Dieppe to London. London is the last in a long line of betrayals.

Suzanne stands at the window: she cannot see the stars. A haze of vague orange hangs above the night city. She is hardly aware of the depth of her own stillness. Who betrayed whom? That's the eternal question.

Always she fantasises the reunion: the moment of recognition, the embrace, the surge of delicious and recaptured love. In deep and repeated dreams she has lived that moment. All bitter misunderstanding washed away.

She still remembers the colour of Maxine's eyes, the feel of the down on her cheek, the smell of her hair. It was only the day before yesterday, after all. Suzanne's passion for Elena is her passion for Maxine; whatever love she feels is what she felt for her.

When he finally comes upstairs he finds her packing. "What are you doing?" he asks.

"I'm taking the Johnny Cash," Maxine answers.

For a minute he stands helpless, watching her fold her clothes.

"Don't you think this is rather extreme?" he says at last.

Maxine lays down the sweater she has been folding: looks Nathan fully in the eyes. "What is extreme?" she asks. "You tell me what is extreme. Is it extreme to fall in love with someone? Is it extreme to leave your native country?"

He stares back helpless.

"You tell me the answer," she says, resuming her packing. "I don't know what means anything any more."

He doesn't know the meaning of anything. He can no longer tell what matters and what is unimportant.

Until now his life has felt weightless, unreal, as though all his actions were carried out upon a screen, distanced essentially from him, a mere performance. He grimaces, watching television downstairs while Maxine is packing. He has become a TV personality.

For a long time it has seemed as though his actions carried no consequences, that he performed in a bubble, following the dictates of some foreign will; truly insensate to the pain of others. As far back as he can remember it has been like this. Even his own pain is no longer real to him.

He has abdicated the plot: that way seemed best. Death taught him a long time ago that he had no volition.

Now all of a sudden events in his life have causes; all of tonight's events have origins. His life, which was previously so light, which was unreal, grows suddenly too heavy for him to bear. Staring at the television screen, involuntary tears roll down his cheeks. His grief is as heavy as lead. He feels his heart will break beneath its crushing burden.

Her suitcase is packed, her essentials are collected; she is eager to leave, ready to get going. How long she has wanted this, how restless she has become. She didn't realise how restless until this evening.

All her life she has wanted to escape, to take with her only that which is essential. She has shed her life like a skin over and over; every time she was renewed and frightened. Each time she feels lighter, as though leached of substance. She grows thin and hard, without context, shedding her memories behind her like confetti.

Time and again she performs this act of betrayal. There is no affair, no midnight assignation. Her only paramour is solitude. Her only secret lover is herself.

Two hundred and eighty-two miles away Suzanne is dreaming. She lies on her side asleep; moonlight brightens her pillow. One hand rests, palm upward, close to her cheek. She smiles as she dreams of a consummated kiss.

Vistas of forgotten happiness, of lost love, open up for her out of the darkness, as though she had woken to find herself in the dream, as though the kiss were at last to be reclaimed, not snatched away at the moment of consummation. They stand in the alcove; they wear the faces of children. Years of longing are sated in their embrace. She has dreamed it many times, but this one is so real, she will hardly believe, when she wakes, that it didn't happen. She will ask of the morning air: Were you really here? It is an epiphany; a night-gift. Joy blossoms in the silence of the dark bedroom.

All night he sits in front of the blank TV. The room strewn with possessions. If he were a drinker he would have a bottle.

He doesn't need to intoxicate himself. He is already drunk on self-reproaches. He opens his heart like a target and takes the blame. Only that way will he ever be forgiven.

His father died suddenly, unreconciled. His mother suffered a long, drawn-out, demanding, vengeful death. Both stand at his elbow with the face of mourning.

He is where he expected to be, at the end of the day. Silence, grief, lost love, loneliness, remembrance. And no music.

The deepest darkness of the night passes, and behind him the window greys with the first light. As if called, he rises and lifts the curtain. She has not returned. It is tomorrow.

Terpsichore
The Muse of Dance

And so on the fifth and final night of the Feast did Terpsichore appear, with lyre and plectrum, and how her dance did pale those seven sisters of the fixed sphere. Thus were the Four nights piping and singing rendered vulgar beside the grace of the fair one, the Whirler. So alluring was her dance, it is said, that all movement did stop within the walls of the city, until the river itself did stay its current in shame.

Cressidia
De Anima, Bk. 3

The Eyes of Horus

Ursula Pflug

PINKA GOT A TAKE-OUT COFFEE and a banana muffin at her landlord's street level restaurant to hitchhike with. A falcon headed dude stopped for her right away. She didn't know he was Horus, the Egyptian God; she took him for a guy going to a masquerade party. Only later, at work, did it occur to her that he squawked, and smelled of wet feathers. He drove her all the way down Yonge, and over on Queen to Dufferin Street. Had she told him that was where she was going? Pinka didn't ask, because a headache was coming on, and she didn't want to betray how messed up she was suddenly feeling. Although she was only twenty, she figured she was getting too old to go to work without any sleep. But had she, actually, ever done that before? Suddenly she was no longer sure, but she figured you had to try everything once.

Horus pulled up in front of The Gladstone Hotel, as if not wanting to be seen at her place of employment across the street. He looked at her sideways out of yellow bird eyes.

"You'll be okay today," he said.

"Hope so," she said, wishing it was noon and The Gladstone was already open, and she could skip work and just go drink with this strange bird headed guy. It felt like the kind of day when scotch for breakfast would not be entirely amiss. And it wasn't breakfast, anyway. It wasn't as if she hadn't eaten her whole banana muffin, evidenced by the lap full of crumbs she was about to disperse all over the floor of the bird headed guy's Camaro.

She checked to see whether he had hands. He did, but they protruded from his wing elbows, like the second set of little talons the South American hoatzin had. He leaned over, snapped open the glove compartment and took out a little vial. Oh, he was going to try and sell her drugs. It figured. All the interestingly weird people ended up being drug dealers. He unscrewed the lid, took her hand, and poured five little eyes into the palm that, curious, Pinka hadn't been able to resist opening. They were exactly like his eyes except smaller, beady and yellow around a deep black iris.

"I don't do drugs," she said, which wasn't strictly true.

"Why is it that in your time people can no longer tell the difference between drugs and eyes?" Horus asked, and added, "You have to try everything once. Swallow them. My eyes will get you through the day and further if you let them."

She'd had such a weird night she obeyed.

Horus's eyes didn't taste like anything. Still, they told her his name, immediately. So there were after all people in the world other than herself and her roommates Roger and Clara who were capable of mental telepathy.

"In twenty-five years I'll offer you another ride. I'll honk my horn three times and you'll know it's me."

"Horus, thanks. I'll look forward to it," Pinka said. Her headache was gone and she felt as if she'd had nine hours sleep. The eyes had it, that was for sure. She got out of the Camaro, endeavoring to get as many of her muffin crumbs out into the street as possible.

"Don't worry about the crumbs," Horus said, "I'll have them later."

"Oh, right." He was a bird after all.

Pinka shut the car door and went in to work. She wasn't reprimanded for being late, because there was a transit strike on, and many of the employees were hitchhiking. Inside the big warehouse, Pinka climbed the stepladder she'd set next to a twenty foot fake fir the day before. She climbed, carefully balancing a big cardboard box of Xmas ornaments on her arm. Ten big green balls down each side, and between each of the green ones, a smaller red one. Pinka liked the reprieve from her previous location at one of the big trestle tables that seemed now so very far below, counting things, gluing things. Wendy the supervisor had for some reason sent her to do the big tree alone; perhaps she'd noticed Pinka compositions achieved the desired symmetry, that her gluing and counting were better than other people's. Pinka reveled in the solitude, free to pursue her work and to think, without having to pretend to pay attention to the other girls' chatter for fear of appearing rude, much as she usually liked the camaraderie.

Pinka looked down at the girls, all busy at their stations. More than half on any given day seemed some combination of drunk or teenaged or pregnant or some other manifestation of disadvantage. And she loved them all just then, briefly, pityingly, wanting to save them from their abject circumstances. She wanted to tuck them in and bring them tea and toast and read to them out of "Winnie The Pooh," as their own mothers probably never had, or they wouldn't be here, would they? Everyone knew having "Winnie The Pooh" read to one at bedtime led to success in later life; there were stats to prove it. But why was Pinka here? Her mother had read to her on a nightly basis, and made her Ovaltine and real porridge in the mornings, gluey as it often was. Being an art college drop out, she could figure out how to space balls evenly, although management hadn't cared to see her résumé. Like Christmas help as a mail sorter at the post office, this job was temporary, without benefits, non-union. But it paid better than minimum wage, and those who had the luck of low rent, and could finagle time off from school or other obligations could pack in lots of hours and put away some cash for winter luxuries. A sale at Brown's Shoes on Bloor Street. Single malt scotch. Absinthe to impress one's friends. Time to play with magic roommates. It was looking like a good year, like she might manage to pull off all of the above.

Pinka set the box of ornaments on the top of the ladder and removed a green ball which she affixed to the big tree using its attached wire, which was basically an oversized twist tie. She measured three hand breadths and attached a second ball below the first, and then did it again. Once she had attached five balls, it was time to gingerly carry the ornaments down the ladder, move the ladder one quarter of three hundred and sixty degrees, and climb up and do it again. When she had done all four meridians at the top of the tree, she had to open a new box of big green balls and continue each stripe till it reached the bottom of the tree's skirts, inches from the floor. The trick was multifaceted: to evenly space the balls in unwavering lines, to not fall off the ladder, and not drop the box of balls, which, being plastic, wouldn't break but might only chip.

She thought of home, where Roger and Clara had probably gone to sleep. She wondered whether they had borrowed her bedroom, or just one of them had, or whether they had opened the fold out couch and were sleeping in it side by side. Pinka's apartment was on the third floor above a greasy spoon. The owner of the greasy spoon, a Greek immigrant who went by the name of Paul, also owned the building, a rabbit warren of apartments: some small, some large, some single rooms that shared a bedroom and a kitchen. Pinka had a bedroom and a kitchen overlooking noisy sooty Yonge Street, and a big living room overlooking a rooftop, where a fire escape led to a confusion of alleyways. She shared the second floor bathroom with an eccentric middle aged artist lady named Ilana and a very young man, an aspiring writer named Jackson. Both kept the bathroom mercifully clean. In the summer they occasionally got together on Pinka's roof for a drink or a pot of tea, and sometimes the three even sat together on a Friday night over a couple of bottles of wine. It was convivial, but Pinka knew that she participated in these gatherings because she was bored and lonely, and so were Ilana and Jackson, and hence, the boredom and loneliness were in some ways made worse, not better. But then Roger and Clara had moved in with Pinka, and all that had changed. Spending time with her new roommates felt like riding the crest of a wave, a wave of almost impossibly beautiful friendship, growing over the course of several increasingly strange, increasingly sleepless nights.

Long walks just before dawn, scraping together enough change for takeout coffees to drink while sitting on the edges of dead winter fountains, and later, when they were good and cold, on greasy spoon breakfasts. They'd come across so many dead November fountains Pinka hadn't even known existed. You thought you knew your city and it turned out you didn't, not really. You thought you had friends but it turned out you hadn't, not really, not till this moment. Just look at them. And Pinka's heart always skipped a pleasure filled beat. It can't be. This much happiness, it just can't.

She'd liked Roger right away partly because he was slender and no taller than she; it had made him seem brotherly and sexy all at once. She'd met him behind the big library near Yonge and Wellesley. He'd offered her a toke and she'd accepted; they'd taken to chatting. His words had seemed oddly weighted, as if she'd heard them before, or words very like them, and from him too. Which wasn't really possible, because they'd only just met. She'd thought about him all afternoon, and then run into him again in the evening, in the bar down the street. She hadn't been surprised. And then who should walk in but Clara, the younger sister of a girl she'd known way back in high school. Pinka hadn't seen Clara for awhile, and she was several things she hadn't been before, most of them beautiful. Pinka invited her to join them, and when the bar closed all three went for coffee, and then Clara said she needed a short term place, and by that time they already felt like the oldest and best of friends, so Pinka said she could share her flat. The next night they went out dancing, all three, and Pinka had more fun than she'd had in years, or possibly ever, so when Roger called the next day to tell her he'd been evicted and could he stay just for a little while, while he looked, of course Pinka said yes. And now Roger and Clara, in spite of not being lovers, shared a pull out couch in the living room most nights, while Pinka kept the bedroom for herself. It had a big white painted old steel hospital bed, and a poster of Marilyn tacked to the wall. It was Clara who had brought these things. Pinka herself had never once in her life pinned a poster to the wall. She preferred to scribble mysterious, evocative and haunting words and images onto large pieces of expensive art paper and tack them to the walls with thumbtacks. They didn't have multicolored push pins in clever geometrical shapes back then, Pinka thought, affixing another big green plastic ball to a big green plastic tree.

Who had thought that particular thought, in actuality? It couldn't be she. Pinka hadn't lived her future life yet. She didn't know about the push pins. Except that she suddenly did, somehow. For instance, she knew she hated the triangular prisms because they hurt her thumbs. She knew the cylinder shaped push pins always broke under the weight of even the lightest hammer. She knew that thumbtacks, about to go out of style, were by far the superior product. Never mind the weirdness, Pinka told herself, just concentrate on work. Although she did pause to wonder whether Horus was sending her these glimpses of the future, a presence now in her mind, just as she had been one in his Camaro.

Pinka mentally complimented herself on her ability to attach balls in such nice straight lines given the fact she'd stayed up all night; she'd already forgotten about Horus's eyes. Moving the ladder to start her second row, she thought of the night before, of walking and talking in what seemed like infinity with Roger and Clara, their shadows stretching under streetlights, playing with them, making them tall and short and then really tall and really short, and–there they were again, the others, terrifying as they'd been since the very beginning, circling above, and this time Pinka's heart skipped a black beat and she sat down, her heart wrapped in a fist, disconsolate on the fountain wall alone while her breath came back in gasps, and Roger and Clara, not noticing, continued to play with their still happy shadows.

Eventually Clara came and sat beside her. "What's wrong?" But now Pinka felt alone and couldn't share it, as if only happiness and pleasure could be shared after all, and that dark premonition was just as isolating as anything had ever been, more so, in fact.

"What is it?" Clara repeated.

Roger came and sat beside them and took an orange out of his pocket. He didn't peel it though, but held it up, and Pinka saw it as their planet, their Earth.

An orange ball.

A juicy fruit.

"What?" Pinka asked, sensing that Roger was about to tell a story, a very important story, using the orange as a prop. And he wasn't going to tell it using words, but through telepathy, which they had discovered, much to their delight over the past week, was increasingly possible amongst the three of them. "What?" she asked, just as they had asked what, and then she saw the source of her discomfort, quite clearly in her mind's eye: alien warlords, reptilian, toothed and clawed, poised to eat the lovely fruit, to section it off, divide it amongst themselves, to chew each morsel, and each mortal, perpetuating a kind of eternal slavery of the soul.

Not all infinities were pleasurable as telepathy. Not all telepathy was pleasurable as infinity.

Pinka saw it all clear as day, and it rattled her with a doom filled terror worse than anything she'd ever felt. It must be the sleepless nights, Pinka told herself, the lack of nutritious food. They hadn't been eating well; it was just a little schizoid moment; it would pass; nothing more to it than that, and then she met Roger's eyes. They were drained of all emotion except fear, and his usual paleness had turned whiter still, and he said, "I'm sorry, I didn't mean to show you that—I didn't even know I was going to—it just happened." Just now he looked so frail Pinka wished, for his sake, he were a big strong man who'd brush away what had just happened instead of slender and possessed of an elfin grace.

"You seemed so unhappy," Clara suggested, "that he wanted to help, he wanted to see if he could find out the reason you were feeling that way, and so he opened up, and that's the picture that came in."

"Maybe it isn't true," Pinka said.

"You hope in vain," Clara said, and crossed her pretty green stockinged legs and buttoned the buttons of her orange corduroy blazer. She wasn't wearing nearly enough for the weather, Pinka thought. They really all had to start taking better care of themselves.

"And now we all see together," Roger said.

"It's so amazing," Pinka said, for it was amazing, what had just occurred, if unexplainable, and certainly not verifiable in any way, and while scary, also beautiful beyond compare because, because of what Roger had said—and now we all see together. Pinka looked at Roger to see if he might be feeling as elated as she suddenly, inexplicably was–talk about mood swings—but he looked pale and tired, almost corpse-like in his sudden exhaustion and said, "let's go home. I feel sick."

And so they did. And as they left behind the dawn lit streets to climb the stairs to the third floor, dragging themselves, wishing for once they lived on the second floor and not the airy eyrie of the third, Pinka said, "Oh shit, I have to go to work. I forgot." Clara laughed, although Roger was still so silent and grim Pinka worried for him.

You hope in vain.

Pinka went back out and walked down to Wellesley and stuck out her thumb, waiting for a red light and the ride she knew it would bring, and wondered what Clara had meant. Were the reptilians real? It was one thing to say the same thing at the same time, to successfully experiment with tossing balls of thought one amongst the other, to go dancing till dawn and have the floor clear not because they were particularly expert dancers but because they shone with a faint but clearly visible light they themselves didn't understand, but believing in monstrous depraved aliens was the kind of thing that got you incarcerated.

And then the bird headed guy pulled up in his Camaro, and everything changed so much again, almost immediately, that she lost that particular train of thought.

Far below, Wendy was calling up to her. "They're evenly spaced, and the lines are straight. You're a genius, and those are in short supply around here." Pinka was on the last of the four stripes.

It was the first time Pinka had ever heard Wendy say something that wasn't insulting, either to herself or any of the other girls. "Thank-you!" she called witlessly, and then hoped immediately none of the other girls had heard, especially not Patty, the tough native girl. Saying thank-you to the supervisor was a bit like sucking a teacher's dick. It might get you good marks but there'd be hell to pay in the schoolyard later. She meant it figuratively, of course. Pinka had never sucked a teacher's dick, and didn't know anyone else who had either, although there were probably a handful at art college who had. And anyway, the schoolyard had changed. What felt like several lifetimes ago it had been about cheating at "Red Light, Green Light," but now it was about getting a ride from a falcon, eating his eyes, and battling illegal alien reptilians. The new schoolyard was a lot harder to puzzle out than the old one, that was for sure.

Pinka balanced the empty carton on her arm, and began to climb back down the ladder. She couldn't help herself: she turned to bask in the thrilled look on Wendy's face, who was beaming up at her, reaching out to pass her a new box of twenty balls. Sucking the teacher's dick was always a big mistake. Pinka missed her step and fell off the ladder. So much for the eyes of Horus.

Unconscious, Pinka dreamt they'd gone dancing, all three, as they so often did. In her dream she wanted only to dance with Roger and Clara, because of their shared magic, but Roger danced with any woman who asked, which were many, because of his dark haired good looks, his slender insouciance, his sexy moves. Pinka turned down the guys who asked her, preferring to sit at the bar and sip scotch and watch her friends. A strange man asked Clara to dance too, and she said yes, but then she danced as if alone, staring into ancient infinities, both elating and terrifying ones, and flapped her huge wings all the while, and he backed away, frightened, leaving her to dance alone. She wasn't the bimbo he'd taken her for. But then, Pinka wondered even in the dream, what was she? What were any of them? What, what, what? But no picture came from Roger's mind into her own this time to elucidate the matter.

And then Roger woke her up, said, "Get dressed, we're going dancing." Clara gave her coffee and put on music, what did they listen to then—was it The Stones, Miss You—or was it later, The Smiths? Pinka was getting used to it now, these little news flashes from the future. Clara gave her a blue vintage silk dress to wear; Pinka put it on, only a little begrudgingly. It was hard to get her out of jeans and sweatshirts, but she knew Roger liked going out with a babe on each arm, and she liked him so much she didn't mind humoring him. Clara herself didn't change out of the torn cotton tights and green wrap skirt she always wore.

"It doesn't matter," Roger said. "You have such beautiful eyes. You always look more dressed up than anyone else, just by having those eyes."

"You should see them from this side," Clara retorted. "Then you wouldn't like them so much."

Roger laughed, but like the reptilians, it gave Pinka a sudden sinking feeling of foreboding, like it might not after all be the winter of new boots and absinthe and magical companions she'd foreseen. And at the door, Clara suddenly turned around and climbed back up the stairs.

"It won't be fun without you," Roger called, but Clara didn't turn around. Pinka met his eyes. "Let her go," he said, "she's just tired."

"No, I'm going to go and talk to her," Pinka said. "I'll come and meet you later. We're going to Larry's, right?"

"Okay," Roger said, and kissed her on the cheek.

It felt so good she had to wonder.

By the time Pinka got back to the third floor, Clara was already in bed, in her own white hospital bed in Pinka's bedroom. She must've run the last flight. She must've gotten under the covers in her clothes.

"He's right it wouldn't be fun without you," Pinka said, feeling Clara's forehead which wasn't warm but seemed instead a little too cool. "He loves you more," she said, for it seemed to be true. Roger seemed lately more and more smitten by Clara. She was the coolest, a cosmic punk poetess, with her Egyptian stare and scruffy pretty hand me downs. Clara figured she herself was too butch to be the woman he wanted, in jeans and boots and sweatshirts, unkempt hair.

"Oh, just take him," Clara said. "Tonight when you come home. He'll have you, whether he likes me better or not. He's a man after all. And then you'll have him, which is what you want."

Pinka felt blessed, only now realizing she'd been doting on Roger all week while they played celestial mind games; thought, but secretly, he'd never have her, he who could have anyone, could have Clara. All the usual insecurities, well traveled by billions, nothing unique in her feelings at all which was part of her problem; Pinka could usually armor herself behind steely originality and here Roger had the rug pulled out from under her. She was used to being chased, and wanting someone badly was so hard to take she'd kept it secret even from herself. But obviously, not from Clara.

"Of the two of us, if I were Roger, I'd pick you every time," she said. Clara looked at her pityingly. Still Pinka wanted him so, and

Clara had seemingly given him to her, wrapped in silver, tied with ribbons and balloons. "And what will you do?" Pinka asked. "Who do you love?"

"I loved a boy called Sylvan last year, still love him. He wouldn't have me. I love you," Clara said, "but like a sister."

"I don't know Sylvan," Pinka said, surprised: they all knew the same crowd, more or less. She was shocked; thought they knew each other's hearts, removed them at night, playing with them like beloved pets. Thought she knew all there was to know, except whether Roger could love her.

"I'm going to sleep. I'm very tired," Clara said. "Pleased don't worry or try and make me come dancing, not tonight."

Pinka kissed Clara's forehead, worried she was coming down with flu. Reality sneered at her. Who could think Goddesses such as they could catch flu? "Sleep tight," Pinka said, and went out to meet Roger. It wasn't the same as going out with Clara at all. It felt more like a date, which was what she'd wanted, wasn't it? And when they got home they indeed made love on the pullout; Roger was Pinka's lover after that, just as Clara had prophesied.

The next morning Clara didn't get out of bed. Pinka brought her coffee and a banana muffin from Paul's coffee shop downstairs. "Tell me a story," she said, even though she knew she'd be late for work again.

"Oh," Clara said, surprised, seemingly happy, smiling at last: "It was so beautiful when we were priests and priestesses of Isis, before they came. Those rooms where we communicated with our star families, where we grounded heaven to earth through the apex. You were there. We were best friends just like now."

It seemed possible. "What else?" Pinka asked, remembering how, walking home the week before, they'd heard people's thoughts and the sidewalk had descended several inches so they could float. Like the horse that knows the way, the air currents had carried them home so they could use their time more profitably: staring at the reflections of stars in one another's eyes and not just any stars: always the Pleiades.

"They came," Clara said. "They took our temples, our power, our initiations and made them their own. Rituals enacted for peace and beauty were stolen, made into rituals for control."

"That's very sad," Pinka said, smoothing the hair out of Clara's eyes. "Your mother phoned last night, just before I left. I didn't want to wake you; you seemed so tired. She said to let you sleep. She'd like you to call. I did your laundry. We're starting to run out of money. If you want I can try to get you a position at the warehouse. The supervisor likes me; I'll tell her you're as good as I am. It's pretty fun there in a lot of ways, for a shit job." Like Clara's mother on the phone, Pinka was starting to think maybe all her friend needed was a job. Maybe all that was the matter was having too much time on her beautiful hands.

Clara ignored all this. "You have no idea how sad. Actually you do; you've just forgotten. Convenient that, how I wish I could. But I've been cursed with a good memory since before I was born."

"But we're together now. We're trying to fix it all."

Clara answered in a rhyme: "But can you do it on your own, who are you when the spirit's flown?"

What spirit?

That night after work Pinka stayed home with Clara, while Roger went out alone. Clara couldn't sleep at all, it turned out, nor get up. Pinka sat half the night in the darkened bedroom with her. Not speaking for an hour Clara stared unblinking at the poster of Marilyn on the wall, whose beauty and tragedy she already imitated, the prettiest girl Pinka had ever known. Refusing to get up. Muttering, when she at last spoke, about Egypt.

"Egypt Egypt Egypt. Sadder than you know."

Pinka stopped arguing. She held Clara's hand a little less tightly. She began to fear. At last Clara rolled her eyes, a little secretive smile on her face as if it was all part of some cosmically ironic joke too abstruse for the likes of Pinka, winked at Marilyn, went to sleep. Outside the night cars and street cars went by on Yonge Street, noisy even in the middle of the night. Pinka stayed up, worrying about Clara, waiting for Roger to come home. Roger and dawn straggled in at the same time. Pinka didn't ask questions, but she still stayed awake, listening to time go by. Later she washed the kitchen floor and wrote scraps of poems here and there, stealing Clara's best line.

But can you do it on your own, who are you when the spirit's flown?

Did Clara know about Horus? She hadn't told either of them. They were the two people she thought she could tell absolutely anything on earth, or they had been till a few days ago, when Clara had started to withdraw, and Pinka had never gotten around to sharing the story of the bird-headed god. But he was Egyptian. And hadn't Clara been talking about Egypt a lot lately, as she withdrew even further?

Clara went to work without any sleep again. It was the week before, only turned on its ass. Wendy and Patty and all the others were clever and fun to be around. The girls who had never shown the slightest ability to count or space, were suddenly quite competent. The floors sparkled not just with ground glitter but, it seemed, with fairy dust. Pinka found a torn cardboard carton of plastic Egyptian gods under one of the trestle tables, where she and Patty surreptitiously rummaged at lunch. It was too coincidental, and too unlikely to be true. And yet there it was. She was torn between the urge to question Wendy, ask about the little gods' provenance, what lesser mall project they were leftover from, and putting them in her large tote bag and sneaking them home. All the girls came to work with enormous tote bags. When Wendy was gone from the room they'd stuff their bags with junk, mini lights and Santa Clauses and reindeer and plastic pine cones to decorate their own apartments with. Pinka thought their boldness and their theft were sure to be discovered and get them fired, but which of them cared if they got fired? Equally bad jobs were free for the taking, all over town. And perhaps even management didn't care if they stole. Perhaps management was at core softhearted, and knew the girls needed a little sparkle to jazz up their pathetic lives. But of course she wouldn't ask Wendy. It was a moment for sneakiness, like cheating at "Red Light, Green Light." If she gave Clara Isis and Set and Horus and Hathor, Clara would get better. How could she not? It was a miracle, after all.

"It won't work," Patty said.

"I beg your pardon?"

"You can take them, but take them for you, not for her."

"What? I thought only Roger and Clara could do that."

"Do what?" Patty asked.

"Telepathy," Pinka said. "What you just did."

"Shut up or they'll hear you," Patty hissed.

"Who?" Pinka asked.

"The aliens, stupid," Patty said. "They hate telepathy, more than anything else. They can hear our words, but not our thoughts. So we have to be real careful about what we say."

"Talk in code, kind of like?" Pinka asked.

"You got it, " Patty said. "They've already got her, like it or not. You still have a chance. Don't try and save her, you're not nearly strong enough yet."

"Will I ever be?" Pinka asked.

"Maybe in twenty-five years," Patty said.

"Horus said something like that," Pinka told her.

"Who's Horus?" Patty asked.

"The bird headed guy who gave me a ride that day? I told you about that, didn't I?"

"Oh. Your hallucination," Patty laughed. "Let's go across the street for a beer. We still have time. And if we're late back, what the fuck, who even cares."

Now and again the girls went across the street to the Gladstone, where draft beer could be had for the seemly price of three for a dollar. When they got back, Wendy smelled the beer on their breaths and scolded them. It seemed strange. They were all of age. All the guys at TSE had double martinis at lunch and no one complained. Yet the girls drank watery draft with their fries and Wendy admonished them as if they were teenagers at boarding school. Or interred in some kind of work house. Which was more or less what it felt like.

"Wendy will take a fit," Pinka reminded her.

"Wendy will not. She worships the ground you walk on. Because of you, she filled her big order early and got a huge bonus."

It was true the giant trees, all of which Pinka had decorated quite alone, were gone. Shipped out. She'd barely noticed. She'd been too busy worrying about Clara, and having sex with Roger. And beginning the new shipment, mercifully smaller trees of a nonetheless garish shade of silver. Pinka thought of the little Egyptian gods, how she'd love to sneak in early the morning this order shipped, replace all the gaudy blue plastic balls and ribbons with Isis and Horus and Set and Hathor and what was the jackal headed one called again? Anubis, that was him. And how come she knew so much about Egyptian deities suddenly? Was it a news flash from the future, like multicolored geometric push pins, or from the past? Maybe, at eleven, Pinka had been obsessed with Egypt, had learned the names and faces of all the gods, kind of like Clara now, only saner. Maybe, between "Winnie the Pooh" and dinosaurs and Bauhaus, both the band and the art movement, it had once seemed important. In twenty-five years, would she care about Bauhaus? Remember any of their names, either the guys in the band or the guys in the art movement?

It depended. It depended on a lot of things. Like whether Clara would be okay. And whether Roger, beloved by women, would be able to resist this balm to his ego and be faithful to her. And whether she'd go back to OCAD and finish her degree. And whether she'd be able to stop getting Patty to sniff the glue she used to glue things. And. And. And. It depended on so many things, was the fucking problem.

"Cool," she asked. "Do we get a share?"

"Are you fucking kidding?" Patty asked. "What do you think this place is, a democracy?"

And they went across the street and ate French fries and drank draft beer and watched some guys playing pool. Eventually one of the guys came over and asked whether either of them would like to suck his dick in the alley for twenty dollars and Patty hurled such a stream of epithets at him that he turned quite pale and looked like he might retch before turning back to his friends.

Pinka thought Patty had gone overboard but when she next glanced at the guys she noticed they all had a decidedly reptilian look to their skin. As well as tails. Claws. Scales. And then they were just guys again, offensive yahoos. She glanced at Patty.

"You have to be harsh with them, or they'll keep coming at you," Patty said mildly, before tossing her Export A butt into the dregs of her third, now empty draft glass.

That night when Clara called, Pinka asked Roger to go in to her. She washed a week of dishes and re-organized the coffee table clutter while she waited, sketched Clara's face on scraps of paper wherever she went. Wrote things under the faces. Nice things.

Roger came out. "What did she say?" Pinka asked.

"She's crackers. She thinks she's Isis." Roger insouciantly applied blue eyeliner, staring into the mirror that hung above the sink, and not thanking her for the done dishes, either. And went out, not saying good-bye. Pinka looked in on Clara; she was sleeping. When Clara woke near midnight and called, Pinka brought her rosehip tea she didn't drink and said, "He thinks you think you're Isis."

Clara sighed.

"Well, do you?" Already taking his side.

"Of course not. What do you think, I'm crazy? It's just that's every man's choice, to be Osiris or Set. Most choose Set, for obvious reasons. He's the one with the power, or so he says, and is unfortunately usually believed."

Osiris. That was the other one.

"What about Horus?" Pinka asked, armed with her new or old found wisdom. "Horus killed Set after Set killed Osiris. It took awhile, but he did it. He lost an eye for his trouble, and Thoth gave him a new one. But Horus missed his dad, or his brother, depending on which version you believe, and so he gave the eye to Osiris, who came back to life and then descended to the underworld to preside over the dead. And ever since, the eyes of Horus have given protection. The right eye is rational, the left eye is irrational; Thoth's eye, eye of midnight and magic. Having both kinds of eyes is useful," Pinka said. Maybe Clara had only the left, had lost her right eye. Pinka wished she'd kept some of Horus's eyes back; she could've made Clara eat them. There must have been at least one rational eye in the lot.

"By the way, how are you finding him?" Clara asked, changing the subject. Pinka felt a little ill. Just days before she'd felt she'd won the prince of stars, and now it was as if Clara had tossed her an old gnawed bone, no meat left on it.

"It's fine. He's fine; we're fine. It's you we're worried about," Pinka said and went back to the other room, back to Roger. She'd heard his key in the door and was ready to ask where he'd been, as she'd be doing for years. News flash.

"She doesn't think she's Isis," Pinka explained, "not literally, not at all. She said every man has the choice of being Osiris or Set, the good or the evil twin. It's kind of interesting and intellectual and metaphorical, really. I wish I knew that story better, then I'd be able to explain it more clearly." Maybe she'd go across the street to the library one evening and look it up. It would beat watching Roger putting on make-up and going out without her. It would beat holding Clara's hand while she stared unblinking at Marilyn for what seemed like hours, her mouth twitching a little every once in awhile. It was the unblinking part that bothered Pinka the most, she had to admit. Did Clara really never blink? That would be dangerous, if it were true. You weren't supposed to not blink. It was bad for your eyes, Pinka was sure.

Right. As if not blinking was Clara's biggest problem.

"Crackers," Roger said.

"How come you never ask me to go with you anymore?" Pinka asked.

"Well," Roger said. "You have to get up for work."

"Did I tell you about meeting Horus?"

"Is this more of her Egyptian bullshit?" Roger asked.

"No. I'd go with you," Pinka said, "I'd just come home at midnight."

Roger rolled his eyes. "None of the good clubs open till eleven."

"Well," Pinka said, "if you could get a job maybe we could go out together on Friday and Saturday nights like normal people, and we could buy groceries and cook instead of spending my whole paycheck on restaurants, and—"

"—It's my UI check that pays for our meals. Yours goes to the rent and phone. She doesn't contribute anything at all. We're supporting her between the two of us, you and I."

"I don't mind, Roger. She's more fragile than we are. Although I did suggest I'd try and get her a job at the warehouse."

"That job will be over before Christmas. You said so yourself. It's seasonal, like mail sorting at the Post Office. I think she should move out. Anyway, what happened to my witty Pinka? You're usually so clever and sharp. This conversation is such a downer." And he leant towards her, open mouthed. Pinka opened her mouth in return, misgivings and all.

Was Roger Set, or was he Osiris? Pinka figured she probably

knew, but just didn't want to look at that just yet. Come to think of it, Osiris was a pretty crappy deal too, nice as he might have been. After all, he got dismembered, in both meanings of the term. Set was the original serial killer, hiding the body parts so there'd be no evidence.

All women wait for the prince of stars to dance with, and Set steps into the space made by their longing, leans openmouthed towards them.

News flash.

Roger headed for the door.

"Where are you going? It's four o clock in the morning."

"I'm sleeping at my friend Zak's. The pullout is uncomfortable; there's a nice bed in your bedroom. That's where we should be."

"It's a three quarter. And it's hers."

"We could get another. Sleeping in the living room is ridiculous."

And he shut the door behind him.

Pinka wondered why he'd reapplied his eyeliner for Zak.

She looked out the tiny kitchen window and watched him walk alone down Yonge Street, away from her.

Clara called.

Pinka went back in to her after all, even though she didn't much feel like it. She argued with Clara this time, as if her friend had chosen. "How can one go mad," she asked, "when the world is round, what edge is there to fall off? Our minds are the same."

"They watch for those who try to regrow their wings," Clara said. "They're the first to be destroyed, lest we tell the others."

"Do you believe this is all true?" Pinka asked. "I mean literally?"

"You might still be able to save me if you opened his eyes."

Pinka was a little annoyed by all the deflection. "But I do need to know whether you remember other lives," she said stubbornly.

"You should do it too."

"People will say I'm crackers," Pinka said, didn't add: just look at you, and lay down beside her till Clara's eyes closed, to sleep or other times or worlds she didn't know, before going back to the living room to see if Roger had changed his mind about Zak's and come home. He hadn't. But then, he hadn't said he would, either.

In the morning rumpled purple sheets remaining, shrouding only absence. Clara had taken Pinka's favorite shoes, expensive blue velvet platforms. Pinka didn't mind, although if Roger had been there, she might have woken him, said, "she took my shoes without asking."

She knew. It sunk inside her like a heavy heavy stone, her knowing. It sunk and sunk and sunk. She stopped paying attention, knowing it would never hit bottom, there was so far to go. She went downstairs for coffee, opened her notebook and wrote. Before that morning she'd sometimes written for pleasure and sometimes, she had to admit, tried to sound haunting and evocative and profound in the hope of impressing her art college pals, but at that moment she held her blue book as she might a life raft. Words a line thrown from the shore, through heavy seas. Seas heavy as the stone inside her, still falling. It would be falling there forever inside her, she knew. And wrote and wrote and wrote, as if it could yet save her.

To each of us, the "you" was Roger, at least at the beginning. Just like in that old song, he probably thinks this story is about him. So be it, for he's right, it is, if only in a quite small part, smaller than he'd intended, small as he deserves in fact. What I wonders now is how Roger pulled that off, making Clara and I less consequential to one another than he was.

Him. Sometimes I want to call him up and say, "Do you remember what we saw together?" Maybe he didn't see it at all. Maybe I saw alone, but wanted company so badly I believed he didn't just see beside me, but received those visions from some celestial library, and projected them into my mind. She was right. How glad I was to have a mage for a lover, handsome and profound.

When did I fall in love with him? Or, as she would later ask, why?

He and I spent a few short years together. We had our moments of peace and joy and pleasure but in the end I knew my deepest dreams were broken glass at my feet, not just illusions but able to hurt, not just me but her. Shattered crystal visions. Me. Him. Her. Said good-bye. Went west, kept writing. What else is there to do? Now and then I try and send her some of my equanimity, as if it might yet help. Here, girl, take as much as you want. And these words: the stone nears the bottom, falls to rest at last among shredded wings, drowned and devoured purple. I remember her words then.

But can you do it on your own, who are you when the spirit's flown?

Can I mend these broken wings by writing? I have no choice but to try, for her sake and for mine. The all-seeing eye of Horus is so powerful it cuts the bearer who hasn't trained to carry the burden of sight.

We were children, just over and just under twenty. Roger was born the same year as me. Clara was two years younger. How often in the intervening years I have thought of Clara, and sometimes wept for her. Or is it myself I'm weeping for when I think I weep for Clara? Or all of humanity? A doomed plant populated by sleepwalkers, no knowledge of their enslavement. We are all little more than prey, the indoctrination so near complete no knowledge beyond nightmare leaks through to daylight consciousness.

There is a Them. There was one then, there is one now. Seeing it again and again, you chose madness. If madness is the right word for remembering.

You. There, at last I have called her by her rightful name. Should've done it then. Poor child all alone. Please come home.

Please stop being crazy. We'll value your sight this time, I promise, and no longer burn you dead for it as we did so many times before. Before.

Within the week she called from a psych ward, medicated. She sure did like her drugs, that girl, any way she could get 'em. Much more than me.

This is all have left: a quill, these bones, probably all I ever had. I still have dreams of that apartment I left at twenty-one, with you, she lost. Lost lost lost. I learned to work there, before I invited the two of you to share my home, my life. It was full of quiet and wholesome solitude and blank white pages I learned there, for the first time, to fill one after another. If I'd known how good for me those rooms were, I might not have been in such a hurry to welcome you in, to give you my power.

The prettiest girl I ever knew went mad.

All that was years ago. Some mornings now I wake with hope in full bloom, feel more than I've ever felt. Do I mean in this life or all the others too? How can I know? Yet it feels like first hope.

Like automatic writing, except it wasn't information from the spirit world, but from the future. News flash after news flash, but pouring out through her hand; Pinka didn't know any of it till she saw it on the page. It didn't seem to pass through her mind at all on its way in, or was that its way out?

Things were getting out of hand. Maybe she shouldn't have eaten so many of Horus's eyes. Maybe she should have pocketed most of them, saved them for later.

Which later?

And if the futures she had just written were probabilities and not prophesies, which was the good future she hadn't yet seen? Could she write that one instead? Or better yet, live it?

Even more on the bright side, Horus's eyes seemingly made her capable of going to work not just once on no sleep, but day after day after day.

The place was empty, all the orders shipped. No girls, no chatter, no sparkle. Had they told her the day before the job was finished for the season and she'd just forgotten? What was happening? At least she could take the little Egyptian gods home. Pinka rummaged under one of the trestle tables where she'd stashed the tote bag and then another, and then another. As she pushed cartons aside under the last table she heard footsteps, and Patty's voice saying, "You won't find them."

"Why ever not? I left them here. Did you take them?"

"I wouldn't do that, " Patty said, "You left them in the other reality. Now come out from under there," and reached her a hand. Pinka took it, and let Patty pull her out and up.

"Wendy's coming," Patty said, "And I'm sorry, but I have to do this or the realities won't bridge properly. I wasn't supposed to have to, but you're getting stuck. You're letting them get to you," and pushed her, hard. Pinka knocked her head on a table and blacked out. Her last thought was she'd known right from the start Patty had it in for her.

She woke to look into Wendy's face. "What's your name again?" the supervisor asked. Pinka wondered whether she was worried about concussion or really didn't know. Wendy being a boss, the second seemed more likely to be true.

"I'm not sure," Pinka replied. "I'm looking for a new one. Got any?"

The woman laughed. "You're crazy, all the girls say so, but you can space the balls evenly, and you know the difference between white and green."

"Red and green," Pinka said. "Red means stop and green means go. We all remember that from the schoolyard, playing "Red Light, Green Light." Although I have to admit, I used to cheat."

The supervisor laughed and helped her up. "Look into my eyes."

Pinka looked. Wendy's eyes were blue. She wore gold tone cat-eye glasses, but just now these hung from a chain around her neck. Her upper lip was lined. She smoked. Her hair was permed and dyed. She wasn't young. "Can you work through lunch? We're behind."

I have a concussion and no sleep and you're asking me to work through lunch, Pinka thought but did not say. "Get the night shift to do it," she replied instead.

"Even if I had one, I doubt they'd know the difference between red and green," Wendy said.

"You should've put up ads at the art college. Every girl in here is drunk or pregnant or on drugs or some combination of the above. Much as I love them, and in any case my lifestyle doesn't allow me to claim any moral superiority, only a superior ability to count and space," Pinka said, aware the same lippiness would get any number of the other girls fired.

"After Christmas," Wendy said, "we'll get started on next season. You'll be in the art department. But lay off the drugs."

"And the streets are paved with gold," Pinka said, and turned her back on Wendy. She made her way to a stool at one of the sorting and gluing stations. In spite of the ventilators the place was thick with dust. The dust on the floor sparkled. It was made of ground glass and plastic and glue and feathers, particulated into dust. And skin. Don't forget the skin. Pinka didn't smoke, but just then she wished she did. In those days you could still smoke in the workplace. There it was again. In those days, unlike now. Or was it that now she wasn't supposed to, but in the old days it had been alright? The last time she'd thought a thing like that she'd fallen off a stepladder. There was nowhere to fall to now, except to the floor from her stool. She leaned her elbows on the work table for extra stability. She squinted her eyes at the floor, wanting to make it sparkle some more. It was like the milky way. Up north where the spruce trees were real. It had been so long.

She heard Wendy still chortling behind her. She looked up from the felt Santa Clauses someone had been gluing onto already fraying red polyester satin ribbon to see Patty approaching her. She was scared. But Patty smiled and said, "You look like shit, about forty-five years old."

"No wonder. You punched me out."

"Wrong reality." Patty lit a cigarette. "Wendy's such a bitch but she laughs at your jokes."

"Maybe no one told her any good ones before," Pinka said, wondering vaguely whether this would get her beaten up in the schoolyard at lunch.

Patty asked what was wrong with her.

"Don't you mean what's left of me?" Pinka asked.

It was too abstruse for Patty. Ralph would've understood. Or Clara.

"What's wrong?" Patty asked again, as everyone was asking her recently, everyone except Wendy and Horus, who had supervisory positions, and expected great things from her. Working overtime on no sleep. Eating eyes. The hell with them.

"Tell Wendy I'll call Workmen's Comp on her if she doesn't lay off," Pinka told Patty. "I'm going home."

"You'll get fired," Patty said, but she said it as if she didn't believe it herself, as if it were a test.

"I will not," Pinka said. "She can't afford to fire me."

"I think you're right," Patty said. "All this crap gets shipped Friday. And you do seem pretty fucked up."

"I fell off the ladder and knocked myself out. My ride to work had a bird's head. I didn't get any sleep. And last night I learned that evil reptilian aliens have it in for every one of us." Only after she'd said it did Pinka remember Patty had already let it slip she knew about the reptilians. Or was that in another reality?

"Ya gotta watch the reptilians," Patty sighed. "They're the worst. But the bird headed guy I don't believe. The way I see it, you were just hallucinating."

Pinka left, taking the bag full of little gods someone had kindly left by the door for her. The streets were largely empty of traffic, it being mid-morning. She had to walk most of the way home; the transit workers were still on strike. It was cold. She only fainted once. A guy in a weird outfit woke her up. For a brief second she hoped it was Horus, but it was a guy in a clown suit, handing out flyers for a discount carpet cleaning operation, which not only didn't make any sense, but then he had the nerve to ask for her number.

"I fell off the ladder at work and knocked myself out. My ride to work this morning was a bird. He gave me little eye shaped pills and said I'd be fine if I took them, which, as you can see, was a big fat lie. I didn't get any sleep. And last night I learned that evil reptilian aliens have it in for each and every one of us. So that's bloody rude of you to hit on me."

"But I know about the reptilians," the clown said. "I knew you knew about them too. That's why you keep blacking out, not knowing what day it is when you wake up. They're after you, because you saw. I know how to fight them. You need to make a screen, so they can't see you, try to harm you in any more ways. I know how the screens are made. If you don't want to give me your number, I'll give you mine." And he scribbled on a matchbook and gave it to her. The matchbook said, "Success Without College."

"I'll drop by sometime," she said, pocketing it. She didn't mean it, she thought, but Pinka was at the same time a little curious. "We can have a meeting. Invite a few others. I know two. How many do you know?"

"They don't allow me visitors at my group home," the clown said sadly. "Next month I move to another one, once I've proved I'm stable enough."

"Best of luck with that," Pinka said and walked north on Yonge Street, but she didn't throw away the matches.

At home Clara was putting on tea and rolling a joint. Pinka gave her the bag of gods, waited for her reaction.

"These are very cute," Clara said, "but why Egypt? You said you'd bring me a string of lights in the shapes of strawberries."

"Hmm," Pinka said, not remembering that ever having happened. "Anyway, I'm glad you came home."

"Where did I come home from?" Clara asked, and Roger laughed as if he got it and Pinka never could. They were playing cards. Clara was wearing her favorite mauve sweater. She'd found it at the Salvation Army. It went so well with the mauve in her eyes. Maybe Roger was secretly Clara's boyfriend, Pinka thought out of nowhere, and they only had sex when she was at work, for fear of offending her. After all, she gave them largely free rent, and she might not want to do that anymore if she knew. Maybe. And maybe they were after all just friends. Occasionally they held hands, occasionally Roger pecked Clara on the cheek. But Pinka did that with both of them too, so it didn't mean much. Still, they snickered over their cards in an exclusionary way, but then Roger said, "Get dressed, we're going dancing. We'll eat on the way."

Clara gave her coffee and put on music, first early Stones, then Roxy Music, then The Smiths, then Tom Waits. "The music was so much better when you were young," she said. "You're lucky, Pinka."

"Tom Waits was when I was young," Pinka said, "and now too. The Stones as well, although no one I know listens to them anymore. And who has any idea what the Smiths are up to now?"

News flash, only this time it had come out of her own mouth, as if, as if—

On the way to the bedroom Pinka stopped; Roger had pinned the rent to a bulletin board using multicolored geometrically shaped push pins. The main thing, Pinka thought, was she was getting used to it now. Clara brought her a blue vintage silk dress to wear, although she herself didn't change out of the torn cotton tights and green wrap skirt she almost always wore. "It doesn't matter," Roger told her. "You have such beautiful eyes. You always look more dressed up than anyone else, just by having those eyes."

"You should see them from this side," Clara retorted. "Then you wouldn't like them so much."

Roger laughed, but like the aliens, it gave Pinka a sudden sinking feeling of foreboding, like it might not be a winter of new boots and absinthe and magical companions after all. On the way to the door, she looked in the mirror and almost passed out for the third time that day, if you could even call what time had become days anymore. She was old, Wendy's age. She'd stayed thin, could fit into the dress which was oddly still beguiling on her. There were a lot of dry cleaning numbers stapled to the inside of the lapel. Aside from the horror of being suddenly aged and seeing herself as ugly, which a more careful examination told her she was in fact, not, Pinka found herself wondering whether it was a good thing or a bad thing. And had it happened when she'd fallen off the ladder, or when she'd eaten Horus's eyes; when Patty had knocked her down, or when she'd fainted and the clown had helped her? Or was it, as the clown had suggested, an attack on her by the reptilian aliens, in revenge for discovering their existence? Maybe it didn't matter, even if that was the case. Maybe the trick was she had to find a way to use it for good.

Out on the street a horn honked three times.

"The taxi's here," Clara said. "You look beautiful, Pinka."

And at last she saw it all in her mind's eyes, the eyes of Horus he'd made her swallow all those years before and had been waiting all this time, patiently, for her to open, just as Clara had asked her to do: in the life where they'd all three been young at the same time, Clara ended up in the crazy hospital, Roger married Pinka and cheated every chance he got, and the aliens put chips in everyone's foreheads. It was better this way, to be Wendy's age, one of the supervisors. She could help keep the young people implant free and out of nuthouses.

"I've changed my mind," Pinka said. "I've got some paperwork to do. Enjoy yourselves. And if the driver has the head of a bird and gives you little eyes to swallow, don't turn him down. His eyes will help you to see. And remind him it's my ride, but that you guys can have it."

They kissed her on the cheek, the middle-aged bohemian landlady, and went out without her, just as Pinka and Roger had gone out with Clara that dreadful day so many years before. "Other reality," Patty's voice said in her mind, and Pinka missed Patty terribly, wondered what had become of her, and wished her well. Patty had been so helpful even though she'd never believed in Horus, unless she'd been lying to help keep them all safe, or maybe Horus had another name in her religion. Just then Horus's eyes told Pinka she owned the building now, and that she did indeed still work at the ornament firm, but as head of design. In her current reality she'd stayed on after Christmas that year, taken on more and more of the design work, not just fulfilling other people's concepts but creating her own. Because she was good, Wendy and the owner had been able to secure contracts from better clients, not just cheesy faded malls in the middle of nowhere, but up and coming independent design stores, and even Brown's Shoes on Bloor Street. Now Pinka too wore cat eye glasses on a string, but she wore them with irony. Wendy had died last year, of lung cancer. Pinka had visited her in her hospital bed, and said, "If you hadn't complimented my work that day, I'd never have fallen off the ladder, and I'd never have agreed to keep working for you after the season was over, and I'd never have risen through the ranks and been able to buy my building and rent it out to magical youngsters in need of shelter."

Wendy had looked puzzled as if she didn't know anything about that. Maybe in Wendy's version, things were slightly different. Still, Pinka continued. "I'd never have seen push pins replace thumb tacks. The aliens would've gotten me."

And Wendy had said, “Phone your friend,” and Pinka had asked, “you mean Horus?” and Wendy had replied, “No, although he runs a cab company now. He calls it the Egyptian Taxi Company. Or The Wings of Isis or something. You should be able to find it. He has extra services.”

“I think I know all that,” Pinka said.

“But I meant your clown.”

And in her current reality which she had to figure was probably the best of the lot, Pinka listened to Horus start the engine and drive the kids to their party. She went to the coat closet and took out first her old jacket, and then the matchbook that had stayed in the pocket for twenty-five years, gone in the wink of an eye, vanished in an Egyptian god’s wing beat. It was time to call.

“Hello?”

“Success without college,” she said.

His name was Randy, Horus’s eyes told her. He knew immediately who she was. “We won,” he said. “And we didn’t even have to have that meeting.”

Polyhymnia
The Muse of Sacred Poetry

At the same time, several Polyhymnian sects also thrived. Composers of sacred poetry all, the more devout members took a vow of public silence. Some scholars claimed the sacred poetry was a mere diversion from their investigations into horticulture, meditation and geometry (including numerous studies on the then-called blending of floral and edible species) which were meticulous and infamously disseminated. Indeed, the sects were banished in ignominy under persecution at the hands of the Pythagoreans.

Margaret Fitzgerald-Dent
Proceedings of the Society for Presocratic Studies:
Special Symposium on Women in Ancient Science, 1967

Ask For Her Hand

Victoria Elizabeth Garcia

MY SISTER CANDACE BANGED on the door, then walked straight in without waiting for us to answer. Patent-leather stilettos lengthened her legs, and her camel-hair trench-coat swirled at mid-calf. With her was a delicate man in pinstripes, wearing an inky purple shirt and a bow-tie. He towed a wheeled case that said "Western Culinary Institute."

He had to be the fiancé.

"Welcome home," I said, hurrying through the old living room. The clip in my hair had come loose. It hung from the back of my head at an angle. I prayed she wouldn't notice.

I had spent the last two days cleaning, but I had forgotten about the upstairs. We all had. Now, watching Candace, as she took in the dusty flowers, the clutter, and the old furniture, I could see how horrible it must look.

She let me help her off with her coat, and I got a breath of her cologne, spicy and fresh. She'd started wearing men's fragrances when she was in middle-school. Clearly, she hadn't stopped. The delicate man smiled at me. He wasn't much taller than I was.

"Where are Gil and Lil?" Candace asked. "Where's Dad?" Her eyes swept across the room, as though she didn't really expect to find evidence of them.

"They're downstairs, getting ready."

My sister smirked and nodded, then the basement door banged open and it was Lilly, our stepmother, wearing her office-lady make-up and her office-lady shoes. Her yellow church-blouse had a corsage of blue silk flowers pinned to it, and she was holding a midnight-blue bottle of Polish spring water.

Her rose-pink lips split into a smile.

"So *this* is the young fellow!" She raised thin eyebrows. "Hello!"

I watch the young fellow compose himself. Shoulders shifted for a second, and he pulled his chin up before coming forward to take my stepmother's hand. There was a moment of hesitation, and I suspected that he was trying to decide whether to kiss it or not. I decided I might loathe him if he did.

"Mrs. Konzhaurr. Very, very pleased to meet you. I'm Stewart Clench." He flashed a grin. His teeth were white, and regular as graph paper. "I'm looking forward to getting to know all of you." Then he turned and winked at me.

I knew was being worked, so I winked back. I winked like a half-broken Western Barbie, heavily and mechanically. Maybe I would loathe him, after all.

I followed my stepmother into the basement. Behind us I heard my sister and her fiancé as they stepped onto the warping, hollow stairs. His Western Culinary Institute case bumped along beside them.

Two years ago, we all started living in the basement. My father thought it would be safer, and my stepmother and aunt agreed. Aunt Gil built us a new kitchen where the laundry room used to be, and the rec room, with its football-team wallpaper and its heavy red shag, became the bedroom. We divided it with partitions that we got at the office-liquidation store.

For this homecoming dinner, we'd moved the futons, clothes bars, and office dividers into the upstairs kitchen. The rec room, once again, was long and wide. A string of card tables looked surprisingly regal under piles of tablecloths.

Hours before, when my father had come downstairs with the electric Christmas candles, I'd told him they were too much. Then Aunt Gil had snapped at me to remember to defer to my father, and she had set them out herself. Their jerky flicker made the football logos on the walls seem to move.

Only two dividers were left, and they cut off the far end of the room, the part that normally belonged to Aunt Gil. Behind it, I happened to know, were two chairs and a pair of brandy snifters. That's where dad and the delicate man would go, if the delicate man asked to marry Candace.

At the foot of the stairs, Mamma Lilly turned and smiled at me.

"Why don't you give Candy and her young man a tour?" she said. "Candy hasn't been here since we remodeled." Then she scooted off into the kitchen to join Aunt Gil and Dad, who were bent over the roast.

When Candace had lived with us years before, during the height of our Charismatic phase, she would have made a crack about the remodeling. This time, she didn't. She was a trainer at the Small Business Administration now, and it seemed that she'd acquired a kind of personal shellac. It kept her hair in place and her nails from chipping. Maybe it kept her mouth shut, too.

The delicate man looked over my shoulder and into the kitchen.

"That looks beautiful," he called. I didn't know how he could see whether it looked beautiful or not.

My father stood, turned, and met his eyes. Dad was a tall man, with a thick middle and a fringe of golden hair around a shiny bald pate.

"You must be Stewart," he said, his face breaking into a grin. "Did I hear that you're a chef-to-be?"

"That's right," he said. "Can I be of any help?"

Dad gestured at Lilly and Gil. "They seem to think the roast might be coming out too dry. Me, I say it looks perfect, but—"

"Mushroom soup," said Aunt Gil. "I told you three hours ago, mushroom soup. You didn't listen, and now look."

"It may not be too late to bard it a bit," said Stewart, breaking away from Candace's side. "You don't have any duck fat, do you?"

Candace leaned toward me and whispered, "A minute, alone, now."

We went behind divider, to the engagement chairs. Candace sat on the recliner and kicked off the stilettos. Noticing the cognac, she picked up the bottle and poured herself several inches. I wondered if there would be enough left for the proposal.

"Okay," she said, leaning back and closing her eyes. "I know things have changed, because you folks have booze in the house now, but what the hell's up with all the flowers?"

"They make the house welcoming to spirits," I said, shrugging.

She let out fragment of laugh and shook her head.

"I asked you how much Jesus to expect. You told me none."

"There isn't much, really. They stopped going Latter Rain almost a year ago."

"But angels. . . ."

"Well, now they're going to Ephenia Carter. She has lots of stereogram cards and talks to dead people. Last week, she helped Mamma Lilly to talk to her ex-husband from before Dad. It's not a religion, exactly. Ephenia does massage, too."

"They're paying her, of course."

I shrugged.

"A lot?"

I shrugged again. "I don't think it's more than they can afford."

Aunt Gil had a small pension from the Burlington Northern railroad, and Mamma Lilly had half of her ex-husband's retirement from the county. Dad worked part time for a smoke alarm company, managing four salesmen. He made decent money some months. I knew all of this, because I'd been taking care of the finances for about a year, but that was not something I have any desire to tell

Candace.

Candace drew her legs up and took a sip from her snifter.

"You can't let them do these things," she said.

Stewart's face popped up like a puppet over the office divider. "I'm going to run to Ettinger's for some duck fat, love. Back before you know it." His black hair was glossy as a show-dog's coat.

Then he disappeared. Candace stared after him for a moment. When she turns back to me, there was a look on her face that was half smile and half smirk.

"Do you love him?" I asked.

Her eyebrows rose. "He's a bit short," she said, resting her chin in her hand. She held the cognac bottle out to me.

"Have some. Have a lot."

I eyeballed the liquor level. There were about five inches in the bottle. I could afford a swallow or two.

I poured a glass and brought it to my lips. The fumes penetrated my nose and make me want to sneeze. It smelled astringent and woody, like a varnish. At Ephenia Carter's, we had wine sometimes, because the spirits liked it. But the wine we drank there was syrupy-thick and purple. I didn't think I could drink the cognac, and I didn't think Dad would be able to either.

A tremor of laughter passed through Candace.

"Bottoms up, little sis." I met her eyes over the top of the glass; then I open my mouth and knocked it back.

There was a tingling numbness, and then a hot splash on the back of my throat. I closed my eyes and strained not to gag. When I open my eyes, she was still staring at me.

"Good girl," she said. "A woman who can't drink can't possibly have the stones to lead the old farts out of here. How's that going, by the way?"

In the kitchen, I heard banging, then Aunt Gil's voice saying, "You can't keep pulling it out and putting it back in."

Candace nodded toward the kitchen and snorted. "I'll say," she whispered.

"Well, how can I tell how cooked it is if I don't pull it out? If you ask me, we should just shut off the oven and wait for the young man to come back."

Candace clamped a hand over her mouth. Her eyes bulged, and I could hear her choking on laughter.

"I don't know why we're trying to eat this at all," said Gil. "I have that lovely raw food book, after all."

"I'm not going to plunk a bucket of blueberries in front of the man who's come here to ask for Candy."

I looked back at my sister and saw that the shellac over her smile was beginning to flake away.

She leaned forward.

"They think I'm going to marry him?"

I winced.

"Did *you* think I was going to marry him?"

"Well..."

She slumped in her chair and tilted her head back to stare at the ceiling.

"Elisabeth, why?"

"You never come back here. They figured it had to be something big—like maybe you were getting ready to settle down, have babies, and become a member of this family again. It's not like they don't know that you're embarrassed by them. They aren't that damned dense."

"They thought I would want ask their permission before I got married."

"Why did—"

Candace stood up.

"Because if you must know, I've been dining out on stories about this place. I went on five dates with the guy. Conversation slowed; I trotted out this shit. He was fascinated, and who wouldn't be? You all are living in a slow-motion train wreck. Fuck it, Liz. I'm getting out of here."

I stood up too.

"Candy, they can hear you."

"I know they can. I mean them to."

Candace popped her head over the divider and looked into the kitchen. The aunts and Mamma Lilly stood there, staring. Aunt Gil wore an apron spattered with the juice from the roast.

"Gang, I don't think I can handle this scene. I'm leaving. Don't hold your breath waiting for me to come back."

Dad came forward through the kitchen. He had the roast stuck on the end of a fork.

"Candy," he began.

"Jesus," she said, and she turned away before she could hear what he might have to say.

We were cleaning up when Candy's boyfriend came back, white-wrapped package of duck in hand. We weren't really expecting him to return. We'd cut the roast in half and had thrown it into a pair of old margarine tubs. It was still bleeding red in the middle, and no one'd had the heart to try to eat it.

Dad was the one who came out of the kitchen to tell him that his girl had gone.

The delicate man craned his neck to look over our heads, like he didn't quite believe that Candace wasn't there.

"That's, um," he ran his fingers through his brilliant hair, "That's really disappointing."

"There'll probably be a message for you when you get home," I said.

He reached into his jacket and pulled out a jellybean-shaped silver phone, and shook it like an Orangina.

"She knows my cell number. No, no, this is. . ."

Again, he peered into the shadows. "Can I just ask, is this something that she normally does, or—"

Dad took a deep breath.

"Quite frankly, we're not aware of what she does or does not normally do. She's made herself pretty scarce for the last few years."

The delicate man tried to smile. "That's okay. That's—look, can I still make you folks dinner? I know this is all rather awkward now, but I did buy some duck fat, and barding is a very useful technique. Once I teach you how to do it, you'll never wonder what to do with a roast again." He shrugged and smiled. "What do you say?"

We filed into the kitchen. Aunt Gil pulled the margarine tubs out of the refrigerator and handed them to him.

Dad stood behind him, hunched in his striped polo shirt. His fists were shoved into his pockets.

"I don't know why she does these things," Dad said. "In the months after she first left, I prayed on her. I prayed on her every day."

We watched the delicate man, as he opened the margarine tubs and tied strip of yellow fat after strip of yellow fat to the two cold hunks.

Mamma Lilly leaned on the counter and watched him.

"I first met that girl when she was seven years old. I was the court clerk for the custody case over this one." She reached over and gave my shoulder a shake. "You should have seen Candy, sitting in that courtroom. She wanted to sit at the petitioner's table with her Daddy, but Judge Ogburn wouldn't have it. He didn't like the kids to be in family court at all. She looked so lost, sitting there, that I finally gave her a legal pad and a pen. For days, we all watched that little head bend over her pad of paper, with her hair working loose from its pigtails. We thought she was drawing."

Mamma Lilly looked up, and she grabbed my hand. Squeezing it, she looked into The Delicate Man's eyes. "It turned out that she was taking notes. She took down everything that was said. At the end of the case, she stood up and said 'permission to approach, your honor.' She said it twice before he heard her. Judge Ogburn held out a hand to her, and she walked straight up and gave him that pad, with its pages full of her square, fat writing. Judge Ogburn took it from her and asked me to enter it into the record as a bench note. I did. Her little hand was bright red from the writing. I heard later that for a week after, she had to wear an ace bandage to keep her wrist from hurting." Mamma Lilly's squeezing turned into a shaky pulsation, and she twisted her lips.

"There's an alright girl in my stepdaughter, sir. But there are demons too. Everyone in this family's been delivered of demons except Candace."

The Delicate Man's fingers went still in the duck fat. I could feel the floor dropping away.

Aunt Gil stepped forward. "I was delivered of gluttony, profanity, lustfulness, squalor, and asthma."

Mamma Lilly nodded. "I was delivered of willfulness, pride, covetousness, atheism, false piety, pornography and lesbianism. Harold?"

My father stepped forward. "I was delivered of tax evasion, heart disease, sarcasm, sloth, racism, and constipation. Tax evasion was the worst. I vomited up half a gallon of blood and pus, getting that one out." Mamma Lilly pulled me close to her and put her arm around my shoulders. "Tell him about your demons, Lizzie."

The delicate man faced us with his shoulders slack. His duck-greased hands hung at his sides, and I could see his eyebrows cresting above the rims of his glasses. He was in a basement, in Gresham, surrounded by religious whacks. At any moment, we might fall upon him, tie him to a chair, and try to whip the foppishness from him. At any moment, the BATF, in black Kevlar, could come hut-hut-hutting down the stairs.

I stepped forward. "Your name is Stewart, right?" He cocked his head to the side and gave a shallow nod. I turned to my family.

"Guys, I think Stewart wants to go home. He's had a rough night."

"That's ridiculous," said Mamma Lilly. "We haven't even put the roast in." She him a wide smile. "You're not ready to go home yet, are you dear?"

His eyes locked with mine. I backed up, and the semicircle of my family widened. He took a deep breath, smiled, and raised his hands.

"You know, I do think I need to go home. Liz is right, there could be a message from Candace on my home voicemail."

There was a murmur from my father and stepmother. I walked backwards out of the kitchen, drawing Stewart out into the rec room and up the stairs. When we reached the top, Mama Lilly called to us.

"You'll come back, won't you Stewart?" My father was behind her, with a hand on her shoulder.

"You're a chosen vessel," my father said. "I can see it. You were put on this earth to do some important work, for the Savior and for the spirits of those gone."

"Thanks," said the delicate man. He gave a little wave.

He followed me into the old dining room, where I found his coat hanging from a curtain rod. I handed to him, and tried to smile.

"They're really pretty good people," I said.

"I could tell. Don't worry about—I mean, I wasn't weirded out, really. I just feel like I need to get home. I'm not exactly thrilled that Candace ditched me, but I probably do need to be there if she calls."

I walked him past the flower shrines and the book cases full of dusty glass paperweights. When we reached the front door, he cocked his head and looked at me.

"Does your Dad say that to everyone?"

"The thing about the half-gallon of blood and the pus? Uh—"

"No, no. The chosen vessel part."

"Oh, that." I struggled to maintain my smile. "I don't know. I don't think I've heard him say that in a while."

"Well, tell him I'm flattered. Would you?"

"Sure." I offered him a hand to shake. He took it, then he looked into my eyes. Stepping forward, he wrapped his harms around me and hugged me so fast I almost didn't have time to hug him back.

"Thanks, Liz," he said. Pulling on his coat, he gave me one last long look. "I really do want to hear about those demons of yours." He stepped through the open door. "Some day."

Then he was gone.

They were clustered in the kitchen when I came downstairs, peering into the pan at the duck fat-wrapped meat.

For blocks and blocks, for miles and miles in every direction, there were houses full of people to whom rump roast wasn't some exotic puzzle.

"I don't think I like this stuff," said Gil. She washed her hands and then began the process of picking the duck fat off the roast. Dad stood at the sink with his sleeves rolled up and started to wash the dishes. Mama Lilly went to the refrigerator and pulled out our stock pot. When we didn't have company, we kept that pot on the stove day and night. Every evening we add a quart of this; a handful of that. Supplemented with Gil's raw creations, it nourished us as well as we needed, no worse and no better.

I stood in the middle of the kitchen. "I think I'll start bringing down the beds," I said.

Dad looked up from his dishes. "Don't worry about that," he said. "It's late. I think maybe we'll rough it tonight. What do you girls think?"

Mamma Lilly smiled in a way that stretched her lips across her teeth. She didn't like the idea of roughing it, I could tell.

"Sure," said Aunt Gil, without looking up.

I glanced from one to the other. Neither of them would sleep right, if they don't have their cubicles set up the way they liked them.

"I think I will try to bring a few things down, if that's alright with you, Dad. 'Don't put off 'til tomorrow' and all."

"It's alright by me, Junior. Go ahead."

The shades were up on the ground floor of the house, and squares of gray streetlamp light came in from all directions. Candace must have stopped to raise the blinds, before she stormed out. I switched on lights. Through the dust, they shed a yellowish glow. The dividers were in the old dining room, stacked on top of each other in a loose heap.

I found that I could carry the panels two at a time. Their bases bumped and gouged the door frame, but I didn't suppose anyone cared about that anymore.

For an hour and a half I hefted and toted. Gil and Mamma Lilly relaxed visibly as they begin to reconstruct their sleeping niches. Dad helped me with the futons.

At midnight, only my futon remained upstairs, crumpled up against the wall of the old dining room. Dad stood, winded, hair clinging in tiny, sweaty clumps to his forehead.

"Let's take care of that last one, Scout, then you can rest."

My futon had an off-white cover, and there was something about the way it was piled that made it look just a little bit like a cloud. A china cabinet rose to the left of it, and the facets of glassware were visible through the dust.

"I think maybe I'll sleep up here tonight," I said. "I'm beat." In the bedroom that used to belong to Candace and me, there were kids' books, old magazines. The Shakespeare, from when Aunt Gil taught English was there, too.

Dad let out a breath and tilted his head, his lips pursed. Drawing his hands up to his hips he said, "I don't think that's a good idea, Scout."

"Why?"

He tuned and looks toward the window. We'd pulled the blinds back down, but strips of nighttime were still visible between the slats.

"Why? Well because—"and then he turned back to me.

"Are you defying me, Elizabeth?" He drew himself up and squared his shoulders, doing his best to look like a patriarch, one designated by God to stand vigil over us, the wayward female sheep.

We stared into each other's eyes for seconds, and I saw that he was scared. One wrong word. One wrong word and I could blow the siding off the house. One wrong word and I could send the silverware shooting like spears through the air. One wrong word, and I could make the foundations collapse and the earth swallow us, the house, and all evidence that we had ever been.

"I love you, Dad." My voice was quavering.

He stared down at me for long, long moment, the storminess in his face melting into confusion. "I know you wouldn't defy me, Punkin." He opened his arms and I went to him, and pressed my face against the sweaty green cotton of his polo shirt.

Together, we shouldered the cloud-futon, and we struggled down the stairs.

Urania
The Muse of Astronomy

Several patriarchal scholars have noted these early representations of Urania with her staff and celestial globe, attributing her stance to part of a ritual act of obeisance to a phallic idol, an image deeply rooted in the pre-Catal Huyuk Anatolian culture. But I submit to you a different interpretation, one that more fully integrates with our current state of knowledge regarding matriarchy and the place of feminist ritual in that area from which the Urania myth spread: Urania's staff and celestial globe were, indeed, phallic objects. But the Muse did not worship them, holding them up to the stars in veneration. Rather, she held them above her head only to cast them down to earth. And, standing atop the fallen symbols of patriarchy, she would reach upward, to the stars.

Emma Grosskreutz
Celestial Mythos and the New Age of Feminism
Leipzig University Press, 1974
(Passage translated from the original German by Forrest Aguirre)

Skatebirding

Heather Shaw

THE SKATEBOARDERS FLEW around Gretchen like a flock of birds circling, the granite purr of their wheels like a hundred wings flapping. She smiled and closed her eyes as she kept up her steady pace towards her building; without sight, they seemed even more like birds, their baggy clothes brushing against her like feathers. She opened her eyes to climb the steps just as the tall boy with spiky hair rode his board sideways down the railing, grinning at her as he missed her by inches. She felt her smile widen and her cheeks flush as she opened the door to the lobby—*that* one certainly knew how cute he was.

She checked her mailbox and went into her apartment, clicking her tongue to call her cats, even though they never responded. The cats sat in the window, watching the skateboarders with rapt attention, the ends of their tails flicking back and forth, the younger one mrowling low in his throat.

The com unit sounded its mellow tone, summoning her to the screen. She hurried across the room and sat in a soft leather chair before hitting the "accept" key. Her husband's face appeared on the screen in front of her. His bright green eyes and sharp cheekbones were a welcome sight.

"Hi, honey!"

"Hi," she said. His face was bright, his color high, as if he'd just come from some physical exertion. "Nice of you to finally call."

She'd been here for two weeks, in this house where she was being forced to wait out her pregnancy. Two weeks, and this was the first time he'd bothered to call. She was torn between anger and the relief of seeing a familiar face.

He smiled at her and held up his hand in a placating gesture. "It's been busy, sweetie. You know that. There was graduation, and then the job started right away. There's been lots to set up and I've been putting in long days. And com time is expensive—you don't want to waste it on fighting, do you? How are you?"

"I'm okay." She forced herself to smile. She didn't want to hear about the job, didn't want to think about the job, but it was hard to think about anything else. The job had been hers, until two weeks ago, when the doctor at the station clinic had discovered she was pregnant.

"Sweetie, how's the new apartment?"

"Fine."

"Are you settling in okay?"

"It would help if I had some friends in this city. Or a job. Or anything at all to do, really."

"Honey, I'm sorry. I really am. It's for your own protection."

"For the baby's protection, you mean. If I had my way, I'd still be up on the space station, where I belong, doing something important." She trailed off.

She'd worked so hard to get into orbit. She'd qualified for the experimental graduate astrophysics program and was a member of the first class to study directly on the space station. She'd risen to the top of her class, and she'd *earned* her place in the sole research position on the space station granted to a graduating student. It was a once in a lifetime opportunity, and she'd blown it by getting pregnant.

"You know they're still not sure what the effects of long-term time in orbit has on a woman in your condition."

She stood up, furious, and leaned into the screen. "'In my condition?' I'm not an invalid, Robert—I'm not even showing yet. I'm supposed to take it easy, stay at home in a town I don't know, not take any risks or expose myself while I bake up a nice little baby for my husband? As if that's not bad enough, I'm stuck in a stupid bubble town where I don't know anyone and where my family can't even visit!"

"Sweetie." Robert ran his fingers through his short hair before folding his hands in front of him and putting on his "let's be reasonable" face. "The government is recommending the bubble towns now for pregnant women; the open environment isn't safe for a developing baby."

She sat back in the soft chair and seethed for a moment. Robert was glancing at something or someone off-screen, looking embarrassed. He should have told her he wasn't alone.

"Robert, I'm sorry, I'm just so damn *lonely*, you know? I only leave the house to buy groceries and run errands. The only good thing about this town is the library—they still have a real bricks-and-mortar one. It's the best thing about this place, and no one goes to it. Every day it's me and librarian, and she tells me that the only reason they haven't shut the place down is because it's on the historic register." She thought to herself that the other good thing was the skateboarders, but she was holding back from telling Robert about them. He might worry about them banging into her, hurting her and the baby. He'd make a call, send an e-mail, and the boys would be shooed away for good, and she didn't want that. What would the cats watch?

"Well, that's something, isn't it?"

"Hm? Oh, yes, the library is something. I think I'm going to end up reading every book they have twice over before this baby is even born." There were books in the library you couldn't get online anymore—books written by and about homosexuals, books that viciously satirized the government, even one of those books full of moronic quotations by former presidents. The Department of Homeland Integrity didn't even think about old-fashioned libraries anymore, apparently, or they would have cleaned those books out. Reading them gave her the same delicious thrill she got from walking among the skateboards.

"How is the pregnancy going? Any weird cravings yet?"

The image of the tall, spiky haired skater flashed through her mind. She'd been having strong cravings, but not the kind he was talking about. She must have blushed, as his voice became low and seductive.

"Oh, sweetie. I miss you, too. I wish I could be with you right now, I really do. Just hold tight, okay? I'll try to get special leave so I can be home with you before the little one is born."

"Promise you'll come home soon?" she whispered, tearing up. She never used to cry so easily.

Stupid hormones. Stupid life-altering-upheavals.

"Don't cry, Gretchen, you know I can't, oh, I have to go, my com time is up. Don't leave me crying—I don't want to think of you crying."

She wiped away her tears. "Thanks for calling. When will I talk to you again?"

"I'm scheduled for Wednesday."

"Robert! That's almost another week!"

"Shh, I know. I'll try for sooner, ok?"

"Okay."

"Good bye, sweetheart."

"'Bye."

She sat long after the screen went blue, and listened to the rasp of the skateboards outside her window. She felt guilty for burdening Robert with her unhappiness. He had a hard job—she knew that well! —and plenty to worry about. He was going to be an important man. She had been on her way to becoming an important woman, not so long ago, but now she'd have to settle for being one of those women who stood behind a great man. It was not what she'd envisioned.

For want of contraception, the kingdom was lost, she thought. Abortion was illegal, birth control was a controlled substance, and condoms were unreliable—some said the government made sure some percentage of condoms was defective, to help increase population growth and promote family values. They'd used a condom, but it hadn't helped.

Gretchen paced her small apartment, momentarily distracting her cats with the atypical movement. The old tom started meowing for his dinner, and as she opened the packet into his dish, she seethed over her situation. She felt a bizarre, overwhelming urge to put on a dress and heels and do some housework, just like the 1950's housewife she felt like, but the apartment was the latest in modern technology and did all its own cleaning. Even her meals were prepared for her from the ingredients she brought home every day; she'd entertained herself bringing home weirder and weirder combinations of food to see what the machines came up with, until morning sickness had made her give up the habit in favor of milder flavors.

Seized by a sudden idea, she went to the bags of groceries she hadn't put away yet and dug through them. Finding the lemons and sugar she'd bought, she began to make old-fashioned lemonade. She was boiling water to melt the sugar in when the computer interrupted her.

"I can make that for you."

"No, I want to do it myself."

"Would you like assistance?"

"No. Mute, please."

The system shut down its speakers with a hiss that sounded suspiciously like a sigh. *Moody computer*, she thought.

She tasted some of what she'd just made, added some more sugar water, tried it again. *Close enough,* she thought, and grabbed a stack of plastic cups and headed outside.

The boys were pretty used to her schedule at this point, and her reappearance at the door startled a couple of them enough that they stumbled off their boards. She concentrated on keeping herself from blushing as she moved to the steps and sat down, saying "I thought you boys must get thirsty skateboarding all the time, so I made you some lemonade . . . "

They approached her warily, like wild animals, some of them even sniffing in the direction of the lemonade. She sat perfectly still, *just like you'd do for an animal*, she thought, and she noticed for the first time how shabby some of them looked. Most of them were dirty, their clothes full of rips and poorly mended. She'd only ever walked through them before, never stopped to notice what they looked like other than the tall, cute one she favored. As they came nearer she could smell that most of them hadn't bathed recently, and she could see that their skateboards were old-fashioned, beat-up boards, not the newer ultra-light models with the almost-frictionless wheels she'd seen the kids using back when she was an undergrad. She felt a thrill of fear that these boys weren't from her class, weren't of her world at all. It felt wonderful, new and strange and interesting and very different from her life of late.

She smiled and started to pour cups of lemonade, setting them at arms length between her and the boys. The first one snatched a cup and stuck his nose inside, breathing deeply before looking at her with surprise and downing the liquid in one chug. The others snatched up the cups immediately, and those that were still waiting crowded closer to her, wanting to be the next to receive a cup of the freshly squeezed fruit drink. She was surprised by their eagerness.

After all, it was only lemonade. The tall one stood back a little, watching her with a smirk. He didn't take a cup, and when she held a cup out to him he shook his head even as the cup was snatched away by a more enterprising skateboarder. Soon the lemonade was gone and the boys started skating around her again, whooping in joy as they jumped over her, one after another. She ducked her head and laughed—she felt more alive than she had in weeks.

"That means thank you," the tall, spiky-haired one said before taking off on his board.

As the light changed from late-afternoon to early-evening, the boys drifted away. She shivered a bit at the drop in temperature and was reluctant to leave the scene of the most excitement she'd had in this town. She slowly picked up her things and went back into the house.

A few minutes later there was a knock on the door. She peered out through the peep-hole at the spiky-haired skater, who was grinning and holding a bottle of wine out to her. She opened the door, but didn't invite him in.

"Hello?"

"Hi. I just wanted to say, well, that was really nice, what you did for the kids there."

"Oh. Thank you." She felt strangely awkward. The thrill of worlds colliding didn't seem to apply when someone from a completely different background was at her doorstep, and this bothered her. What made her think she was better than these people? She invited him in, almost defiantly.

He sat on her couch, disrupting one of the snoozing cats. "You probably prevented scurvy in most of them with that lemonade there."

"Scurvy? In this day and age... ?"

"It's expensive to live here. The only livable places at this latitude are bubble towns, and we have to freight in all our supplies from up north. It's like we're on an island."

Gretchen hadn't considered the isolation of the town beyond the pain of her own loneliness. She almost asked them why they didn't move further north where it was cheaper, but stopped herself.

If it was expensive to get food down here, it was probably even more expensive to buy train fare north.

"But . . . you're not so bad off? You managed to find some wine, I see."

"Yeah, I'm ok. My grandparents left me a bunch of money, so I don't have to work and I don't have to live on the street either. I like to skate with these guys, though. They're real. The skate parks are full of padding and safety grids. You fall there, nothing happens. It's just not as thrilling as actually risking your neck on the street."

He handed her the wine. "I thought you looked—well, forgive me if this is rude—kind of lonely out there. I thought you might like some company."

She took the bottle, blushing. "Let me just open this in the kitchen."

She came back with two glasses and the open bottle. She sat near him on the couch and poured them each a glass.

He held up his glass to hers. "To company."

She smiled and tinked his glass with hers. "Cheers."

They drank in silence for a few minutes. The boy looked distinctly uncomfortable, and cleared his throat several times before he said, "By the way, I'm Machinery."

"Oh! I'm Gretchen."

"Hi Gretchen."

"Machinery is an unusual name, isn't it?"

"It's a street name. You kind of need one to fit in."

"So you have clothes that aren't all torn up and a home, but you pretend to be poor to hang out with those kids?"

"Sure. I have all the stuff the parents need to see when they visit, but I don't live my life that way. I figure that I've been given a gift, that I'm one of the few people in the world who doesn't have to live his life—well, most of my life—the way someone else says. And, since I can do what I want, I skate. But I don't want to make the kids feel weird, so I don't buy stupid fashion gear or top-notch boards. I like the old school stuff anyway."

"Well, that's nice. But you could be doing so much else with your money."

"What, you mean donating to charities? To hell with that—most of the money you give them goes to keeping the administrative part of it working, or towards their annoying fundraising, and very little goes to those they're supposedly helping. And what, you think I just pretend to be poor and ignore those kids that are starving? Who do you think feeds them? When one of them breaks a leg, I'm there to take them to the hospital."

"And they take charity from you?"

"They didn't like it at first, that's true. But I'm enough like them that they're used to it." He shook his head. "It all makes me sick. The government pushes us to have kids, because the infertility rates keep going up and the third world keeps pumping out babies while the developed nations go into negative population growth. But do they do anything to take care of the kids after they're born? Sure, you get free health care for the first five years, but after that you have to pay for it, and the public schools are worse than a joke... these kids have it bad. I know I can't save them, but I do what I can."

She nodded. "I'm jealous."

"What? Of me?"

"Yeah."

"Yeah, I can see that."

She laughed and playfully slapped at him. "Okay, then, tell me why."

"Well, I can do whatever I want. I don't answer to anyone, don't have to stay put or do anything I don't want to except for twice a year when the 'rents visit for three days. But you—I dunno, but from the look on your face and the way you walk around, I get the sense you're pretty much locked into whatever situation you're in, and there's no way out. Am I right?"

She stared into her glass of wine for a moment and murmured,

"Yeah, you're right."

"Hey now." He reached under her chin and tipped her face up to look into his; she shivered at being touched by a man she barely knew. "I'm sorry. I didn't mean to rub it in."

"It's ok. It's just... god, is it so obvious? I mean, it's bad enough to be alone and pregnant and lonely as hell, but then to know that just anyone on the street can read that off me—"

"Whoah, hey, I didn't say all that! And, besides, I see you everyday; I doubt it's immediately obvious." Machinery sat for a moment, and Gretchen wondered if he was going to ask her about being pregnant; she didn't show yet, so it had to be a surprise to him. Instead he said "Did you know that you're the only one in this building who trusts us enough to walk through us without pausing, without shouting at us to stop or threatening to call the cops? Most of the tenants here, we have to stop when they want to go in and out of the building, but not you."

"Yeah, I like it. It's like walking through a flock of birds."

"Really? We're like birds, huh? Most of these kids have never even seen birds, not after the last big avian flu epidemic."

"I used to watch birds when I was young. I loved them. I've always thought of you guys as skatebirders."

"Skatebirders? I like that. Sweet."

"Yeah."

He sat back and smiled. "Man, for that, you deserve a street name."

"Oh!" She was about to say no, but the thought delighted her. "Really?"

"Yeah. How about, yeah. How about 'Sparrow'?"

"Sparrow. Wow, that's nice." *Is that what he thinks of me as? A drab little brown bird?*

"Thank you."

"You're welcome, Sparrow."

There was a long silence while they both sat with quirky smiles on their faces. A vacuum robot hummed to itself as it made its rounds past them. Machinery seemed to make up his mind about something, set his glass down on the coffee table, and kissed her.

He tasted sour, like old beer and unfiltered cigarettes. His tongue was oddly rough and his teeth bumped into hers as he forced her lips wider apart. He smelled awful this close up and she had to remind herself that from a distance she thought he was cute. Still, it was so interesting, so different from what her life had been like lately that she put up with it. When his tongue finally hit her tonsils, she pushed him off of her.

"No, no. Sorry. I—I mean, I'm married."

"Seriously? Jeez, Gretchen, you should have told me!" He looked around the apartment, then asked, "So, why doesn't he live with you?"

"He works on the space station."

"No shit! Wow, I had no idea you were married to a big shot. That explains your fancy apartment, then."

"Yeah. Well." She told herself she shouldn't tell him the whole story. She hardly knew him and it wasn't appropriate. But the next thing she knew, the whole story was flowing out of her.

"Shit, so he got *your* job when he knocked you up? Sounds like he did it on purpose."

"Oh, no, it was just an accident."

"A couple of pin pricks through the end of the condom, you'd never even have noticed he'd set up your 'accident'."

Her mouth dropped open. She stared at Machinery, who looked back at her sympathetically.

"Good lord. You might be right. I never thought of that."

"Gretchen, I shouldn't have said that. I'm sorry."

"No." Gretchen stood up and started pacing. "No. It actually makes more sense this way. He *hated* me when we started grad school up there, and all my friends said it was because he was jealous of my talent. I was his biggest rival, even. I got the highest score on the entrance exam—and I mean the highest score in the history of the exam. I wasn't there a month before the administration had invented a new award just so they could give it to me. I was *good*, Machinery. Robert was a distant second place. I frustrated the hell out of him at first.

"After our first year, he started paying attention to me. I thought it was just that my friends were all wrong about him, that I'd misjudged his behavior. He told me that he was turned on by my mind. I'd always wanted to be loved for my mind, to find someone who wasn't intimidated by my ambition, who understood my passions, who would like me for my ideas and not because I was sort of pretty and a woman in the sciences. He seemed perfect. We had a lot of fun. But now... what if he courted me because he knew all he had to do was knock me up and I'd have no choice but to return dirtside?"

Machinery stood up and put his arms around her. He led her back to the couch and sat her down.

"Gretchen, listen. I don't know your husband at all, but, well, I think he must love you. If he was just trying to get your job, he could have just abandoned you once he knocked you up. He wouldn't have married you."

"No, I wouldn't have sex with him until I was married. Premarital sex is way too dangerous on a government-operated station, they can kick you out for that if they catch you. He had to marry me. And it would look bad for his career if he abandoned a pregnant wife."

"Okay, but look at this apartment. He didn't just send you back to live with your parents in an unprotected town up North, he bought you a state-of-the-art apartment in one of the best bubble towns in the country. Most women dream of doing their pregnancies here, did you know that? It's not cheap to move in here, at least, not here on the nice side of town."

Gretchen was crying quietly. "I suppose he might have accidentally fallen in love with me along the way. We always did get along until I was sent here. Hell, we were great together. It's just, I mean, he seemed so perfect for me, and now to think he might have done this to me on purpose."

She sobbed, leaning into Machinery's shoulder and allowing him to comfort her.

After a while she stopped crying. He leaned in and tried to kiss her again, and she gently pushed him away.

"Gretchen. Sparrow. We might be able to help you get rid of this pregnancy, if you don't want it. I'm not up on it or anything, but some of the boy's sisters have gotten rid of unwanted pregnancies, so they wouldn't be even poorer trying to care for a baby. I can ask around on different ways to do it. You should let me help you."

"He'd know." Her eyes welled up at the thought of how stuck she was. Her apartment felt small and stuffy, despite the clean chrome and leather, the filtered air. "It would have to look like an accident, and most of those old-fashioned abortions leave obvious medical traces. I have mandatory check-ups every two weeks." She wiped her eyes. "Thanks anyway, Machinery. For listening, for pointing out what I should have realized a long time ago. Thank you. I hate to be abrupt, but I think you should go now." She stood up and walked over to the door.

"Sure, Sparrow. I totally understand." He joined her in the doorway and leaned in to whisper in her ear, "Let me know if you ever feel like coming over to my place sometime, okay?" He kissed her on the cheek.

"Sure." She forced on her brave smile. "Goodbye."

After spending the whole day at the library doing research, she walked home, excited about her life again. She hadn't gotten as far as she had in life by moping around and letting other people decide what was best for her. Getting pregnant had changed her life, but she didn't have to let it ruin everything. She didn't even have to stay in this bubble town if she didn't want to. She'd decided to put her talents to work helping those unwanted kids Machinery had been talking about the night before. Maybe start small, with some after-school tutoring for school-age kids that the government ignored, working up to wider-scale programs. It would be good practice for having her own child. If she had to be a mother, she'd be the best one she possibly could.

She could hardly wait to see Machinery and tell him about her plans. He knew the kids, and could help her figure out how to begin reaching them.

As she approached the skateboarders, they looked at her oddly, staring at her body and muttering comments to one another. She hunched her shoulders as she walked through their circling mass. The touches were stronger than usual today. A hand brushed past her breast, the owner laughing as her nipple stood up at the attention. Another hand spanked her as she passed. The groping became more intense, and she moved faster, fighting her way through the catcalling, manhandling boys to the top of the stairs.

Machinery stood at the top of the stairs, looking down at her with pity in his eyes. She glared at him, but before she could speak, he leaned in and whispered "Protect your head." Then he pushed her backwards, down the stairs, the boys kicking at her stomach as she tumbled to the bottom, their shouts and laugher sounding for all the world like a murder of crows, cawing at her.

Thalia
The Muse of Comedy and Idyllic Poetry

Tennyson be damned, along with his muse. His landscapes have been blasted, and Thalia has done nothing to stop the bullets from flying here, let alone imparting me some inspiration.

Soldier-poet Lionel Musgrave, in a letter to his sister dated January 12, 1916. Musgrave, whose poems have only recently been discovered, was killed three days later after a tree fell into his foxhole as a result of a German artillery barrage.

Spies

Kit Reed

IT'S BOILING OUTSIDE, HOTTER than a bitch's tits after the Peach Bowl game, but here we are on the Moriartys' side porch at high noon on the worst day so far. That's me and my best friend Tessa curled up under their kitchen window, hot and pink as a pair of steamed shrimp.

Heat dropped on downtown Glassboro like a wet beach towel last month and it hasn't quit. Power company can't keep up with it so air conditioners are out and the grownups had to fall back on paper funeral parlor fans. At least in high school you can still run under the sprinkler if you want to, or get a cute boy to ride you around in his car.

It's been hot for so long that the town waits for dark, when you can go outside without sweat running down you like the falls on the water ride at Six Flags. In spite of chiggers and redbugs and mosquitoes, our folks would rather drag mattresses out on the roof than lie there sticking to the sheets. Cats and dogs get all weird and fletchy in this weather and the town's newlyweds are fighting like skunks.

Days are worse. By noon there are tar bubbles popping on Front Street. The white line slides around on the blacktop and heat mirages shimmer in the middle distance like unkept promises. The sun is so high and white that you start seeing things that aren't, long shadows on the horizon—men in black approaching or dark riders, loping in. You shade your eyes and squint into the glare, in hopes.

Frankly, the way things are you'd just as soon somebody did ride on in to slay and pillage or shoot up the town. It's enough to make you wish for a nice big hurricane, a kick-ass Category Five to come in and blow it all away. Anything is better than this.

We like to died crossing Front Street. Tessa was practically puking from the heat and I had to drag her into the shade. Flies are staggering in circles all around us and dropping dead up here on the Moriartys' porch, just plain expiring on the weathered floor while Tessa and I kneel at the kitchen window, looking in through the rusty screen. We are waiting for the fight.

With the Moriartys, it's only a matter of time. They are known for their short fuses, and Ada is the worst.

Nobody knows just exactly when Clo, Lally and their big sister Ada came to Glassboro, not even our moms, and they've all been over to the house. Nobody saw the moving van pull up in front of the Ravenal place on Front Street and nobody saw their furniture going in. It's just, one night lights went on inside the old gingerbread heap and the next day sprinklers started up on a new front lawn. We thought maybe the DeLoach boys came in the night and rolled it out like a carpet, but Oley says no way. It wasn't Pinkney Landscaping either, we checked, so who knows how that yard full of weeds and rusty tin cans turned into beautiful grass? Naturally, our mothers went calling, Southerners still do. Lally came to the door. She said a nice thank you for the lovely pralines and peach pies but you can't come in right now, Clo and Ada are working in the back.

They are always working in the back, but don't ask. Believe me, you don't want to piss them off.

Clo pays the yard boys and shops for food and Lally goes to Claymore's for their stockings and underwear, but the mothers who play bridge on Thursdays are here to tell you Ada runs the show. Clo has thick chestnut hair in curls that rise up in front like she's surprised. She's sturdy but shapely, if you like the type, and from what we hear, Archie Hannibal really likes the type although he is too much of a gentleman to tell. Nice smile on Lally Moriarty, or Bill Claymore thinks so, but when she fixes those green eyes on you, you know she's sizing you up. You just don't know for what. Their big sister Ada isn't all that big, she's just the oldest. She is what our mothers call, "disagreeable," and they should know.

Ada, Lally and Clo are not their real names. If you knew their real names you would gasp and fall down screaming, but with ladies of a certain age, you never ask. We don't even know how old they are. They look old to me and Tessa, but in certain lights they could be younger than our moms. Nobody knows about the loom in the back room, either, except for Tessa and me, and that is for a reason. Or what their day jobs are. As far as Glassboro is concerned the Moriarty sisters are a closed book, and if Tessa and I happen to know what we know about them, well...

We spy.

Right now Clo and Lally are sitting at the kitchen table, talking about Ada behind her back. Clo is sketching, sketching, sketching for the next tapestry, did I tell you we think that's the family business? It looks like Clo is in charge of the designs. All her colored pencils are melting in the heat and even from here we can see the lines smudging faster than she can draw. Her red pencil snaps and she yowls like a cat. "I hate this town!"

Lally slaps her ruler down. "I hate this job!"

"I hate this heat!"

Tessa grins at me. They're starting up.

"You never complained in Athens," Lally says, and I shiver because she does not mean Athens, Georgia, plus, my ancestors came from there. We're one of three Greek families in town.

"Yeah well, that was dry heat," Clo says, glaring.

"Don't blame me, blame Ada."

"She didn't make the weather."

"Yeah, but she made us move."

"Well, she can damn well move us out." Clo adds bitterly, "Since she's in charge."

Lally's eyes narrow to green slits and when she turns, her smile scares even me. "Who says she's in charge?"

"What are you thinking?"

Lally stands, not caring that her bundled yarns slide out of her lap. "I'm thinking we could drop this and go."

"Ada would have kittens," Clo says.

"What do you care? You have Archie Hannibal, and I..."

This frightens the crap out of Clo. "Don't mention Archie," she hisses. "If she knew about Archie she'd..."

Tessa nudges me and I nudge back. We know about Clo and Archie Hannibal even if Ada doesn't, which makes us somehow better than her. We know about Lally and Bill Claymore too, although we've never seen them do any more than kiss over the cash register at Claymore's store.

"Come on, Clo. What's the worst thing she can do to us?"

"Right. What's the worst thing she could do to us?" Seconds go by while Clo thinks. Then she covers her mouth with a little shriek. She knows. "Oh!"

Ada pops out of the back room like the witch on a weather house. "You called?"

Shrinking, her sisters open their hands to prove that they are innocent. "Who, us? Not really. No."

Tessa and I are impressed all over again by how big Ada looks—and how tiny she is. We also know that she has the fiercest temper in all Georgia and to tell the truth, we are shrinking too. You don't want to cross Ada Moriarty. Just smile when she passes and keep going, and whatever you do, stay out of her way.

It is tense out here on the porch of the Ravenal house. It's tense in the kitchen too.

Then Ava surprises everybody present with a grin. "Let's go out and mess some people up."

Oh my God, they're coming out!

As if I don't know what they're up to, my idiot sisters and those fool girls snickering outside my kitchen window. As if I don't know everything that's going on.

As for you, my sisters, my right hand and my left, what were you thinking? Do you think even for a minute that you can put down the work and walk away? This is not a choice we have. Remember, we have moved a hundred dozen times on our way to destiny and this is by no means the last detour. The gods won't catch up with us, but the work keeps pace and there is no escaping, no matter how skillfully we zig and zag.

Meanwhile, my sisters are subject to snares and delusions. Involuntary spurts of hope. Silly women, prone to crushes and distractions. Unless—Lally. Clo, you tramp! —you are supine.

Well, we'll put an end to that.

And you pretty, silly high school girls invading my veranda as if I can't smell you out there, sweating like galley slaves on the fast boat to hell. Do you think I don't know what you're up to? Do you imagine I'm going to let you get away with it?

Understand! I can end this, no problem, any time I want.

Fools. They have no idea what I'm thinking. They're not going to find out all at once, either.

Neither will you.

You will know when it's time. Your time.

Hats, ladies, it's hot today, and don't forget your things, remember that's why we carry matching bags. Hurry up. Stop grumbling. It's time.

We put on our wide-brimmed straws, practical and flattering. Oh good grief, Clo has pinned a flower on hers. Dead giveaway, but she can't believe that I know. There was a man once, a mere mortal who admired me in this very hat, but that's a story I never tell. Wraparound sunglasses. If these hicks see what lies behind our faces, we'll have to move on. Our simple white shifts. Stylish, classic, and the white refracts the glare. I band my waist with my black cord and Lally knots her silken tape measure around hers so I'll think she's still on the job, but Clo—another dead giveaway! Poor Clothos wears a sash she designed, the romantic fool: nymphs and satyrs circling in a mad unending chase. Says it all, right?

Blanch when you see me coming, Archie Hannibal, but do not even pretend to hide. Prepare to die.

Oh God this is exciting, running along the sidewalk behind parked cars while the Moriarty sisters walk right straight down the middle of Front Street without a clue. It's weird out here in the steaming sunlight and me and Tessa are gasping and dizzy from the heat but you'd think those ladies were strolling downtown in midwinter, they are that cool.

The Moriartys go along like walking heat mirages, except that they are white, not black, and unlike the dark men and long riders that never come any closer than the middle distance, these ladies are up close and personal. Real people you can really touch.

As if you'd dare.

Look at them, fanning out like they own the street, the town, the entire state of Georgia. They are going straight down the white center line with Ada in the middle, swinging their bags. Nobody's ever seen all three of them out together like this, not in all their history in this town. In spite of whatever's going on between them, Clo and Lally and Ada walk like a force to be reckoned with, and drivers are swerving left and right to keep from running into them. They'd rather hit trees than get between the three Moriartys and wherever they are going, and it isn't just the outfits or the way they carry their heads. Together, they are huge. Look at them sailing along like they think they own the world.

Well you're wrong. The world belongs to us. You can't just come down from up North and act like you're from here. We are, and you. You aren't from here. You're not from anywhere around here and you are in no respect local. You don't even belong.

Wait.

They're stopping. The three Moriartys hesitate at the biggest intersection, reconnoitering. They turn south and Tessa and I fall into a crouch and skitter after them.

At the last minute Ada swivels and we dodge behind the big live oak in front of Claymore's store, just off Front Street.

Tessa whispers, "Look out!"

I put Tessa behind me. "Duck!"

My best friend is a dancer and, like that she drops into an I'm-doing-Swan-Lake-here crouch. We hold our breath until Ada shrugs and the three sisters turn and move on, which is a relief in a way. Lally has been seeing Bill Claymore and there's always the possibility that Ada has found out but the Moriartys keep moving, which means that Bill Claymore is safe, at least for today.

Tessa grabs my arm. "Where do you think they're going?"

"That's what I'm afraid of."

"What do you mean?"

"Archie." I'm scared shit they are heading for Archie's store. You can tell by the body language Clo's scared too, but she can't let Ada see this, so when they turn off Flagler Street onto Azalea, Clo's shoulders are higher and her back is that much stiffer than her sisters' but she's managing. She doesn't say anything to create a diversion, she doesn't even drag her heels.

Archie runs the French bakery a half-block down Azalea and when he says bonjour mamselle, can I help you, you'd think he was French, even though he was born right here in Glassboro and his great-great-great-great grandfather fought on the Confederate side. Since Clo does the food shopping she sees Archie every day—and then some, we're here to tell you. Archie's place is right above the store.

When they get to Hannibal's Ada opens the door and stands back. She gives Clo a little shove so she's the first one inside. Behind the counter, Archie lights up like a Christmas tree when she comes in. We can see him beaming from here. Then Lally follows and he looks surprised to see her, as in, Clo always goes alone. Then Ada barges in, and Archie goes white. Oh, no!

Ada pushes Clo aside like a swinging door. She is probably saying, "Well, Archie," but I don't know and Tessa doesn't know because we can see through the thick plate glass, but we can't hear.

Inside there is a little psychodrama going on.

Archie is apologizing or explaining, but Ada shakes her head, like, don't even start. Clo is tugging on her arm. From here it looks like she is begging. Ada shakes her off. She lifts her arm, pointing. It's all she has to do. We thought Lally was fixing to rebel but she rummages in her raffia bag like a Christmas elf.

A blind dream weaver could see that Clo is upset. She can't believe Lally is going along and, Archie? Archie is bewildered. He can't for the life of him figure out what these women are doing, all three of them milling in his tiny store.

Outside, Tessa and I bite our cheeks and hold our breath. Archie may not know it, but something terrible is coming down. Ada points again. Lally's face turns paler than that shroud thing she is wearing, but she nods.

We don't have to hear. We know what Ada means. Do it.

Clo grabs Lally's free hand. She's crying, NO, but it's too late. Lally has pulled out one of her skeins of colored yarn. Ada nods. Then her hand darts at Lally's midsection like an adder's tongue and pulls off her sash. It is a humongous measuring tape. Ada hands it to her and points again: NOW.

Weeping, Lally does what she has to. She lays the yarn on the counter and measures it off. Archie ought to be grabbing for his shotgun, running for the hills, but he just stands there blinking.

After all, there hasn't been much conversation. Whatever is happening between the three sisters is simply happening, just the way it's happened since before the history of the world. So the Moriartys go about it and Clo is begging for Archie's life, howling so loud that Tessa and I can hear it all the way out here in the street, and the worst part?

We are helpless. Two kids who happen to be from here. What can we possibly do? "Oh no," I murmur.

Behind me Tessa hums, "Oooooh nooooo."

Ada reaches into her bag. She is about to do it. In another minute—how do I know this?—In another minute she will pull out her shears. She will cut Archie off like a length of yarn and that will be the end of him.

But there is a disturbance on the walk behind me. A shuffle and a desperate tap tapping, action! I turn. It's wonderful. Brilliant. My best friend Tessa is... She's up on the points of her ballerina shoes and she is dancing, whirling, waving her arms higher and wider and ever faster in a brilliant pageant of desperate grace. Tessa is... She's creating a diversion, and even though it's too hot to breathe and much too hot to make a sound that carries she is shouting, "Thalia Chikades, do it. Act!"

I get it, I get it! We are creating a diversion. I turn to her, grinning like the face on the... what is that building? How do I know? I am grinning and shouting at Tessa, "You go, girl!"

So Tessa dances and I move out, gesturing and spinning like a mad thing, tearing my hair and beating on my breast like... wait. Like somebody I don't remember did on the first stage in Athens, long ago. I am taking the classic Thespian attitudes—glory, rage, despair, hand on the forehead, arm just so—and although my long suit is comedy I am doing all the faces: fear and hope, the rictus of despair, the deeply tragic mask. I am a pageant, I am a panoply, I am the Miss America contest and Festival of States rolled into one and Tessa, my best friend Tessa the dancer is a one-woman parade.

We are taking on out here on the steaming sidewalk so powerfully that even the gilded rebel soldier in front of the courthouse can't miss it, and fixed as she is on her evil business with Archie Hannibal and whatever else follows—Bill Claymore? Probably. Fixed as she is on the business at hand, grim Ada Moriarty is forced to drop everything for a minute and check out the disturbance in the street.

Like everyone else in downtown Glassboro, she has to see just what in the name of creation is going on out here.

Ava turns our way like the searchlight outside the state pen at Milledgeville, slow and deliberate and mean. She lifts her head. It is frightening but I keep on ACTING. Gotta save Archie! Gotta stop this thing somehow! I know Ada Moriarty is powerful and it's dangerous to cross her but I press my face to the shop window in a dramatic attitude designed to knock her dead. In that second I am the Medusa. I am Clytemnestra, whom nobody believes, I am Medea, fixing to kill her own kids. I am...

Falling!

Just now Ada took something—a biscuit? a dinner roll?—Ada just hauled back and hit the window where I was waving and grimacing with something so hard that it left a star of cracks in the glass. This round white item slammed into the window of Hannibal's French bakery and I fell backward as if it had come straight through the insulated glass and nailed me smack in the middle of the forehead.

I am flat on my back on the sidewalk, torn up and desperate because all the breath in my body is gone, every scrap of it. Ada's guided missile knocked it right out of me and I don't know if I will ever get it back. It is terrible, terrifying, terr... Everything in my chest burns! Tessa is dancing closer but with all the strength I have I raise one hand and signal: stay back!

And when my squeezed-out lungs open just enough to let the air in and I get enough to produce sound I fight the pain ripping into my chest to croak:

"Get Eula!"

Tessa hears.

Ada has been studying me through the window. She is fingering her scissors, but she looks up to see where I am looking.

"Go!"

Tessa goes.

You fools, you idiot children. As if I didn't know you from before! You with your silly little show. Look at you, taking on as though you have no memory of me. Don't you know we all come from the same place? Give it up, girls. Move, and say goodbye to Archie Hannibal as you leave town. You aren't helping him. Do you really think your prancing and howling can prevent anybody's death? Do you think for a minute that my sisters can bed down with these Georgia hicks and expect them to be the same a hundred years from now? Do you think they can waste their energy making love and still do their jobs? Do you honestly believe that the Fates can be in love and make it last?

It's not our way.

If I thought we could stop time and have our way with them, I'd step down off this high horse and find myself a man! Nothing like a wallow in hot weather to make a girl relax and forget the duty at hand.

For a while. A very, very little while.

Understand, what we do, we will keep doing because our work, like yours—and I mean each and every one of you except perhaps for you, my little actress and my little dancer—is fated. It's not as if we have a choice.

Now get out of my way and let me finish this. Oh good grief. That child Terpsichore was quite enough. And this buffoon of a girl laid out on the sidewalk outside this window, Thalia felled by a dinner roll, but now. Euterpe! The dancer has come back with Euterpe. As if anything stops me at my work.

But I've always been a sucker for a flute.

Oooh, yes I am glad to see Eula, she starts tweetling away before Tessa so much as dances another step and I should add that by this time there are people hanging out of all the windows overlooking Hannibal's, and there are people coming down into doorways and spilling out on front steps because in our own way we girls are as powerful as the three sisters, humid or not, hot as the devil's griddle or colder than we ever hope to be, we know how to put on a SHOW.

Too busy to talk now, really. What we are doing out here on Azalea Street in downtown Glassboro, Georgia, takes all the passion we can muster, which is plenty, and all the energy we have because at the moment our other sisters are out doing what they do in other places and that leaves Tessa, Eula and me, Thalia Chakides, to put on a show fit to save Archie Hannibal because that... OK, that is our function. We can't stop Ada, OK, Atropos. We can't stop Atropos, but we do by God know how to distract her and if I am reading her correctly, she's forgotten about Archie and is watching what's going on out here and believe me, with Eula fluting and Tessa dancing and me doing the Seven Deadly Sins and all the plagues of Egypt with touches of the Oresteia—updated, of course, for the locals—we are as amusing as all hell. And watching! Oh, we are watching the Moriartys as closely as they are watching us.

Behind Ada, Lally's snatched her skein off the counter and stuffed it back into her bag along with her tape measure sash, to hell with what it does to her look, and weeping Clo is running her hand down Archie's cheek in what I know must be a loving farewell because Archie'll be OK, at least for the time being, but whatever they had between them is done and meanwhile Ada watches us performing, shaking her head because it has always been this way between us—Death watching while Art staves her off and in this instance all Glassboro applauds—and instead of being pissed at us Ada is, OK, she is smiling!

Blinded by sweat and throbbing with emotion, we finish our act. Ada walks out of Hannibal's French Bakery and stands before us. She puts her scissors away so we are not frightened when she raises her hand to get our attention. She wants to make certain that we are finished before she speaks.

"All right," she says. She gestures and her sisters come out of the bakery and line up on either side of her. They are waiting for the inevitable, which Ada acknowledges with a nod. "That's it."

Eula smiles and Tessa's face breaks open in a smile. I can't help it, I drop into a little bow. The people of Glassboro don't know it, but we have just saved Archie Hannibal.

Then Ada turns and right before she and her sisters turn to go she says the inevitable, which we acknowledge with a nod and she finishes.

"For now."

The Colors of Tomorrow

Beth Bernobich

When Estelle looked into her stepmother's eyes, she could think of nothing but a starless midnight sky. Justine's eyes were large and black, with flecks of darkest violet. Lovely, cold, dangerous eyes. A person might suffocate in their depths. One already had.

"Of course you cannot go to the ball," Justine told her.

Estelle forced herself to meet Justine's gaze as though she were not afraid. Off to one side, Nadia and Sylvie spoke in quiet tones about gowns and perfume and jewelry, waiting for their mother to give word to depart. Her stepsisters would not help her cause, but neither would they interfere.

"Why not?" she asked, keeping her voice as steady. "You promised I could go, too."

Justine shook her head. "Tch-tch, child. I promised to *consider* the idea, nothing more. But look at you. You are not dressed properly. Not at all."

She flicked her fingertips in Estelle's direction. Bright specks flickered in the air, and the lace along Estelle's hem and bodice curled into rags. Estelle stiffened before she could stop herself, but Justine merely shook her head. Another flick, and ugly blotches stained the gown's apricot silk. *Flick, flick, flick.* Though she kept her face a blank, Estelle winced inside at every spark of magic as

Justine destroyed the costume Estelle had spent months creating for this evening. She heard Nadia giggling, then Sylvie's sharp whisper telling her to behave.

"A pity it's too late for you to sew another," Justine went on. "But even with the prettiest gown in all Auprès-Lune, you would hardly wish to appear like *that*."

Flick. Flick. Flick. More sparks whirled through the air. Magic nipped at Estelle's face, tiny bites and burns that lingered after the sparks had vanished. She could not tell what Justine had done, but she could guess she would not like it.

Justine surveyed her work with a complacent smile. "Such a shame," she murmured, smoothing the dark blue folds of her own perfect gown. "Perhaps it's better that you stay home. Otherwise you might distract your father, and we cannot have that. Make up the bread for tomorrow, as usual, my dear. Oh, and I told Cook that you would clean the kitchen, instead of her girls doing that chore."

Estelle started to argue, but bit down on her lip. Her father. Yes. She did not want her father more distracted than he already was. Justine nodded, as though approving her decision. She glanced back to Sylvie and Nadia. "Come, Nadia, Sylvie. The coach is waiting. Gilles, my love, please do not dawdle."

She glided out the door, leaving behind a delicate cloud of perfume. Nadia followed, but stopped in front of Estelle and stared. Her mouth twitched in some private amusement.

"Leave her be," Sylvie said quietly. "Or I shall tell Mama about the pin—"

"I don't care!" Nadia said. But she hurried out the door.

Sylvie paused, too. She looked as though she wanted to say something, but she only shook her head and went on.

Last of all came Estelle's father. He too was dressed in his finest clothes and fit the part of the wealthy merchant—except for the strange, clouded look in his eye. "Have a lovely evening," he said, kissing her cheek. "A shame you did not wish to come."

Estelle dutifully returned the kiss. No, her father was not dead, but neither was he truly alive. Not since Justine. If only...

"Papa," she said suddenly. "I *did* wish to attend the ball."

Her father paused, frowned. "But..."

The hall clock whirred. Her father jerked his head around, still frowning. Estelle could see him try to recall the truth of what had happened. *Think, Papa,* she urged him. *Remember.* But then the clock's mechanism clicked loudly, and from outside, Justine called, "Gilles. The coach is waiting."

Still frowning, her father turned toward the door. "Yes, my love." To Estelle, he murmured, "Next time, I must try to persuade you."

The doors closed behind him. The butler, after a glance toward Estelle, vanished to his other duties. Estelle stood a moment in the empty foyer, staring at the patterned tiles. Outside, she could hear her stepmother coaxing her father into the carriage. *We do not want him distracted.* She shivered. Justine had used those same words when she first met Estelle, just days before the too-quick marriage.

With a sigh, Estelle turned and walked slowly down the hall to her rooms. It hurt to think of her father with that woman. It hurt even more to think that magic alone had not besotted him so. Justine was beautiful and cultured, in ways that Estelle could never hope to imitate. Even before her mother died, Estelle had felt more at home in the kitchens than the parlor. Tears burned in her eyes. She swiped them away, wishing she could do the same for the ache in her chest.

Once in her tiny bedchamber, Estelle ripped off her spoiled gown and dressed in a plain clean skirt and smock. Her hair felt greasy—more of Justine's spite. She untied the ribbons and brushed out the snarls, then tied the thick mass into a tight braid. Tomorrow she would find a way to soak in hot water, but for now, it was the best she could do.

All the scullery girls had left by the time she arrived in the kitchens. The head cook was drying her hands on a cloth. Anabelle's eyes widened at Estelle's appearance, but she said nothing more than, "Come to make the bread, miss?"

Estelle nodded, not trusting her voice. Anabelle smiled pensively, as though she understood. "Well, then. The ovens are cooling, but I've left the fire going for hot water if you need it. The flour and butter and yeast are out on the table..." When she got no answer, she sighed and shook her head. "Well, good night then, miss."

Alone again, Estelle picked up the nearest mixing bowl and began measuring out flour from the bin. Guests were expected late tomorrow morning—Mistress Gris and her two daughters. Nadia disliked them. Sylvie merely shrugged when their names were mentioned. They would talk about the ball. Who flirted with whom. Who caused a scandal, and who scored a triumph. And how everyone had danced until dawn...

She was crying before she knew it. Huge hot tears blurred her vision and plopped into the bowl. Estelle wiped them away with the back of her hand. It was then she saw the spots on her arm.

Justine, she thought at once.

By tilting a clean bowl this way and that, Estelle could make out her reflection in its polished bottom. Plain brown face. Black eyes, bright with tears. Thick straight black hair. And spots. Tiny red boils covered her nose. She tilted the bowl again and saw more dotting her chin. Estelle touched one gingerly and hissed at the pain.

You would hardly wish to appear like that.

Estelle could imagine them in the carriage, laughing about the trick. No, it would be Nadia who laughed. Sylvie would not say anything. And Justine would smile as though she knew all the secrets in the world.

With a strangled cry, Estelle snatched up the bowl and flung it across the room. The bowl hit the wall with a loud clang and clattered to the floor. The bowl with the flour went next. Then she was pounding the worktable with her fists until a sharp ache made her stop with a gasp of pain. She bent over the worktable and pressed both hands against her eyes.

I hate this house. I hate her. I hate me—

From the nearby tower, she heard the chimes ringing six plus the quarter hour. You cannot run away, the bells seemed to say. No, she could not. Justine had made clear that her father would pay for any disobedience on Estelle's part.

She blew out a breath. *So live,* she told herself. *Make the bread. Clean the kitchen. Watch for a chance to save ourselves.*

A dipper of water from the barrel helped to revive her. She cleaned up the mess of flour. Then she measured out more flour, mixed and kneaded the dough. Plain loaves first—a dozen of those. Fancy loaves with dried fruits and cinnamon and extra butter. The familiar routine soothed her nerves; breathing in the scents of yeast and milk and freshly ground cinnamon, she could almost forget the prince's ball, and Justine's latest unkindness.

She covered the rows of pans with damp cloths and set them aside to rise, then turned to the rest of her chores. Pots scrubbed and stacked away. (Estelle was careful to avoid her reflection.) Silverware polished. The floor washed and dried. By the time she finished, full dark had fallen and the full moon filled the tall kitchen windows with its silvery light. *Auprès-Lune,* she thought, smiling as she gave the counters a last swipe with her rag. *The city by the moon.*

She tossed the rag into the laundry bin. As she turned away, a glitter from underneath the stove caught her eye. Estelle knelt and retrieved the object—a jeweled hairpin whose tiny diamond winked in the moonlight as she turned it over in her hands. Not Anabelle's, she thought. Nor any of the kitchen girls, certainly. Such a lovely object could only belong to Justine or her daughters.

Nadia, she thought. Nadia had come to the kitchens with a

message about dinner. She had lingered a few moments, teasing one of the kitchen girls, before Anabelle chased her away. The pin must have fallen from her hair.

For a delicious moment, Estelle considered throwing the pin into the garbage. Justine would be furious. But no. Justine would be furious with everyone. And if she discovered that Estelle had found and discarded the pin...

Estelle tucked the pin into her pocket and lit a candle. She would have to return the pin to Justine's dressing room and hope that would do.

The upper floors were dark. No one was about. Estelle set her candle on the floor and slipped into Justine's sitting room, where her stepmother entertained her intimate friends. Here, too, all was dark, except for a sliver of moonlight that painted a white line across the dark red carpet. She half expected to find Justine's personal maid here, but the woman had probably retired to the servants' quarters for a few hours of sleep before her mistress returned.

The dressing room lay a few doors beyond. Estelle carefully made her way between the low tables, decorated with expensive porcelain figurines. She gained the dressing room without mishap and carefully set the pin inside her stepmother's jewelry box. In the silence, she could almost imagine the moonlight whispering over the knotted silk carpet.

...whisper...

Estelle jumped and glanced around nervously. No one behind her.

...no one...

Again she started, only to see her own shadow fluttering over the walls.

...is no one but me...come to me...

The voice came from the next room, she thought. One of the maids had left a door ajar, and though it Estelle could see her stepmother's bedchamber, its the furniture edged by moonlight.

Estelle slowly approached the door. Go back, she thought, but curiosity tugged at her. Curiosity and something else. She felt a faint prickling at her neck as she pushed the door open and went inside.

The moon washed the bedroom with its silvery light. All here was still and quiet. All except for a tall black cabinet that stood next to Justine's enormous canopied bed. A strange light, the color of old blood, leaked from around the cabinet doors. From behind its doors, a muffled voice called out. No more words, just an inarticulate cry.

Her heart beating faster, Estelle circled the bed and approached the cabinet. The door was locked, but Justine had left the key in the lock. Unable to stop herself, Estelle reached out and turned the key...

With a crackling explosion, the cabinet door burst open. Estelle stumbled backward and fell hard. Her teeth clicked together, and she tasted blood. Above the roaring in her ears, she heard a triumphant keening. Estelle scrambled back, knocking over stools and a small table. Her hands met a wall. The window? She could not tell. Her eyes burned and she could only see smeared shapes. The air smelled thick and sour. Frantically she rubbed her eyes. Then her vision cleared and she froze.

A woman stood in the center of the room, surrounded by a circle of light. A tall bone-thin woman, with silver-bright hair and eyes the color of hot flames. She stared at Estelle, and her lips pulled back into a smile.

You. Her voice was a hiss. *You are not the mistress.*

Estelle glanced from side to side. The woman stood between her and the door, but if she were quick...

Before she could move, the creature hissed and darted forward. Estelle screamed, but the next moment, the creature jerked back, howling. Now Estelle saw the collar around its neck, a thin braided band that glowed like moonlight. It called out a high sharp voice that set Estelle's teeth on edge.

Why? Why did you call me?

Estelle swallowed. "I didn't call you. I—"

Lies! You called me with blood. With rage. Why?

The coppery taste of blood in her mouth. Her outburst in the kitchen. It must have heard through all the plaster and wood of three floors. "Who are you?" she whispered. "What are you?"

Ys. I am Ys.

A demon, Estelle thought. Justine must have trapped it somehow. Ys was staring at her, her eyes brighter and hotter than before. A hungry look. A desperate one.

You want, Ys said. *I could hear that. From far away I could hear. You want free. You want dance. That is why you called.*

Estelle opened her mouth to protest, then stopped. She did want all those things, and more.

Ys's mouth curled into a smile, as though she could hear Estelle's thoughts. *Come here.*

Her pulse gave a leap. "What do you want?"

Help you. Help me.

"I...I don't know if I can."

Ys tilted her head. With the light falling across her face, her skin took on the pattern of tiny scales, edged in gray. *We try. Come. I will not hurt you.*

It was a chance. *Her* chance. She might not have another. Still, Estelle needed a few moments before she could summon the courage to stand and walk toward Ys. Ys lifted one hand and touched Estelle's cheek. Fire burned her skin, a cold bright fire.

You are afraid. That is good.

Estelle shivered. "Yes, I am afraid. But do not stop."

She heard a hissing—Ys was laughing. Then two burning hands gripped her face, and a wave of agony swept through her. Estelle tried to scream, but Ys pressed her mouth against Estelle's. A vivid fire coursed through her veins. Pain, pain, pain. An exquisite, lovely, consuming pain.

The fire died away. Ys loosed her hold. For a long moment,

Estelle stared into Y's flame-red eyes. Her heart was racing, and she still felt the warmth from the creature's hands.

So, Ys said with a smile. *See what my magic can do.*

Estelle blinked and saw a mirror in Ys's thin hands. Was that her face? Yes, it was hers, but transformed, as Estelle had not believed possible. The lips fuller and redder. The eyes canted slightly. Her complexion lighter than before. And her hair. She touched the soft mass that curled around her face. Only then did she notice the jeweled rings on her fingers. Diamonds sparkled around her neck. And her gown...

"Everything I wanted," she whispered.

Everything, Ys replied. *No one can resist. Now go to the ball, but remember, I cannot do so much once midnight strikes. Listen for the bells.*

Without waiting for another word, Estelle ran out the bedchamber door and down the stairs.

Outside the front door, a magnificent carriage waited for Estelle. Liveried attendants surrounded it; a tall gaunt driver sat with reins in hand. Ys's work, Estelle thought, taking in how the silent attendants all resembled the demon with their patterned skin and burning eyes. One handed her into the carriage with a smile, the moonlight glinting from his teeth.

She rode in state through the winding streets of Auprès-Lune. Except for her own carriage, the streets were empty and quiet. All the merchants and nobles had left for the prince's ball hours before. The full moon hung just above the mountain peaks that ringed the city—a swollen white disc against the violet expanse of sky.

It was like a dream, Estelle thought, touching the jewels at her throat and wrist. Ys had fashioned her a dress of dark gold, edged with apricot lace. Tiny pearl made a constellation in her dark hair, and her slippers... Estelle glanced down at her feet. Slippers made of glass. How foolish. And yet they felt as soft and pliable as silk against her skin.

Estelle released a long breath. Strange or not, tonight was a gift. She would dance. Who knew what else might happen. She might meet—Ah but that was impossible. Best to dance. And watch. And hope for tomorrow.

The bells were just ringing half past nine when Estelle's carriage stopped before the palace gates. One of the liveried attendants opened the door and helped her to descend, while servants from the palace came forward to usher her inside.

She had never seen anything so grand. There were lamps in all the windows, lamps atop the courtyard walls, lamps hanging from the ornate poles that lined the walk. Their light blazed like miniature suns, catching upon the fine gold leaf work that decorated the palace walls, until the whole ran with threads of liquid fire. Estelle took a deep breath and tried not to stare as she passed between the rows of guards, through the enormous double doors, and into the palace.

At the entrance to the ballroom, a herald bowed and asked her name.

For this she was prepared. "Sophie," Estelle said, using the name she had decided upon during the ride. "Mistress Sophie Deylune."

"Welcome to the prince's ball," the herald said, then turned to announce her.

For the next hour, Estelle danced with partner after partner. Her plans were forgotten, overwhelmed by an excess of delight. She had never seen so many jewels, so many rich gowns. Golden light from the chandeliers reflected from the ivory walls; a flash caught Estelle's eye. She half-turned and glimpsed a mechanical bird swooping around the beribboned columns. A laughing girl caught the bird, then loosed it again. Another and another appeared, until a flock hovered above the dancers, their song blending with the flutes and violins. Once, Estelle thought she glimpsed Justine's dark figure amid the bright silks, but the prince's ballroom was enormous, and his visitors numerous. She was safe.

"Mistress Deylune."

A young man, dressed in the prince's livery, bowed to Estelle. "His Royal Highness asks if you would honor him with the next dance."

"The prince?" she asked. Surely she had misheard.

At his gesture, she followed him through the crowds, which parted to reveal the prince standing on the vast patterned square in the ballroom's center. A ring of courtiers stood just behind him, while more liveried attendants hovered in the background. One man stood at the prince's side, tall and heavily built, dressed in gray silk. His face was dark and marked by strong features; his eyes were black and bright and keen. Rings of office glittered from his fingers. As Estelle approached, she could just hear the man say, "You Highness, you might not like it, but I have concerns—"

"—I understand those concerns, Lord Durand," the prince said. "You may tell me about them at length. But later." He extended his hand toward Estelle. "You are lovely, Mistress Deylune," he said in his low voice. "As lovely as the first lilies. Will you dance with me?"

He smiled, his teeth flashing white against his brown skin. Just barely, Estelle remembered to curtsey. "I will, your Highness, and gladly."

There was no comparison, she thought, as the prince led her in the first movement of the dance. Just as the sun burned brighter than the moon, so the prince surpassed all her previous partners. It was not just that he was handsome—he was—but how he guided her deftly through the complicated steps, the way his gaze lingered on her face, the warmth of his hands against her back. Strange that she had never felt this way with the other young men. It had to be Ys's magic, working upon them both. The thought gave her a pang of regret, that magic alone could make her desirable, but when the prince drew her close, she did not resist, and when he murmured that they should go into the gardens, she whispered her consent.

Servants opened the doors leading onto the terrace. Estelle barely noticed who watched their departure. She found it hard to breathe, as though the air had turned thick. The prince put an arm around her shoulders, making her pulse leap. His touch was hot.

He urged her down the stairs and into the garden, along a graveled pathway that led between rows of ornamental trees. They came to a sheltered clearing, where a fountain sputtered in the bright moonlight. The prince put his arms around Estelle and kissed her. "Now we are alone," he murmured. "Come. Do not be shy."

He kissed her again, a strong deep kiss the swept away the last of her resistance. When he ran his hands over her breasts, she gasped and leaned into the caress. Another few moments and he would take her upon the ground. A small voice inside wailed no, even while she opened her mouth to his next kiss.

Through the haze of passion, she heard the bells ring. Dimly, she remembered a warning—something about the hour, and what might happen.

Estelle pushed the prince away. "What is the time?"

He wiped his hand across his mouth. "Does it matter?"

When he tried to grab her wrist, she dodged away. How many times had the clock struck? Ten? Eleven? But as the quarter bells finished, and the first notes of the hour bells echoed through the air, she knew. It was midnight. Already she felt a prickling all over her skin, like tiny hot pins. The prince frowned, as though he too sensed something not right.

Estelle spun around and fled into the garden. The prince called after her. She covered her ears and ran faster. More voices rang through the air as the prince called for his guards. They would hunt her down, laugh at her ugly face and clothes. And the prince himself —he would stare at her as he would stare at a toad.

She veered off the path and plunged into a thicket of rose bushes, ignoring the thorns that tore at her face and gown. In the heart of the thicket, she curled up into a ball, hoping the guards would not spot her.

Her scratches stung fiercely. Rain from the day before soaked through her dress. The air smelled strongly of wet dirt and musty old leaves, overlaid by the fainter scent of roses. How hard would they look? she wondered, as the heavy tramping came closer. First the prince, then Lord Durand, called out orders, telling the guards to search here and there amongst the shrubbery. One man even poked a stick into the rose bushes. Estelle saw the pale wood stab into the ground not three inches from her nose.

The searchers eventually moved on. Estelle waited until she was certain they would not double back, then crawled from the thicket. Her hair had fallen from its coil. Her gown, the plain cotton one now, hung in muddy tatters. Somewhere she had lost one slipper. She took off the other slipper and limped down the path, away from the palace. Bells rang one o'clock. She had perhaps two more hours before Justine and the others returned home.

But escaping the prince's gardens was not as simple as she expected. Estelle wandered from path to path, searching for a gate into the streets. She knew they had to exist. Surely the servants and gardeners did not come and go through the palace itself. But shadows and moonlight made all the paths look alike. She turned here and there, only to find herself crossing her own footprints for the third time. Too weary to continue, she leaned against a tree, thinking how the moon had washed away all the colors in the world. She glanced down at the glass slipper, still clutched in her hands. In the moonlight, it looked as insubstantial as she felt.

"Mistress Deylune."

Estelle smothered a cry. One of the prince's attendants stood a few feet away. He must have just rounded the bend. She edged away from him. Her legs felt like water, but if she had to run, she would.

"I won't hurt you, Mistress Deylune," the young man said. "I won't give you away."

His voice was a soft alto, as soothing as silk. True, he had not moved toward her, but Estelle could not bring herself to trust him. "I'm not Mistress Deylune," she said as steadily as she could.

"But you are lost. I can show you the way out."

Her breath caught at the pity in his voice. *A way out. You cannot possibly understand how much I want a way out.*

But he was waiting, patiently, and at last she thought she might believe him. "Please. Yes. I've lost my way."

"Indeed," he murmured. "At least this much I can set right."

Sooner than she expected, he brought her to a narrow gate, set deep into a wall covered with vines. The young man opened the gate with a key and pushed it open. Not once had he touched her, for which Estelle was grateful. "Thank you," she whispered.

He shrugged. "Go home. Stay safe."

Estelle passed through the gate and heard the lock click shut behind her.

The clocks were striking two before Estelle reached home. Exhausted and footsore, she crept through the dark house to her rooms, where she hid the glass slipper at the bottom of her clothes trunk. Then she pulled off her muddy torn clothes and tumbled into bed.

She spent the next morning twitching in fear of discovery. Had Ys closed herself into the cabinet? Had the maids locked its doors and returned Justine's room to order? What about the magic itself? Could Justine detect its presence?

Justine, however, gave no sign that she noticed anything amiss with her jewelry box or her bedchamber. No one mentioned the scratches on her face, but Nadia did stare at Estelle as they passed in the hallway, and once, Estelle came across her stepsisters whispering together in the parlor. They were speculating about the diamond hairpin, she told herself, but she found it hard to concentrate on her tasks.

News came with their expected visitors that swept any worries from her mind.

"The prince," said old Mistress Gris, as she stirred her tea. "He's sworn to marry the girl with the slipper."

"What slipper?" Nadia demanded.

Justine smiled a lazy smile. "The slipper that marks his one true love."

"How did you know?" Mistress Gris said. "That is the case exactly."

She went on to relate all the latest gossip. How the prince was besotted with a particular woman from the ball. How Lord Durand, the prince's chief mage, had stated his misgivings, only to be ordered from the palace. The prince declared he would find the young woman, no matter how long the search took. He did not know her name or her family, however. All he could say was that she had vanished at midnight, leaving behind one glass slipper.

"How odd," Sylvie said.

"Very," Justine agreed, with a glance toward Estelle, who had lingered outside the parlor.

Estelle drew back quickly. Surely they would only think her curious.

She retreated to the kitchens, where Anabelle and her girls were preparing the noonday meal. Estelle took up a batch of pastry dough, which Anabelle had set aside for later. With practiced fingers, she bent the dough in fanciful twists and curls, but her thoughts were upon the prince and his quest.

I have the missing slipper, she thought. *I have Ys's magic, what's left of it. I could...*

Could what? Marry the prince? The thought nearly made her laugh. Ah, but if she could speak just a few moments with the prince, perhaps she could beg for his help.

And tell him what? That Estelle had seduced him with magic? And would he please forgive her long enough to help her father? He or Lord Durand would arrest her first.

Marry him and be free, whispered a voice.

But then she would be like Justine, who had trapped her father.

One of the kitchen girls tapped Estelle on the shoulder. "What are you doing?"

With a start, Estelle glanced down at the twisted blobs of pastry dough in her hands. She let out a long painful breath and flexed her fingers. Then she gently set about working the pastry dough into a single mass and started over.

The next few days brought more rumors, and Estelle learned that Lord Durand had returned to favor with the prince. Soon new reports circulated, saying that Lord Durand and the prince planned to visit every household, searching for the mysterious young woman.

When she heard that, Estelle took out the slipper, intending to smash it. Whatever Ys claimed, the demon's magic lingered here. She felt it buzzing just beneath the slipper's polished surface, which seemed to bend and flow between her fingers, though her senses told her that the glass remained solid. She saw its effects in how her cheeks turned hot with remembered passion. *You cannot resist,* Ys had told her. That magic worked in both directions. If she destroyed the slipper, the prince would go free.

But then she thought of Ys, trapped by her silver collar. She thought of Justine and her father, and she put the slipper back in its hiding place.

Nearly two weeks later, the prince arrived in their neighborhood with an enormous train of attendants and squires and servants and lackeys. Estelle could mark his progress from house to house by the maids' gossip. Even Anabelle was so distracted that she spoiled the roast intended for dinner. To everyone's surprise, Justine shouted her displeasure but did nothing more.

Mid-morning. Then noon. Then the three o'clock bells rang.

"His Royal Highness, Prince Henri Donatien. Duke of Arzel and Longuemont. Heir to the King."

Standing in the servants' corridor, hidden from view, Estelle listened as the herald's announced the prince in clear ringing tones. She could not see, but she could imagine Justine's smile as she welcomed her royal visitor. She could picture Nadia and Sylvie dropping into graceful curtsies before the prince. She held her breath as the prince explained his quest.

Go to him now. Go free.

Break the slipper. Do not be like Justine.

The next moment, she was racing to her bedroom. She dug out the slipper and hurried back to the parlor. It was only when she reached the threshold that she stopped.

For one long moment, the scene lay frozen before her. Estelle took in the sight of the prince kneeling before Sylvie with the second glass slipper in his hands. Justine stood behind Sylvie's chair, tensed as though to spring. Sylvie herself seemed as dazed as the prince. In the background, Lord Durand observed everyone and everything through narrowed eyes.

Estelle slammed the slipper against the doorjamb. The slipper shattered with a loud crack, leaving just the heel itself in her hands. Without giving herself time to think, Estelle raked the heel's jagged edge over her palm and down her arm. *Blood and passion,* she cried out. *Come to me Ys.*

With an answering cry, Ys burst into the parlor. Nadia screamed. Guards and servants and attendants fell back. Through the confusion, Estelle could see that the prince had drawn his sword. He crouched over Sylvie, who lay motionless on the floor.

Ys darted toward Justine. Justine's lips moved rapidly. Ys howled, clawing at her silver collar. Still muttering, Justine edged toward the door while Ys danced a horrible twitching dance. The dance jerked Ys away from Justine and toward the prince.

Before Estelle could think what to do, a man's voice rapped out a command in odd clipped tones. A loud crack echoed through the room, and Ys's collar broke into pieces. At once, Ys flew toward Justine. There was a keening, a high-pitched shriek, a ripping sound. Then Justine fell limp to the floor.

Ys turned to the rest of the room.

No, Ys! No! Estelle cried.

Ys paused. In that moment, Lord Durand spoke again. A shimmering light filled the room. Lord Durand held up a hand, reciting more words in that peculiar language. Ys's eyes grew wide as bands of light wrapped themselves around her. The bands spun in an ever-shrinking circle, taking Ys with it, until nothing but a small bright sphere remained, which Lord Durand took into his hands.

For a moment all was still. One of the guards picked himself up from the floor. Sylvie stirred and drew a sobbing breath. And the prince passed a hand over his eyes, as though he were waking from a dream.

Only then did Estelle wake to her own situation. She turned and fled down the hall, though the kitchen, ignoring Anabelle's startled exclamation, and out the door into the courtyard. The gate's latch stuck. She rattled it hard, but it refused to budge.

Estelle sank to the ground and leaned her head against the bars, weeping. Blood spattered her gown. Her arm ached all the way to her shoulder. Shivering, she turned over her hand and drew a sharp breath. The wound had already closed. Only a wide silvery scar remained. Ys's last magic at work. "Almost," she whispered. "You were almost free, Ys."

"So you were the one who broke the spell."

Estelle started. One of the prince's attendants stood at the kitchen door, arms crossed, leaning against the doorframe. A young man dressed in neat blue breeches, white shirt, and livery coat. His face was shadowed by the doorframe, but she could tell he was tanned, with long dark hair pulled back into a queue. The young man stepped into the courtyard, and the sun fell across his face.

Her face.

The woman held up the heel of Estelle's slipper, which she must have dropped it along the way. "Am I right? Does this belong to you?"

Estelle nodded, then shook her head, still weeping. The woman crossed over to Estelle and handed her a clean handkerchief. Estelle dried her face. The cloth was soft, and smelled faintly of summer herbs. A water flask came next, and she gulped down the clear cold water, which soothed her throat. "Thank you."

Clair shrugged. "Call it pity. Or duty. I was in the kitchens, talking to my cousin, when I heard the uproar from inside. Then you ran past, and I recognized you from that night in the palace gardens. My name is Clair, by the way. Here, let me help you up."

She set the slipper's broken fragment aside and helped Estelle to her feet, then kept a hand on her elbow, as they walked to a pair of benches underneath the courtyard trees. Estelle sank onto the sun-warmed stone. She was still lightheaded from shock, and it took her a few moments to take in what Clair had told her. "Anabelle is your cousin? You heard what happened?"

"She is. And I did." Clair took the seat beside Estelle. "Tell me what happened. Everything. Starting with your father."

Estelle opened her mouth and closed it. Though she heard kindness in Clair's voice, she had not missed the cool assessing look in the woman's eyes. Yes, she would have to tell someone. Confess. And soon.

"My mother died," she said slowly. "My father remarried. Justine does not care for me. She—She has done something to my father. He works. He eats. But it's as though he were dreaming about the world, not living it."

Unexpectedly she started crying again. Clair wordlessly offered Estelle the water flask again, and Estelle drank down the rest of the water. When the first handkerchief was soaked, Clair gave her a dry one, and with a gentle touch, she brushed the hair from Estelle's face. Her clothes smelled of the same summer herbs as her handkerchiefs, overlaid by the scents of leather and horse. She said nothing, but her quiet presence gradually soothed Estelle, who told her in halting phrases about the night of the ball. How Justine had ruined her dress and threatened her father. The diamond pin. Ys. The interlude in the garden.

"We both wanted to be free," she whispered.

Clair nodded. "And you thought the prince might protect you from Justine."

"I don't know. But I never meant to deceive anyone. I just wanted—"

"—to save yourself and your father. I understand." Clair retrieved the broken remnant of Estelle's slipper and turned it over in her hands. "Strong magic," she said softly. "Strong enough to seduce the prince and nearly wreck the kingdom." She glanced at Estelle, her dark eyes turning serious. "You must speak with Lord Durand. You must tell him everything, just as you told me."

Estelle nodded, her mouth going dry. "Of course."

"I cannot promise how it will go," Clair went on. "But we can explain about your father. And about Justine." Her mouth thinned again. "Justine has punished herself, in a way, but the matter does not end with her. There will be an investigation and a trial. The Court and King will examine you and everyone in this household. Lord Durand will want to search the house itself for evidence."

A trial. With judges and sentences. Estelle's thoughts veered directly to prison cells and long days without the sun. Her mouth went drier, but she had emptied the water flask. "What about my father? What about everyone else?"

At that, Clair's expression softened. "I don't know. It depends on whether your father recovers. From what you tell me, he needs special care. Lord Durand can dispel the magic, of course, but..."

"...but he might never be the same," Estelle whispered. Her throat squeezed shut. She had hoped too hard, she thought. No one should ever hope that hard. "What about Ys? I promised—"

Clair laid a hand on Estelle's arm. "Ys is a demon," she said softly. "She cannot roam our world without causing harm, whether she means to or not. Lord Durand will contain her until he finds the means to return her to her own realms."

Estelle glanced into Clair's eyes, dropped her gaze to her lap. "At least one of us goes free," she murmured.

"Most likely you both will. You might be required to give testimony, and then vow your loyalty before the king and his Court. That would be my recommendation."

She studied the woman beside her. Not so very young, but surely too young to give advice to any prince.

Her expression must have echoed her thoughts, because Clair laughed softly. "I've served the prince for ten years. He does not always agree with me, but I know he will listen." And then her smile faded. "But whatever the outcome—with you, with your father—you will need another home, however temporary. Do you have friends or relatives where you might stay?"

Estelle shook her head. "Not in Auprès-Lune."

There were relatives, to be sure. Distant cousins. She thought about her mother's family, who lived in a far-off corner of the kingdom. Would they make her welcome or would they resent this stranger? And what if her father did not recover? Would she spend the rest of her days in a land far from the city by the moon?

Next to her, Clair continued to turn the slipper's heel this way and that, but her gaze had turned inward, as though she examined something other than the object in her hands. Then she shook herself and glanced at Estelle with those wide dark eyes that seemed to take in everything about her. "Anabelle tells me you are quite good with kitchen work—especially with baking. Do you like it?"

The question took Estelle by surprise. "I do. Why?"

"My sister owns a bakery. She needs assistants—clever sensible ones. You could work for her while your father recovers. And afterward, if you like."

"Those are too many *if*s," Estelle murmured.

Clair smiled. "Not too many, surely. However, to continue—*If* she takes you on, you would have Sunday mornings free and Tuesday afternoons. You could rent a room from her, or we could find you one in the neighborhood. We can talk to my sister as soon as Lord Durand permits."

We again.

Estelle glanced toward Clair, whose warm smile eased the tightness from Estelle's throat. Perhaps she meant they could be friends. That would be something new. A friend to talk with. Someone to share conversation and hopes. Or maybe...

"When do you have days free?" she asked, her cheeks warming as she asked.

Clair's smile widened. Her teeth flashed white against her dark brown skin. "I thought you might never ask," she said. "Sunday mornings and Tuesday afternoons."

Estelle laughed. She took the fragment of glass from Clair and tossed it at the trash heap. The glass spun over and over, catching the sunlight and sparkling with all the colors of tomorrow.

Erato
The Muse of Love Poetry and Mimicry

Boil me down
Shoot me up
Let me drown
In your veins.
Slice your wrists
To bleed me out.
Call it love.

Faith June
From *Erato Screams*
Love Poetry of the Beat Women
Pleiades Press, 1981

Without the Dreaming

Jai Clare

TALIS HALNAKER WALKS INTO a provincial town almost hidden in redwoods, where, in front of a launderette covered in lurid posters, and a discreet bar, an argument between a sturdy clean blonde woman and a fat-shouldered man is in progress. As he moves forward, shuffling in the mud-filled road, listening to the calling of birds high in the trees, the couple shout and push at each other as if they can't bear each other's proximity. They sidle up to each other like scorpions. Danger, like sweat, exudes from them.

When Talis was born in the middle of a dell, in the centre of the island, in the centre of the ocean, no one thought he would survive, for he was born delicate, with transparent skin like water tinged with milk, and his cries were hesitant fragile whimpers. Everyone predicted he wouldn't last the year.

He grew quietly. His flourishing took people by surprise. It was almost as if they hadn't seen him for his eighteen years of growing when suddenly he presented himself to them fully mature.

When he left, the island seemed too large.

His had been a precocious introduction to adulthood. He had to leave or die. There was no other way. He had just turned twenty, when everything he thought about and everything he imagined he could achieve there in that place and with Sarah had come to an end.

Talis took to traveling as if he'd been born incapable of sitting still. He always travels south, wondering how long it will be before he finds himself back where he started and at Sarah's door.

He sees the woman again later in the bar; a short woman with golden blonde hair, and muscular arms, wearing only a dark-stained sleeveless top and shorts. She is quieter now, though occasionally she looks up, asks the barman for something, usually matches, which she uses to light up her endless cigarettes before pounding the matches into the glass ashtray, turning the delicate wood almost into pulp. It is obvious she is waiting. She touches her belly and winches.

When Talis first left home he went to the other islands around him, far from this interior wooded place he finds himself in now, thinking that surely there he would find another like Sarah.

Through barrooms and clubs he walked where women smelt of coconut oil, and the air was imbued with pallid hope. He saw bright colours, he saw smiles, felt sly touches on his arm, and tore himself away from mouths that kissed him smelling too powerfully of desperation.

Sometimes he thinks of Sarah at home, maybe with a family now. He sees her watching for her husband from the door at noon, looking for him. He thinks of her naked by the river, sitting on the diving rocks, washing between her legs, painting her hands with henna at holiday times, and sleeping after a long day's work, and wonders if the boat she had been making, to sail around the island with, had ever been finished. Such desire she had, to make her own boat.

When Talis dreams of her she is always smiling. Sarah had long dark hair, which she kept in a braided ponytail, and bright blue eyes, a tanned skin freckled almost indiscriminately, and she walked like she had forever to get anywhere. What he had loved about her was her back, the way it tucked in and curved into her hips, curved round into her arse and out again. And at the point where he back became her waist, became her bum, was a beauty spot, a beautiful large chocolate brown mole, which he loved to touch when they had worked together by the sea, her telling him to fetch wood for the boat but never asking him to help her make it, for it had been her project, and he had been eager to help her achieve it. When he left on a dove-grey day, the boat was still a shell on the beach, half-born, with waves drifting past it casually.

In the corner of the bar someone is shouting and fighting over a beer bottle. The woman looks up and watches, clinging to her glass as if ready to throw it. The barman takes the two men fighting and pushes them out the door. Without Sarah and the dreams he doesn't feel whole. But most people when they see him they see this tall man exuding confidence. They cannot see the core of him that without Sarah prevaricates, shakes, doubts, needs. They see a man who can cope with most things, who without her can live but is possessed by fear that moves him forward constantly, always searching, always looking. A fear that Sarah was the only person he would feel this affinity with; that this comfortable, erotic feeling of dream-sharing could never be repeated again.

Hope keeps him going, moving on. On hopeful days he mills about the towns with enthusiasm and puppy-like cheerfulness. Only at night does he feel the distance between him and the mind that once he could feel so intimately that it was like exploring another part of him. Sharing his dreams with her had been like opening up her mind and pouring them inside as if dreams were liquid; images seeping into her pores, into her bloodstream and up to her head.

Often he dreams of another woman; but this woman is always faceless and her back always resembles the unique contours of Sarah.

Wood-ash blows through the room as the door opens. Someone coughs and music begins again. Talis wonders if Sarah's husband ever gives her his dreams. He doubts it. Talis knew the moment it had first happened that Sarah was unique, that he was unique; out of the whole ocean of islands no one could ever do what they had achieved. It was so addictive: to be able to dream, and to communicate those dreams to another person by just dreaming them. This astounded him, unable at first to comprehend how such a phenomenon could happen and if indeed it was happening. For a long time he believed that he was merely dreaming this transference. Until Sarah told him the next day the dream she had received from him. Strangely she accepted this affinity between them with greater ease than he did. It made their parting at night more bearable. She would say, "Night is more thrilling than day."

Sometimes now when he is traveling—always taking diversions to different lands and different cultures—he tries to send a dream back to her but the dream is empty; it goes nowhere and Talis can't find her.

Talis sleeps by silent lakes, beneath mountains, the size of which frighten him. He likes to be hidden in fresh aromatic forests, when rain comes. He sees lynx, mountain lions heading deeper upland, and strange silent girls walking to school in thin hollow valleys. Standing above the village or town he just sits watching the people moving about below, always listening and probing. Then he sleeps, stretching out his long thin legs into rye grass full of pink ragged robin, and wild garlic, and sends out his dreams but nothing happens. The transference doesn't come. The night is sated with strange noises, harsh birdcalls, heavy trucks, and pitiful cries of dreaming children. He moves on to the next town, the next village. He can no longer bear to see Sarah again.

Talis could have stayed to watch her wedding under boisterous skies, on the edge of typhoon season, and then watched her settling into the new house at the back of the town, growing fat on contentment and children, watched her being touched by her husband; he could have stayed to feel her push away his dreams and change from the vibrant women he wanted and loved to someone ordinary, squashed by contentment. It would have killed him to be so close to her, to know he could share his dreams with her and yet never to do so again. At least this way, there was still a chance of another like her.

In the bar he talks to Georgia, who fells redwood trees, and yet hates wood. Talis is fascinated by her shapely, muscular arms, and wants to touch them. Her hands pull at wood splinters in the surface of the bar, and contorts matchsticks and sifts speedily through peanuts in a dish before tossing her cigarette packet about in her hands; the skin on her arms tanned but reddened as if recently scrubbed. She shifts in her seat, tucks hair back behind her ears. The scars on her arms are like signposts.

The bar smells of green wood, diesel oil, and tobacco smoke; most of the people are light-skinned as if bleached by the air clogged with wood ash; Talis can see dust particles in Georgia's blonde hair, like white spiders. He longs for the sound of skin touching skin.

Georgia keeps looking towards the door, which makes Talis wonder whether she would smile at the figure she expects to wander in, or wince? Talis just wants to take her to a bed, pick the dust from her hair and sleep peacefully after what he imagines would be innervating sex. He touches her arm. She says, "I need food."

He takes her to a table and carries fried chicken in a wooden bowl, a selection of appetizing salad comprising pine nuts, dark lettuce and ripe avocado cut into thin segments. They share, nearly touching as they reach for the food. Georgia tears the lemony chicken with her brawny hands, getting covered in light-coloured olive oil, but her mind is elsewhere. Music cuts through the conversation and she lifts her head to the door again as if the words reminded her of something. She mentions her boyfriend briefly, hesitantly before changing the subject. Talis wants to know more. A story here. She is someone into whom he can delve. He wants to part her mind like he would her legs.

He tells her about his journeys. From the coast he had moved down to the country of wars, sleeping in disused factory sites amongst the smells of destruction and chemicals, and stood covered in a light dusting of cement powder and sand. Sand stuck in his fingernails but it wasn't the sand of home. Traveling and seeking has given him satisfaction but after a while he is still left by himself and without Sarah and without the dreaming. Sometimes the desire for her is so great he wants to cry. He takes himself away, to run through woods, swim a river, borrow a gun and go out shooting pigeon, or just work hard upon whatever laborious task he's become involved with.

He filled his eyes with sights, sounds and cultures of others, gorging himself on images of the desert, painted beads, coloured rugs and low-slung squat houses clinging to the orange earth. The desert made him ache for the sea. He said: "Sarah, take my dream and you will see all of this."

Talis has tried all types of women, but his preference is for women whose dark hair holds the odour of stinging salt and damp coral, seaweed and the white crash of waves against rock. But the farther he went into the mainland, this smell faded, replaced instead by the smell of pine trees, earth works and gravel pits.

Sex with Georgia is raw and without sophistication; she is yielding and strident in almost the same sharp movement. She is thick-waisted, with legs to bend metal, but with breasts he adores: neither too big, nor small, but round and fat. He waits until she quiets and snuggles into the duvet. He hadn't been sure she would stay long enough to sleep. She looks at him from beneath his chest and he closes his eyes, pretends to sleep, waiting till her eyelids twitch, her chest heaves, watching her breasts moving which he can just see if he leans above her, pretending to move in his sleep. She lies on her side away from him, but her breasts are exposed. Dark aureoles peek over the top of the sheet; an image that turns him on more than her arms, more than her legs; vulnerable and yet trusting.

He decides to dream about her nipples pressing against the palm of his hands, to his instinct of there being something about her. She stirs in her sleep.

Early next morning he is up and into the shower of his boarding house room before Georgia wakes. Sunlight slashes through the bathroom window highlighting sections of his body. He looks pure, untouched and tanned in the light. Then he her brings a glass of orange juice, which he sets on the tiny table beside her slightly open mouth. Her mind is as empty to him now as it was the night before. But he touches her hand and her eyes open: grey like layers of slate, her lashes curl upwards, bits of sleep in the corner of her eyes, blonde bits of wood ash. She touches his arm in return, takes the juice, sips gently, and still holding his arm pulls him towards her while rolling the empty glass to the floor.

The sun has grown even more in the sky now and Talis is sleeping. He is not dreaming with Georgia, but through her that he feels so relaxed. She is somehow his conduit. Maybe because she is Sarah's complete opposite, almost eerily symmetrically the opposite, is the reason he can do this. Sometimes he is conscious in dreams and is now but he cannot question what makes this happen, what force of god knows what enables him to be conscious a little of who she is, without being able to send her his dreams or she him. But being near Georgia thrills him more than he has felt in the last few months.

In his dream he sees Sarah. A pale copy of her, not tanned from the sea breezes as he remembers her, but standing hovering between the inside and the out; between the world of the sun and the world of domestic harmony. Her husband, as lively as twitchy sandpipers on the beach, is outside, chatting to a neighbour, and yet he looks reduced: shoulders smaller, hands more delicate, his head more swallowed by his neck; definitely smaller. Talis doesn't quite believe this though he knows it has to be true. How can such an impressive man suddenly look so ordinary? A Herculean man—a man to awe horizons, and here he is reduced to mere splinters. Sarah looks to call to her husband but her voice is mute. Her mouth open. Nothing issues. Once she was like electricity: sharp, untouchable, radiating. Have these people changed, or has he, or was it just the delusions of love that had made him believe these images? Could he have been carrying the wrong image in his head all this time?

Sarah moves into the orange-coloured house, the hem of her dress brushing against the rosemary bushes at the entrance, and Talis follows her. The house is chillingly beautiful. Clean, sharp vivid objects on limed driftwood furniture, odd-shaped white rocks glitter under striking downlights; well-made sofas whose depth of coral colour invites lounging. Around the walls are wooden boards and banisters in pale blue, while white muslin fabrics blow in under the sidewards sun, creating an ethereal light smelling of poignancy. The house looks sea-washed.

Sarah's rough hands smooth down her pleated skirt. Talis tries to imagine her strong legs hidden there and her pubis bone and the curly tufts of her unmanageable pubic hair. Somehow it doesn't belong to the woman here before him. A child comes running from the outside and nearly sends Sarah flying as she turns round, tripping over the child who is like a dog underfoot hustling in front of her, head down, chewing on something in its hand. Sarah picks the child up, but nearly drops him; it is a boy. He can see the almost indefinable Adam's apple.

Sarah can barely hold the heavy child, who is about five or six and Talis realizes that yes he has been away that long which makes him suddenly homesick. His bones are suddenly fed up with deserts and wood ash air and cities of marsh and mountains full of soldiers, of asking endless questions and searching for Sarah's replacement when Sarah is still living, breathing and looking in need of his help. If she would have it.

He looks at her and she seems to look right back at him with tired eyes, very little life in them. All her life has gone into the bundle sitting on her hips—into the cleaning, the tidying and trying to keep the boy amused. She fills the boy with all of her vivacity. He seems a handful, running and shouting, climbing over furniture. This is her life. The boat is still on the beach, untouched.

Georgia stirs and Talis lifts gently out of the dream. He sees Sarah, burdened and smaller; contentment has crushed her. She seems concave, everything pointing inward whereas before everything about her had faced outward to the light and life. And now the child sits in the boat, scratching at the surface, indenting his name into its surface, like a conqueror in waiting.

Beside him, Georgia wakes and looks at him, "Can you tell I'm two months pregnant? Can you feel the lump?" She touches her belly and Talis is numbed.

"Isn't it a little soon for that? There's nothing there to show. Is it his?" She nods, and looks away.

"He wants me to have it but I'm not sure. He says I'm unnatural for even thinking of not having it. I think he's obsessed with the idea of being added to. I'm not. I don't need something else to make me feel that I am me. Not yet. One day yes when I am ready."

Talis listens as she tells him about her desire not to stay here, not to be like her mother and sisters, who were all tied to children and lost their dreams. Georgia wants to see the ocean, and to swim in ocean water at night naked and alone, the cool water between her legs, calming her face. She wants to eat fish under a pier, feet in the water, hair wet. Talis holds her hand, smiles and she relaxes. Her warmth and receptivity almost consumes him, like air. From the distance he feels Sarah's breath on his cheek.

Georgia says her boyfriend is pressurizing her and she doesn't feel capable. Should she get rid of it? Whatever she does will be awful, but she has to do it otherwise it will be worse for both of them. All of them. They touch as they talk. The walls become imbued with the deep cathartic hues of her conflict.

Talis lets her go. He doesn't book the appointment, but by listening to her he has allowed her to create a space in her mind where she won't feel a monster if she does what she naturally wants. They part in the darkness, smiling and washed of emotion.

She climbs into the parked truck of her waiting boyfriend. She was but a conduit, Talis thinks, an angle of himself let loose. He looks upwards to the sky, east to the mountains and war, south to where from here it gets cooler again, or north back to where he came from, or west. North is Sarah. West is he doesn't know what.

The sky fills with wood-ash as the factory blows its whistle and people hurry into the night. Cars whistle by him, bicycles, people in groups chatting, hair full of blonde dust.

He walks east, backtracks, walks west, despite of the war, despite the absence of Sarah, but thinking maybe it would be interesting, maybe it would be useful to head back to the war. People are more vulnerable in times of trouble. He thinks of Sarah as he heads out of the trees and into the flat land before the mountains, thinks of her in his dream. How lost she looked. Never would she accept his help. He imagines her standing in her pristine house, scrubbed, clean and flattened, and as the years progressed she and the house would merge so that her husband and child would not see her in any other way; Sarah and the house would be synonymous, just as if she had become one with the sunless world of bricks and mortar.

He gets a lift quickly, in a slow comfortable truck. The mountain air is cool. He pulls a jacket about him, smiles to his companion, before settling back, as outside the wind hurries by, into the well of the blue leather seat, for a quick dreamless sleep.

The Teasewater Fire

Sarah Totton

MISS ANNA-LISA EVANS WENT by that name all her life. Marriage never arrived to alter it and when she had her only son she saw no reason why he shouldn't bear it also. Even on such a short journey. Thus, he was buried, three days after his birth, under a stone marked 'Midway Evans.' She'd called him Midway on first discovering her pregnancy as she'd declared his mere existence as "midway to ruining my reputation"; having a child out of wedlock in that era was not looked well upon. The boy's arrival as a stillborn fairly completed the journey, as it took the delicate edge of her eccentricity and twisted it like a Celtic knot.

From the hospital, Anna-Lisa retreated to the house in Telltale Close which she shared with her bachelor brother, Marlow. Here she resumed her occupation as a model-maker and freelance illustrator, busying herself pinning insects and tramping along hedgerows at dawn, eavesdropping on birds. None of which were unusual activities for her. However, the character of her paintings began to shift subtly from realism to surrealism.

A request to draw a likeness of an indigo bunting was met with pictures of the striking bird in various odd and improbable circumstances: drinking tea at a table on the patio, or sitting on the wrist of a cherubic child. A commission for a spotted salamander was duly filled, but rather than posed in its natural habitat, the formless creature was pictured clutched in the hand of same cherubic child.

Her brother, Marlow, spent most of his tidy life successfully avoiding reality by using his unique gifts to simulate it as nearly as possible. At first he coped with his sister's growing obsession by ignoring it, but eventually the unsold artwork began to spill out of her studio and into his life. He found one of her paintings gracing the bottom of the bathtub one evening. Nor was this to be an isolated occurrence. Scattered over the kitchen table at breakfast the next morning, he found several more. All of them featured, in one pose or another, the same young child with golden, curling hair and overlarge blue eyes that hadn't quite settled comfortably in his fleshy face. In one picture, he held a meadow vole in his cupped hands. In another, a frog drooped, its grotesquely long legs hanging and dripping from his hand as he stood, knee-deep in pond water.

Marlow was emotionally stunted in many ways, but he wasn't obtuse. He knew well enough that the inspiration for these sad paintings lay under several feet of cold topsoil in the Teasewater Cemetery. Marlow had always wanted a son, in the vague, wistful way that middle-aged bachelors with no experience of actual children sometimes did. In his idealized imagination, children appeared only when necessary, when surnames and heavy parcels were to be carried, while at other times they became unobtrusive, feeding, clothing and amusing themselves. In his own way, Marlow had been happily anticipating the birth of Anna-Lisa's child. Who else would have looked after them in old age and inherited the family fortune?

Marlow was concerned for Anna-Lisa, but also at a loss as to what to do about her. He reasoned that in time, her grief would lessen and life would resume in its own quiet way. But as the months passed, the paintings and sketches began to multiply. Marlow noticed a difference in these newer drawings. Though the animals never completely disappeared, they were no longer the focus. And the cherubic child was ageing unnaturally swiftly. He had shed the androgynous appearance of infancy and was now clearly recognizable as a boy; his hair had darkened to a deep bronze, though it was still curling. The eyes looked less out of proportion in the face which had shed the chubbiness of babyhood. When he smiled now, a tooth, slightly twisted, showed beneath his upper lip. One of his eyebrows was completely white; his newt-slender fingers sported gnawed-on nubs of fingernails. In one drawing, he stood with one foot balanced on a broken tree stump half-submerged by the bank of a river, playing out a fishing line that ran into the water—no rod, just a line—and watching intently. This picture, Marlow took up to his bedroom and placed on the top of his bureau. He was not one for pretty pictures, but this one, he thought, was worth keeping. It provoked troubling questions in him. What if Midway—silly name, really—hadn't died? What if he had come home to the house and they had raised him? What kind of man would he have become?

Marlow roused himself from his reverie and, feeling somewhat overcome by a motive he didn't want to analyze too closely, he put on his coat and went for a walk. He chose a route that took him through the park. It was that time the day when most people were at work and their children at school—Marlow's preferred time to walk. Of late, he had found that seeing children bothered him a great deal. It had been weeks since he had seen a real child. But this day must have been a school holiday, because they were everywhere. The wind was gusting in the playing field at the park. Marlow saw a young boy running in circles tugging a kite string while his mother, a young woman, yelled encouragement. The boy was intently hauling on the string and there was a look of joy on the mother's face. Marlow stood on the pathway watching them, his head full of the roar of the wind.

He returned home, if anything, more agitated than when he had left. He sought solace in his workshop. Lately he had been working on a life-sized damselfly. Anna-Lisa had designed the model so that it was impossible to distinguish it with its bead-blue body and clear wings, from a real damselfly. Most of her models she sold to universities, schools and museums. But in this particular case, Marlow, seeing what she had done, had asked that she make one for him. He had it in mind to push the envelope in his imitation of nature. He had been designing intricate machinery within the body to allow the damselfly to not only fly, but also catch mosquitoes. And so far, he had succeeded. Now, he was improving on nature; he was designing her to recognize and hover near one particular person. Better than insect repellent, this jewel-bodied servant would be.

When Marlow finally killed the lights above his workbench, it was well after midnight. On his way to bed, he passed Anna-Lisa's studio and found the door open and the lights still burning. Inside, Anna-Lisa was working at her dissecting microscope. She used this for illustrating smaller specimens, mostly insects. Tonight, though, she was not illustrating; she was sculpting another model, and there was a particular intensity in her expression, like the boy in the park with the kite, as though what she was doing hurt her more than it hurt the modeling medium. She was plying it with a sharp instrument, and Marlow was reluctant to interrupt, so he went to bed.

The next morning found Anna-Lisa drinking tea in the kitchen and chewing her toast distractedly. It put Marlow in mind of the days before Midway, peaceful, contented mornings when they would eat breakfast and discuss their various projects or plan collaborations.

"You're up early," said Marlow.

"I haven't been to bed yet," she said. "Come and look what I've done."

She led him upstairs, not to her workshop, but to the room at the end of the hall that had been locked for nearly a year. Despite the passage of time and the now open windows, it still smelt of fresh paint. In the sunlight, the room was bright with the wallpaper Marlow had put up in preparation for the baby who had never come home. Midway's father, whoever he was, had been either indifferent to Anna-Lisa's condition, or more likely, had never known of it. There had been no question of raising Midway anywhere but here in Telltale Close.

"It hasn't dried yet," said Anna-Lisa, leading him to the window by the crib.

Sitting on the sill was one of Anna-Lisa's model animals. This particular one lacked the realism that all of her previous creations possessed. Though it was recognizable as a meadow vole, it stood on its hind feet, exposing its grey belly. Its almost human expression was one of musing, as though the dead flies on the sill held its entire interest.

"Well?" said Anna-Lisa.

"What's it called?" Marlow asked.

"*He* is the Teasewater Vole," she said.

"He's...perfect," said Marlow.

"Not yet," said Anna-Lisa with a meaningful look.

No. What he lacked was spark inside. Marlow had, in a way, been saving himself for a challenge like this. Anna-Lisa was not asking him to make the creature simulate nature; she was asking him to give it something which nature could never do.

"You read my mind," said Marlow.

Both of them laughed, and their bodies and spirits, so unused to feeling joy for so long, ached with it.

After the Teasewater Vole came the Teasewater Otter—who carried a fishing pole and a pipe. Then the Teasewater Frog (a spring peeper with an ornate 'x' on its back). And finally, the Bird of Teasewater—an indigo bunting, the only bird mad enough to sing on a midsummer afternoon. In all, the work took Anna-Lisa two months. When the last stroke of blue had been made on the Bunting, she took him to the nursery and set him to dry on the wooden board in the window. She parted the curtains, letting the sun into the room.

Outside, the red maple tree enclosed the house in its wine-tinted light. She had chosen this room to be the nursery for its view of the trees in Telltale Close. The back garden was wild scrubland with none of the Close's majestic feel. What a world was outside, she thought; she had not properly looked at it in so long.

"Left a bit. Left a bit. There." The Bird of Teasewater perched on the arm of Marlow's desk lamp, peering down at him, giving him unsolicited directions. The Teasewater Otter lay on its back, spread-eagled on a wax-bottomed dissection tray while Marlow adjusted its voice box. He'd learned with the Bunting, having fitted him with a syrinx, the bird's equivalent of a larynx in mammals. If the Bunting was capable of speech and song, Marlow thought, why on earth shouldn't the Otter be as well? It wasn't as if he were compelled to follow nature's design; the Otter's miniature size, (It was a mere four inches in length.) to Marlow's mind gave him license to tweak nature's nose. As he was doing so, a soft hum filled the room as the damselfly flitted in. The Bunting cocked his head at her.

"Leave her!" said Marlow. "Or I'll clip your wings."

The Bunting peered at Marlow, beak gaping, and gave a gesture reminiscent of a shrug. Marlow suppressed a smile and went back to work.

Later, as he prepared lunch, he heard the front door click shut and looked up to see Anna-Lisa taking off her coat.

"You've been out," he said, surprised. Apart from her bird-watching excursions at the crack of dawn, he had not seen her leave the house since Midway's funeral.

In answer, she gave him a sly look and held up a white shopping bag. She pushed his plate aside, put the bag on the kitchen table and reached inside. She brought out an ebony case, the size of a briefcase with three silver clasps in the shape of mouse heads. The case was inlaid with silver and set with an amber locket in the middle of the lid. Inside the locket was a key. With the air of a magician's assistant, Anna-Lisa unlocked the case and lifted the lid. Inside, the case was...empty, but in quite an interesting way.

Anna-Lisa pulled back the green baize flaps in the lid to reveal a compartment within. Set in the foam lining were silk-trimmed burrows the size of egg cups crossed with straps like seatbelts. Beneath each one was a hand-lettered nameplate. At the very top, the same flowing script engraved on a plaque proclaimed: *The Teasewater Quintet.*

Anna-Lisa, still smiling, still silent, pulled back the black velvet cloth covering the bottom of the case. Under it was a landscape that Marlow recognized as a scale model of the grounds behind the house. The creek was represented by a piece of mirror cut in a serpentine shape; the grass and flowers of the banks were suggested with delicate dabs of paint. Some colored pebbles had been glued along the banks to represent boulders and a willow made of blown glass hung over the creek, its long icicle branches almost touching the mirror.

"It's a better place for them to sleep than in your drawer," she said with a trace of pride. She left the case on the table and went upstairs.

Marlow took the case downstairs. Pulling the light switch in the workshop, he was greeted by the song of the Bunting. He'd forgotten to shut it off. The rest of the menagerie, he pulled out of his fittings drawer.

It was only as he was placing them in their silk-lined burrows, buttoning the straps across to hold them in—Otter, Peeper, Vole, and Bunting—that he realized: *Quintet means five.*

Upstairs in her workroom, Anna-Lisa peered through the eyepieces of her dissecting microscope creating what was to be her masterpiece. The animals were wonderful, but they had been mere flirtations.

Permitting neither food nor sleep to interrupt the flow, she allowed her hands to move as though by divine force. So the time passed until at last she sat back from the bench, finished. In a daze, she took the figurine from the stage below the lenses and brought it to the nursery. She was so tired, she stumbled into the doorframe, but her work was protected from harm in her cupped hands. She opened the nursery window, set the piece in the window well and immediately sought her bed. Through that night and all the next day, she slept.

On the evening of the fourth day, Anna-Lisa awoke terribly thirsty and dizzy with hunger. She cupped water from the bedroom sink and took a few swallows. Then she remembered why she had slept for so long. She hurried to the nursery. The curtains lifted gently in a whisper of summer breeze. She parted them and picked up the figurine. She found details she did not remember putting there. It was as though someone else's hands had made him, not hers. She took him back to her room and peered at him under the microscope. His blond hair, tangled as though he had slept on it, (Much as her own must look, she thought.) the short upper lip under which his twisted incisor gleamed. His eyes had lost their babyish hue and were now a metallic yellow-brown. The white-browed eye looked naked. He stood no taller than a hen's egg, with the slight build of young adolescence. He was absolutely perfect. For the first time in a long time, the world seemed right again.

Marlow had a different opinion. He sat chewing his dinner and staring at the boy next to his plate. He showed no surprise, and made no move to touch the figurine, nor would he meet Anna-Lisa's eyes with their look of pleading hope.

"No," he said.

"Why not?"

"Because," said Marlow, and hearing the anger in his voice, he softened it. "It isn't real."

"Then what harm can it do...?"

"The same harm as any lie," he said.

"Would you turn your back on someone who needs you?" Her cupped hand hovered over the figurine as though to coax it toward him.

When Marlow didn't answer, she sighed and left the room leaving the figurine behind. Marlow set down his fork. He donned his reading glasses and, without touching the figure, examined it. She had sewn clothes for him out of scraps of fabric; he wore a matching blue shirt and trousers. She had outdone herself this time, he thought. The detail was so fine, so lifelike, he looked a breath and a twitch from animation. The boy seemed to stare at Marlow with reproach, the expectation of life implicit in his bearing. Marlow *could* do it. But should he?

"No," said Marlow firmly. He draped his napkin over the figurine and continued to eat. When he had finished, he picked the figurine up, still wrapped in the napkin and took it to the Teasewater case. He laid the boy in the empty foam burrow. It was only then he noticed the words on the plaque beneath the burrow: *Midway Evans.*

Anna-Lisa didn't beg or plead with Marlow. That wasn't her way. Instead, she withdrew to her room, emerging only to glean food from the kitchen. The luster and life in her, rekindled momentarily with the creation of the figurine was now fading.

At first, Marlow thought it was simply the final and necessary stage of the grieving process. Acceptance. But it became clear as weeks passed that Anna-Lisa had entered a different stage altogether—apathy, the kind of apathy that precedes the end of a terminal illness.

It was a coercion of the gentlest and most inexorable kind. If the alternative was her premature death, was granting her this wish, however illusory and false, not a kindness? Was false hope worse than no hope? These thoughts, along with the memory of the figurine's reproachful eyes, haunted Marlow. Had she indeed caught the merest trace of resemblance with the baby who had left her womb in silence?

Marlow decided at last, waking late one night from a dream of those eyes. Before he could change his mind in the light of morning, he took the case to his workshop. Brimming with excess energy, he almost expected the figure to come alive at his touch.

There was more to it than that, of course. And Marlow found himself contemplating the concept of a human soul, examining it as though it were under his own lenses and he were fumbling with it like a wet fish. Marlow was a recluse. He had no deep understanding of anyone other than himself. He had no one else to draw from.

Anna-Lisa's workmanship on the figure was exceptional. Breathtaking even. Marlow could do no less than match it. The Bunting had been his crowning achievement. Until now.

It took him four days, four glorious, tooth-grinding, frustrating, anxious days channeling the life that burned within him into the figurine. It was more than just his mind which he shared; it was his soul, his memories, all of it, melded with his sister's own essence which she had poured into its body. When it was over, Marlow felt the boy stir in his palm. He noted the movements of its belly as it breathed deeply, as though to fill itself to bursting, and felt a stab of triumph.

Marlow took the boy upstairs, wanting to see him in sunlight. On an impulse, he picked up the case from the living room and took it into the conservatory. He opened it. At the edge of the case, on the surface of the glass creek rested a tidy little rowboat. A pair of swizzle stick oars lay shipped inside. Marlow set the boy in the boat. The boy slumped there, limp, head bowed, still breathing deeply. After a time, his hands found the oar handles and he gripped them.

He lifted his head, blinked and then peered over the side of the boat. He tapped the surface of the mirror with his oar experimentally, then looked up at Marlow.

"Who are you?" said the boy.

"Your...uncle, I suppose you could say. Uncle Marlow."

Midway shipped the oars and braced his bare feet one on each of the oarlocks. "I need a proper pair of shoes," he said.

"Right," said Marlow. "I'll have your mother make you some."

"Is this all?"

"Is what all?" said Marlow.

"This!" He gestured, wide-armed, at the contents of the case. "I'm bored already."

"Right, I'll...wait a minute." Marlow opened the flaps in the lid and considered for a moment or two. The Bunting was likely to have a jealous sulk, the Vole to bore the boy rigid with his theories on religion, the Peeper was too small. So Marlow chose the Teasewater Otter. They were comparably sized at least, which Marlow, remembering his childhood days, believed to be the primary requisite of a suitable companion. In other words, someone unlikely to beat one senseless, and vice versa.

Marlow animated the Otter and set him on the dock next to the boat. The Otter immediately cast his fishing line into the creek. "Cheers," said the Otter.

"You're not going to catch any fish in that mirror, I hate to tell you," said Midway.

"Catching fish is not the reason I go fishing, young man," said the Otter. "I find it stimulates my imagination."

"It would have to. Reality's got sod-all to offer."

Marlow, satisfied they'd struck up some kind of rapport, however tenuous, went to the liquor cabinet across the room and poured himself a double scotch. He gulped it in three swallows and poured himself another. *Was I angry when I was working on him?* he thought. *Resentful? Cocky?*

Two drinks later, Marlow recalled that the boy didn't have an off switch. Hopefully, he would need sleep. Or at least pretend he did, for Marlow's sake.

"Right, ah, lights-out time, boys," said Marlow. He let the Otter reel in his line before deactivating him, then, hesitating, he picked up the boy and set him in his silk-lined bed. As an afterthought, Marlow tucked his handkerchief around the boy.

"I'm tolerating this under duress," said Midway.

Marlow bit back a curse. He oughtn't to swear in front of the boy. "Try to sleep," he said, and he made sure the straps keeping the boy in were buttoned securely. Then he closed the case, flicked the clasps and for the first time, he locked it with the key. He took the case up to his bedroom and stared at it for hours in a daze before sleep finally overcame him.

The next morning, Marlow took the case down to the kitchen and put it on the table, still locked. He was apprehensive about opening it, so apprehensive that he left it there and went to his workshop where he spent an hour twirling a pencil and staring off into space. When he went upstairs, he found Anna-Lisa sitting at the table, case open before her. She looked up and smiled a rare, radiant smile.

"He's perfect, isn't he, Marlow?"

Marlow had the power to shatter her hope by telling her what he thought. And he couldn't do it, because he saw in the sunlight that the hollows around her eyes were deep and her cheekbones sharp beneath her skin. Though she was only forty, she looked old. She could not take another devastating blow. So he said, "I suppose so."

"He wants a pair of binoculars for his birthday," said Anna-Lisa, "which would be today of course. And I'm going to make him a proper wardrobe. I'll get my sewing box. Watch him, would you?"

Midway balanced himself in the boat which bobbed in the kitchen sink. He was training his binoculars upwards at the curtain rail where the Bunting was perched.

"I can see *right* up your vent," said Midway cheerfully.

"Bloody twitcher," said the Bunting.

The Peeper, sitting opposite Midway in the boat, cocked his head and chipped in his high soprano. "What did he have for breakfast, then?"

"Eggs," said Midway. "Hard-boiled by the looks."

"Now look here," said Marlow. "Any more of that and I'll let the water out of the sink."

Across the kitchen table, Anna-Lisa held a piece of black velvet under a thimbled finger as she put the sewing needle through it. She went at the work with a blissful air.

This morning, Midway sported a suit of royal blue velvet. His boots were ungainly things, draw-string bags made out of muslin. They came up to his knees. The boy looked like a fop in them.

"Hasn't he got seven outfits already?" said Marlow.

"This is for the Peeper," said Anna-Lisa. "And I'm doing up a shawl for the Bunting next." She noticed Marlow's expression. "Why not?"

"It's biologically preposterous," he said. "Animals don't wear clothes."

"You're the one who made them able to speak," she said. "That wasn't my idea."

"I'm thinking that might have been a mistake."

"No," she said. "You'll leave them be. They're Midway's friends now."

"Look, lads," said Midway. "Lover's tiff."

Marlow's head whipped around, but Anna-Lisa stopped him with a hand on his elbow. "Outside," she mouthed, and got up.

As he walked past the sink, Marlow plunged his hand into the water and loosened the plug. The water gurgled down the drain and the little boat spun in circles. Anna-Lisa took Marlow's arm and led him into the hallway outside.

"I wanted to say," she whispered. "I think it's time you talked to him."

"About what?" said Marlow.

"About...you know. The facts of life."

"You're his mother," said Marlow, and realized how appalling that sounded.

"And you're a man," said Anna-Lisa.

Marlow's face reddened. "Is it really necessary? It's not as though he can get into any trouble—"

"Marlow, he needs to know these things," said Anna-Lisa. "Do this for me. Please?"

"All right. But not now. Later,"

As it happened, Marlow's talk with Midway had to be postponed indefinitely. That night, Marlow was woken from a troubled sleep by a noise downstairs. As he lifted his head from his pillow, he heard it again. A sharp report, like a cap gun firing. He shuffled into his slippers and turned on the hall light. The pop came again, this time like a hailstone landing on a plate. Halfway downstairs, Marlow caught a whiff of smoke. He stopped and sniffed again. No, he wasn't imagining it. He charged downstairs and immediately found the source of the smell. In the dining room, the buffet was on fire. Marlow snatched up a handful of magazines from the den and proceeded to bat the flames with them. When that proved futile, he made for the kitchen. He took two steps when his foot leapt out from under him and he crashed flat on his back on the hardwood floor. What looked like a ball bearing drooled loudly across the boards. Marlow picked himself up and bolted into the kitchen. He dumped out the fruit bowl and filled it with water then ran back to empty it over the buffet before he finally convinced the flames not to set up house there.

Examining the mess, he discovered an overturned candlestick, its wick still warm. He coughed and was answered with another sharp pop. Something struck his tailbone and ricocheted.

"Woops, sorry Uncle," said Midway. "Meant to hit the fondue pot."

Marlow turned around. The Teasewater case was open on the dining table. Standing amidst what looked like a pile of ball bearings were Midway and the Peeper. Midway, dressed in his best white linen suit, was holding an oar from his boat and...Marlow leaned closer. Between his lips was a thin taper from which a tiny tendril of smoke was curling.

"What the hell do you think you're doing?" Using his finger and thumbnail, Marlow plucked the smoking thing from between Midway's teeth. He sniffed at it. Cigar smoke. His eyes lit on the case of his best cigars which sat in pride of place in the middle of the table. The box had been opened and one of his cigars protruded over the rim. It had been eviscerated.

"You're *smoking*?" said Marlow. "*My* cigars?" He didn't know which was worse.

"The Otter's got a pipe," said Midway. "If he can smoke, why can't I?"

"Because it'll stunt your gr..." Marlow stuttered, at a loss.

"Gosh, and here's me hoping to crack six inches by my second birthday. Thanks, Uncle Marlow. That was a close one. Sorry about the fire, but, you know, I had a job lighting it from the candlestick and it sort of...fell over." Midway's facade of contrition disintegrated as he burst out laughing. Beside him, the Peeper slapped him on the shin warningly.

"And what's this mess here?" Marlow, grabbing a handful of the ball bearings. He recognized them as a string of silver plastic beads used to garland the Christmas tree. He realized belatedly that someone had cut the end of the string. As he lifted them, they slipped off the string and bounced onto the floor.

"I was teaching him to play cricket," said the Peeper.

"If you'd stop throwing me googlies—"

"Oooo! That's very leg-before-wicket, Mr. Evans," said the Peeper, winking and shoving him playfully.

"Here, I'll show you how I'd hit one properly." Midway picked up one of the beads, tossed it in the air and winding up, gave it a whack with the plastic oar. The bead ricocheted off the buffet table, hit the wooden floor and bounced.

"Marlow?" Anna-Lisa called from the doorway.

"Mind where you step," said Marlow. "Your son's dropped ball bearings all over the floor. And he's almost burned the house down."

"Midway?" said Anna-Lisa. "Are you all right?"

"I thought we'd agreed that nighttime was bedtime," said Marlow sharply. "I'm too tired to deal with this. He's all yours." Marlow splashed through the water on the floor and went up to bed.

After the cricket incident, Marlow drew up a set of house rules which Midway promptly broke. Anna-Lisa forgave him every transgression. By definition, he could do no wrong. Anna-Lisa refused to de-animate the animals or to separate them from Midway, thinking it cruel to deprive him of his friends. Marlow had other ideas. One afternoon while Anna-Lisa took Midway out in the back garden to show him the world outside, Marlow took the Peeper out of the case and brought him down to the workshop.

"What are you doing?" the Peeper demanded.

"You're a bad seed," said Marlow. Really, of all the Teasewater animals, he was the worst influence on Midway. He shut the Peeper off and began making painstaking alterations. He knew he didn't have much time. Anna-Lisa would be bringing Midway inside soon enough, and he would demand to know where his companion had gone. It was not a simple matter to change the Peeper's attitude to one of rigid obedience. It involved identifying the twisted energy that must have leaked out of him and into the Peeper in the first place.

Marlow had never had to undo any of his work before. It was a blow to his pride. Sounds overhead distracted him and guilt made him twitchy. In the end, he was not sure whether he had succeeded or not. When he reanimated the Peeper, it immediately sat up and leapt out of his hand. The next thing he knew, it had hopped behind a wall cabinet. And that was the last he saw of it.

The Otter perched on the edge of the sink beside Midway. Both of them paddled their feet in the water. Midway clutched a fishing pole. "Uncle Marlow, chuck in a couple of minnows for us, would you?"

Marlow remained seated. He tipped himself another glass of whiskey. It was two days since the Peeper's disappearance and no one had said a word about it, other than Anna-Lisa, who'd been quite upset. Midway was as depraved as he'd ever been, perhaps more so. And the Otter was beginning to fall under his influence. The worst seed of the Teasewater Five wasn't the Peeper at all, Marlow realized. It was Midway.

Marlow had to work up the nerve to even consider his next move. Altering the animals was one thing. But Midway was more than an animal. And yet, so much worse...

Marlow took another swallow. He only drank when he was losing his nerve; drunkenness gave him an excuse to dither.

"Marlow, you shouldn't do that in front of Midway," said Anna-Lisa, coming into the kitchen. "You're setting a bad example."

"Fine," said Marlow and he drained his glass and left it sitting on the table. He slunk upstairs. *Tomorrow,* he thought. *I'll deal with him tomorrow.*

Tomorrow came a bit late for Marlow. It was just past noon when he finally emerged from a coma-like sleep. He splashed himself to wakefulness under the bathroom taps before he remembered what he had planned to do today. *Midway.*

He shuffled downstairs, taking each step carefully. He comforted himself that he could do nothing while his head ached and his hands trembled. Downstairs in the kitchen, he found his whiskey glass still on the table. Upside down inside it was the Teasewater Vole. Marlow tipped him out onto the table. He wobbled a little, shook himself and hiccupped. He was wearing the vicar's costume, Anna-Lisa had made him. Marlow noticed that the table was covered with a sprinkling of what looked like dried parsley flakes.

"What the hell...?" Marlow said.

"We didn't have any proper confetti," said the Vole. "So we improvised. But I don't suppose that affects things."

Marlow noticed that the Teasewater case gaped emptily on the counter. "Where's Midway?"

"On his honeymoon," said the Vole. "I married them last night."

"On his *what*?! Married to whom?"

"The Bunting," said the Vole.

"But he's..." Marlow spluttered. "He's not even a mammal!" Then heard what he'd just said. "Where is he?"

"There's no point in looking for them. They've gone. After what happened to the Peeper, I can't say I blame them."

Marlow fumbled a bit with his hands; they seemed to be working independently of his brain. He scooped up the Vole and put him back into the whiskey glass and paced back and forth in the hallway. There was a breeze blowing through it. He followed it and found the French doors wide open on the garden.

Anna-Lisa searched for Midway for days, even sifting through the earth in the garden and in amongst the plants. Each morning she stood on the patio and called for them; the French doors were always left open now and Marlow spent sleepless nights envisaging thieves strolling in and looting the house. He had an alarm system and locks installed on his workshop. He felt no regret over Midway's disappearance, only shameful relief. Though it was hard to see Anna-Lisa suffer, he told himself it was for the best, and at least he had had no hand in it and therefore bore no blame.

Eventually, Anna-Lisa's searching came to an end. She cried for two days running and on the morning of the third, she buried the Teasewater case (with the Vole and the Otter inside) in the back garden next to the sun dial.

"One coffin, five bodies," she said. "Six, really."

Marlow turned over the last spadeful of earth and said nothing. There was nothing to say. And that was the end of the Teasewater Five, although some nights when he was trying to sleep, Marlow thought he heard peeping coming from inside the walls of his bedroom.

A week later, Marlow found Anna-Lisa eating at the breakfast table. Beside her plate lay a life-sized hand, long-fingered, with bitten-down fingernails. Golden hairs glazed the back of it where Anna-Lisa stroked it. She looked up and seemed to see Marlow then. She smiled. "It's a good start, don't you think?"

Meeting M.

Jessica Treat

AT NOON I CHECKED OUT of the hotel. We were supposed to meet at Delaney's at one; I had already traced the route to get there. I knew her only from her book cover. I assumed I would recognize her—or she, me—we had exchanged books some months ago, then agreed to meet in this city—her city. Of course I would not stay with her—I was not on those kinds of terms, we had only written each other letters, e-mails. I had admired her books of stories, the elliptical way she had of writing. I'd come across an interview with her in a magazine somewhere, was attracted to her modesty, the painstaking care with which she wrote stories; I must have seen myself in her. "When you fall in love, you fall in love with yourself, when you kill yourself, you kill someone else." That silly refrain was stuck in my head now as I deposited my luggage in the trunk of my car, locked it and walked toward Delaney's. I was wearing new shoes, my feet felt tight and on the verge of blistering. I felt self-conscious about my weight; I was heavier than in my jacket photo.

I arrived at the restaurant before she did. At least I did not see her anywhere. I sat by the window so that I would see her approach—in a long skirt, I imagined, as in her photo, feet in something like Birkenstocks? I kept thinking she was late, but it was really me who had arrived too early and was now drinking cup after cup of coffee. I pictured myself in a sidewalk café in Paris rather than this sprawling city which I happened to be visiting (happened to be?) in Eastern Canada. It was not very attractive—the faint smell of sulfur, which reached me, it seemed, even inside the restaurant. She lived in an upscale neighborhood. Her husband (yes, she did have a husband) was, I think, a doctor.

I had told her I was en route to—what had I said?—a conference, which might have been true, except I doubted that I would ever arrive there. I would visit M. and then return home, or I would visit and then drive around aimlessly, pretending I had another destination. I would not let on that I no longer wrote, did not think myself a writer any longer.

"You're Clare, aren't you?"

I nodded, pulled out a chair for her. It bothered me that I hadn't seen her approach. She was not wearing the long skirt I had imagined, but sandals, yes (though not Birkenstocks), a summery blouse, pressed jeans.

"Did you sleep well? Was the hotel comfortable?"

We began with such pleasantries, inanities before ordering lunch from our hovering waiter.

She had this annoying habit of twisting a strand of her hair as she listened. It should have been charming, adolescent girl-like, but it made me think she wasn't paying attention. I wanted to tell her to stop it. She neither looked nor acted as I'd imagined she would—a woman nearing 40—she seemed more like an uncertain girl.

Later I would realize that this was perhaps a defense mechanism on my part: a way not to fall in love with her. Concentrate on her flaws and I would not lose myself to her. But why drive more than 500 miles to reach that conclusion? I could not see it then.

Of course when I drove away I regretted that it hadn't gone better. The fact that she wanted to talk mostly about writing hadn't helped of course. I carried on some patter about the novel I was writing and watched her as I spoke, twisting a strand of hair round her finger—she seemed nervous, almost desperate.

Did she believe me? Could she tell I was fabricating everything, that writing was for me just the discussing of it? She had nice things to say about my previous books, carefully crafted phrases I did not take too seriously. She was flattered of course by my interest in her, in her work, in the stories that she wrote so beautifully.

"Will you try a novel?" I asked her.

"Oh! It takes me so very long just to write a story.... Some have taken me years, you know I start them, go back to them, get stuck... I suppose I might, but I haven't really any "novel" ideas, I'm more of a poet, really, masquerading as a story writer..."

I thought she had a point there. "Shall we order dessert? Coffee?"

She ordered the crème brulee; I followed suit. "What about you?" she asked. "Tell me about your own life..." as if we'd been talking about hers. We hadn't. I'd learned nothing of her husband, her daily life. I reminded myself to ask.

"Oh... quite dull really.... I'm divorced, have been for over five years. My life is really uneventful, the life of a small town..." The thought of my town made me feel ill suddenly. I'd lived there since my ex and I had left the city, then stayed on after the divorce when quite obviously, like a patch of poison ivy or a slice of moldy bread, it didn't agree with me. But then nothing seemed to agree with me. I was aware of that. I'd grown, more than ever, hard to please.

"It's a charming little village," I heard myself tell her. "You know, where everyone knows everyone else, the postmaster knows who's writing you letters and sending you packages, the neighbors check in on your cats while you're away..."

"Oh!" she said, "I might find that stultifying."

"Not at all! Reassuring really. To feel part of something—connected..."

"Well, yes, I suppose...though one has a bit of that here too, in the neighborhood..."

And so we continued in this mundane vein until "Is it influencing your fiction? Small town life?"

And I'd said yes, said some more about the novel I was writing (as I suddenly saw it): a thinly disguised village appearing at its center. I knew from previous publications how being a writer in a small town was both a curse and a blessing, and decided to shift the conversation to more solid footing. "Everyone wants to read what you're working on, then sees themselves in it even when they're not. The town wants to own you—this writer in their midst—as if you could bring some coinage to the town, put in on the map... but they rarely like what you've written. It's rather awkward. One misses the anonymity finally...."

"Yes..." she said. "I can see that..." and then after a pause, "Do you ever get stuck? Lose the thread, find yourself unable to write?"

I shifted uncomfortably. How much should I tell her? "Well, yes, sometimes.... I find a long walk helps, or reading... What about you?"

She mumbled something I couldn't hear, spooned the last of her crème brulee from the china dish. "It's always a struggle. One long struggle. Nothing enjoyable about it." She smiled then and I saw that she was really quite stunning.

I remembered to ask about her husband, the "quality of her days." I wanted her to be unhappy, but I cannot honestly say that she was. She professed a good marriage, a love and respect for him. I felt myself wilting. She had everything going for her, and it didn't look like any of it was going to rub off on me, the smell of this sulfur-city notwithstanding.

"Shall we walk for a bit? Before you head off? You're heading to Halifax today is it?"

I nodded. We paid our bill, splitting it quite fairly and without too much awkwardness.

It felt good to be out of the restaurant, the clinking of china and silverware, the tinkling of conversation.

Strangely, we had trouble saying goodbye to one another. We spoke of letters we would write, e-mails, another visit possibly. "If you like, if you don't mind...you could send me part of the novel you're working on? I'd like to read it..."

I told her I'd consider it, that I didn't usually show anything until I'd reached the end of it, and I was nowhere near the end of my novel, was finding it very difficult, troublesome, in ways the other novels hadn't been..."

We said goodbye, a kiss on the cheek, a light hug on the street corner. I watched her walk away. Was she really 40? She looked no more than 26 to me.

It wasn't something I had planned to do but as soon as she'd left me, walked two blocks or so west, I began to fall in step behind her. I thought I would see where she was heading to: was it home? Or did she have another appointment? I knew, like me, there were no children; at least she had never mentioned any—. I had nothing else to do, and the thought of my car, the long drive home or some meandering drive to nowhere, disheartened me.

She did not seem in a hurry, stopping now and then to take in a store window: brightly colored leather purses and shoes; now a bookstore (would she venture in? No, she did not—). Not at all in a hurry to get back to home and husband—of course he must be at work. Her writing would be done for the day. She was a morning writer, an early riser. How clear her conscience must be—able to take in shoes and handbags! I envied that. I was in a muddle—that much was clear—or I would not be following her. And if she saw me? I had to take care that she did not. It would be the end of me. Exposed. The roots of a tree thrown up for all to see; the ugly veins beneath the opaque stockings...

And now she was stopped before a chocolate shop. Was she really so self-indulgent? Or would she buy a gift for someone else—surely not her husband? I watched from a distance, took out my cell phone, dialed a random number as I slipped into a doorway, one that still offered me visibility.

She emerged, must have been ten minutes later—I didn't time it but so it felt—with a small package. What if it were meant for me? What if she sent it to me? This was crazy, she had no reason to indulge me....but I felt a flutter: a moth, not yet a butterfly of hope—and then I lost her. It could be argued that hope—however small—does that. It obscures reality. She had been in front of me, just two blocks away, and now I could not see her anywhere. Another store perhaps? A cross street? I pondered the possibilities and just as quickly lost interest. It wasn't right to be following. Quite wrong, intrusive really.

I went into the chocolate shop; I'd stock up for my long drive—I loved chocolate as much as the next person, more perhaps—especially the gourmet variety—wrapped as they were in blue and gold tinfoil. I felt strangely elated as I paid for my gift box, as if, in fact, she had already given it to me.

About the Authors

Beth Bernobich is a writer who likes to reinvent herself, often in several directions at once. Most recently, her fiction has appeared in Full Unit Hookup, Beyond the Last Star, Polyphony 2, and Strange Horizons.

Jai Clare is currently working on a PhD at the University of Gloucestershire. Her work has appeared in *The London Magazine, Agni 60, Bonfire, The Barcelona Review, Nemonymous, Night Train, Redsine,* the *Pedestal Magazine, Three Lobed Burning Eye, Cadenza, QWF.* She is also featured in *Foreign Affairs, The Erotic Travel Tales Anthology.* She has a website at www.jaiclare.co.uk and a blog at www.thecuspofsomethig.blogspot.com.

Victoria Elizabeth Garcia lives in Seattle with her husband, writer John Aegard. There, she listens to The Mountain Goats, cares for a surly but loveable little dog, and dreams of grad school. Her fiction has appeared in *Polyphony* and *Rabid Transit*, and will soon appear in The Indiana Review.

Elizabeth Hand is the author of seven novels, the most recent of which is *Mortal Love* (Morrow, 2004) and two short story collections, *Bibliomancy* and *Last Summer at Mars Hill.* Her work has received numerous honors, including the Nebula and two World Fantasy Awards, and she is a longtime contributor to the *Washington Post Book World* and *Magazine of Fantasy & Science Fiction*, among other publications. She lives with her family on the coast of Maine, where she is working on a new novel called *Generation Loss*.

Catherine Kaspar is an assistant professor at the University of Texas at San Antonio. Her work has been published in such journals as *American Letters & Commentary*, *The Colorado Review*, *Mid-*

America Review, *Leviathan 4*, and *3rd Bed*. Her chapbook, *Blueprints of the City*, is available from Transparent Tiger Press in Chicago.

A former assistant English professor in the picturesque town of Freiburg on the edge of the Black Forest, **Ruth Nestvold** has given up theory for imagination. The university career has been replaced by a small software localization business, and the Black Forest by the parrots of Bad Cannstatt. She lives with her fantasy and her family and her books in a house with a turret and has sold stories to numerous markets, including *Asimov's*, *Realms of Fantasy*, *Strange Horizons*, and the anthology *Realms of Wonder*. Her novella "Looking Through Lace" made the short list for the Tiptree award in 2003 and was nominated for the Sturgeon award.

Ursula Pflug is author of the novel "Green Music." (Tesseract Books,(2002). She is also a playwright, arts journalist and short story writer.

Kit Reed's new novel, *Thinner Than Thou,* is an A.L.A. Booklist Book of the Year and a winner of the A.L.A. Alex award. *Publishers Weekly* calls her "one of our brightest cultural commentators." *People Magazine* cites her "ear for dialogue and a truly wild imagination," and *Entertainment Weekly* says of *Thinner than Thou*, "*Super Size Me* meets *Soylent Green*."

Dogs of Truth, her new short story collection, is due out from Tor this fall. *The New York Times Book Review* has this to say about her last collection: "Most of these stories shine with the incisive edginess of brilliant cartoons... they are less fantastic than visionary." The *NYTBR* describes *@expectations* as a "poignant new novel about love, life and loss in the age of the Internet." Her other novels include *Captain Grownup*, *Fort Privilege*, *Catholic Girls*, *J. Eden* and *Little Sisters of the Apocalypse*. As Kit Craig she is the author of *Gone*, *Twice Burned* and other psychological thrillers published here and in the UK. A Guggenheim fellow, she is the first American recipient of an international literary grant from the Abraham Woursell Foundation. She's had stories in, among others, *The Yale Review, The Magazine of Fantasy and Science Fiction, Omni, SciFiction* and *The Norton Anthology of Contemporary Literature.* Her books *Weird Women, Wired Women* and *Little Sisters of the Apocalypse* were finalists for the Tiptree Prize.

She and her husband, Joe Reed, live in Connecticut. The current Scotties in residence are Tig and Bridey, a.k.a. McTeague and MacBride of Frankenstein.

Dianna Rodgers is a writer, artist, social worker, adjunct professor, and a coach. A precocious reader, she constantly got in trouble for reading ahead in the Dick and Jane books. She was convinced that the good stuff must be further ahead, but alas, she was always disappointed. So she began to write her own stories. Her work can be seen in *Dead on Demand*, *Best Women's Erotica 2001*, *Myths Fantastic*, *MOTA 2002*, *Truth*, *Polyphony 2*, *Moist*, and *Blowing Kisses*. She recently edited *Ghosts At The Coast* which will be released in fall 2005.

Despite her penchant for sex, risky fiction and midnight walks, **Heather Shaw** is just a nice girl from Indiana, now living in the San Francisco Bay Area. Her fiction has appeared in such nice places as *Strange Horizons*, *Polyphony 3* and *5* and *The Fortean Bureau.* Her poetry has been nominated twice for the Rhysling award. She edits the erotic webzine, *Fishnet* (www.fishnetmag.com) as part of her day job and co-edits *Flytrap, the little zine with teeth*, in the evenings with her fiancé Tim Pratt. They live in Oakland, CA with the requisite two cats.

Sarah Totton is a Canadian veterinarian and wildlife biologist. Her short fiction has appeared in or will be appearing in the anthologies *Tennis Shorts*, *Polyphony 5*, *Tesseracts 9* and

Fantastical Visions III. She is a graduate of the Odyssey and Clarion workshops.

Jessica Treat is the author of *Not a Chance* (FC2, 2000) and *A Robber in the House* (Coffee House Press, 1993), both story collections. Her fiction has appeared in various journals and anthologies, among them: *Ms.*, *Epoch*, *Black Warrior Review*, 3rd Bed, *Quarterly West*, *Writing Women* (UK) and *Wild Cards* (UK). She is the recipient of a CT Commission on the Arts Award and an Associate Professor of English at Northwestern CT Community College. She is completing a third story collection and lives with her son in the northwest corner of Connecticut.

Tamar Yellin is the author of numerous short stories which have appeared in a wide variety of publications, including the anthologies *Leviathan 3* (Prime) and *Best Short Stories* (Heinemann). Her first novel, *The Genizah at the House of Shepher*,'was published in April 2005 by The Toby Press, and her collection, *Kafka in Bronteland and other stories*, is forthcoming, also from The Toby Press.

About the Editors

Forrest Aguirre is a recent recipient of the World Fantasy Award for his editing of the *Leviathan 3* anthology. His fiction has appeared in *Flesh & Blood, Indigenous Fiction, The Earwig Flesh Factory, Redsine, 3rd Bed, Notre Dame Review, Exquisite Corpse, The Journal of Experimental Fiction* and *Polyphony 4* and *5*, among others. He has work forthcoming in *3rd Bed, All Star Zeppelin Adventure Stories*, and *The MacGuffin.*

Locus Magazine calls Forrest "... an interesting writer, worth watching, whom I think could benefit from disciplining the wilder flights of his imagination a bit." Forrest spurns such disciplinary measures.

A collection of his short fiction titled *Fugue XXIX* will be published by Raw Dog Screaming Press in 2005.

Forrest lives in Madison, Wisconsin with his family.

Deborah Layne founded Wheatland Press in 2002 and has been co-editing (with Jay Lake) the *Polyphony* anthology series ever since. Her own fiction has appeared in *The Fortean Bureau, Flytrap 3* and *Indiana Review.* In 2004 and 2005 she was nominated for a World Fantasy Award for *Polyphony.*

She is a member of the Wordos Writers Workshop of Eugene, Oregon. Having earned degrees in history, philosophy, history and philosophy of science and law, she is content to focus on speculative literature. Deborah lives in deepest, darkest Oregon with her family.

Also Available from Wheatland Press

The Beasts of Love:
Stories by Steven Utley
With an introduction by Lisa Tuttle. Utley's love stories spanning the past twenty years; a brilliant mixture of science fiction, fantasy and horror.

Polyphony 5
Edited by Deborah Layne and Jay Lake
The fifth volume in the critically acclaimed slipstream/cross-genre series will feature stories from Jay Caselberg, Ray Vukcevich, Jeff VanderMeer, Theodora Goss, Leslie What and Nick Mamatas.

TEL: Stories
Edited by Jay Lake
An anthology of experimental fiction featuring Greer Gilman, Jeff VanderMeer, Tim Pratt, and Brendan Connell.

Polyphony 4
Edited by Deborah Layne and Jay Lake
Fourth volume in the critically acclaimed slipstream/cross-genre series with stories from Alex Irvine, Lucius Shepard, Michael Bishop, Forrest Aguirre, Theodora Goss, Stepan Chapman and others.

Polyphony 3
Edited by Deborah Layne and Jay Lake
Third volume in the critically acclaimed slipstream/cross-genre series with stories from Jeff Ford, Bruce Holland Rogers, Ray Vukcevich, Robert Freeman Wexler and others.

Polyphony 2
Edited by Deborah Layne and Jay Lake
Second volume in the critically acclaimed slipstream/cross-genre series with stories from Alex Irvine, Theodora Goss, Jack Dann, Michael Bishop and others.

Polyphony 1
Edited by Deborah Layne and Jay Lake
First volume in the critically acclaimed slipstream/cross-genre series with stories from Maureen McHugh, Andy Duncan, Carol Emshwiller, Lucius Shepard and others.

All-Star Zeppelin Adventure Stories
Edited by David Moles and Jay Lake
Original zeppelin stories by David Brin, Jim Van Pelt, Leslie What, and others; featuring a reprint of the zeppelin classic, *"You Could Go Home Again"* by Howard Waldrop.

LaVergne, TN USA
04 October 2010
199532LV00001B/17/A